THE FAERY REHISTORY SERIES

THE
RAVEN
LADY

THE FAERY REHISTORY SERIES

THE RAVEN LADY

SHARON LYNN FISHER

BLACK STONE
PUBLISHING

Printed in the United States of America

First edition: 2020
ISBN 978-1-982572-79-2
Fiction / Fantasy / General

1 3 5 7 9 10 8 6 4 2

CIP data for this book is available
from the Library of Congress

Blackstone Publishing
31 Mistletoe Rd.
Ashland, OR 97520

www.BlackstonePublishing.com

For Robin and Beth, who work so much magic on my behalf

"If thou wilt not, Count Oluf, dance with me,
Then sorrow and sickness will follow thee."

She struck him a blow across the heart,
Never before had he felt such smart.
    —Catherine Martin,
        "Erlkönig's Tochter" ("The Elf King's Daughter")
        from *The Explorers and Other Poems*, 1874

GLOSSARY OF IRISH TERMS AND NAMES

Absinthe: Anise-flavored alcoholic spirit also referred to as "the green fairy;" drinking absinthe allows some people to see into the fairy world.

Alfakonung: Old Norse and Elvish name for the king of the Icelandic shadow elves; also referred to as the Elf King.

Argr: Old Norse and Elvish for "cowardly."

Battle of Ben Bulben: Fought between the Tuatha De Danaan, allied with the people of Ireland, and their enemies the Fomorians and Icelandic elves.

Barrow-wight: A reanimated corpse or ghost from an ancient tomb.

Connacht (KAH-nucht): Region and ancient kingdom in the west of Ireland.

Diarmuid (DEER-muhd): A legendary warrior of the Tuatha De Danaan.

Diarmuid's seal: A centuries-old boundary between Ireland and Faery, broken before the Battle of Ben Bulben so the two could fight together against their common enemy, the Fomorians.

Draug: Old Norse and Elvish word for a reawakened dead thing.

Elvish: In this text, Old Norse, the language of the Icelandic elves.

Faery: Land of fairies and Irish immortals; also refers to the collective races of fairies.

Firglas: Irish woodland fairies and guardians of Knock Ma; literally "green men."

Fomorians: Ancient seafaring foes of the Tuatha De Danaan; often portrayed as a race of monsters; sometimes referred to as the Plague Warriors.

Freyja: Norse goddess associated with love, fertility, and magic.

Gap, the: A space-like void between the overlapping worlds of Ireland and Faery.

Gap galleon: A type of sailing ship that can travel inside the Gap, between Ireland and Faery, and inside Faery.

Gap gate: Means of travel between Faery and Ireland before the seal between worlds was destroyed.

Grace O'Malley: Sixteenth-century pirate queen of Connacht; ghostly captain of the Gap galleon that served in the Battle of Ben Bulben; and ancestress of Duncan O'Malley and Queen Isolde.

Hidden Folk: Icelandic equivalent of Irish fairies; includes elves, dwarves, and trolls.

Hrafn: Old Norse and Elvish for "raven."

Isolde, Queen: The Queen of Ireland, descended from the mythological figure Queen Maeve; cousin of Duncan O'Malley.

Knock Ma: Connacht court and stronghold of the fairy king Finvara.

Lady Meath (Ada Quicksilver): Englishwoman descended from Cliona of the Tuatha De Danaan; a scholar of fairy lore who married Edward Donoghue, Earl of Meath.

Loki: Norse god of mischief; blood brother of Odin; in this text, father of the Icelandic elves.

Lord Meath: Irish earl, Edward Donoghue, descended from Diarmuid of the Tuatha De Danaan; cousin of Queen Isolde and Duncan O'Malley (a.k.a. King Finvara).

Morrigan, the: Irish goddess of war; crow shapeshifter; also called "the battle crow."

Odin: Most revered of the Norse gods; also called All Father; blind in one eye and associated with ravens.

Oisin: A warrior, poet, and historian of the Tuatha De Danaan.

Shadow elves: Icelandic Hidden Folk; in this text, descendants of the Norse god Loki and allies of the Fomorians; sometimes derisively referred to as "goblins."

Skaddafjall: Stronghold of the Elf King on Vestrahorn Mountain in Iceland; Old Norse and Elvish for "shadow mountain."

Tuatha De Danaan (Too-AH-hah day DAHN-uhn), abbrev. Danaan: Ancient supernatural people of Ireland, often associated with fairies; people of the Celtic goddess Dana.

Notes: With regard to the Tuatha De Danaan, this text conforms to the naming conventions and spellings used by W. B. Yeats.

For more information about the fairies' return to Ireland and the Battle of Ben Bulben, see book one in The Faery Rehistory series, *The Absinthe Earl*.

PROLOGUE

Craters of Laki, Iceland—1785

Njála waited.

Her light blue eyes scanned the mist-shrouded horizon, wind whipping her hair against her woolen cloak. Cold seeped into her boots from the so-called "church floor," a rock formation near her village that looked like flagstones set into the turf. She would have taken some comfort from waiting inside the *actual* church, where Pastor Jón had delivered the sermon last summer that had stopped the devil's fire from destroying the village.

But it was the devil she now waited for, and he would not set foot inside a church.

The dreaded visitor was late, and the longer she waited, the more her heart misgave her. Njála, like her countrymen, was a Christian. Also like her countrymen, she knew the Hidden Folk lived among them—elves and other earthy beings, making their homes in the rocks, caves, and crevices of Iceland. Her visitor was in fact one of these beings—the Elf King himself. But he was born of shadow and might as well have been the devil.

She had refused to marry him, intending instead to accept the yoke of shame bestowed on a woman for bearing an illegitimate child. A child that would create a bond between Icelanders and the Hidden Folk and prevent the elves from ever threatening her countrymen again. Last year, the Laki craters had been made to spew poisonous vapors into the air. Though her village had been spared, the eruptions had caused rivers of fire to overrun farmland, resulting in the death of thousands of Icelanders, and even more of the animals upon which their lives depended. In the Elf King's plot to rid Iceland of its mortal population, he had all but rendered the country unfit for the habitation of his own people, and that, in the end, had helped persuade him to go along with the peace.

Such calamity was perhaps inevitable, descended as they were from the old gods—from Loki, who'd been imprisoned beneath Iceland by the All-Father, Odin.

The proposed treaty also offered a prize the Elf King could not refuse—Njála. The elves held Icelanders in contempt, as they possessed neither the resources nor the ambition to be warriors. But Njála—one of the last descendants of the mighty Gunnhild, an ancient Norse queen and sorceress—presented an opportunity to enrich the elven bloodline.

So that the people of Iceland might never feud with the Hidden Folk again, Njála was to bear a child—an elven prince or princess. A child that would be the only thing left in the world to her. For she well knew that while the villagers lauded her sacrifice now, one day, when they were again safe and thriving, they would scorn her as a fallen woman, tainted by her unholy union with the Elf King.

If she survived the ordeal to come.

The wind shifted, blowing her hair back from her face,

carrying with it a smell like gunpowder. She shivered. The choking gray mist swirled, and from the direction of the Laki craters to the north, a shadow approached.

Njála was a milkmaid, a simple farmer's daughter. But she knew her history—her own mother had made sure of it, even over her father's objections. She thought of her powerful ancestress now.

Lifting her chin, she stepped off the flagstones into the grass and strode out to meet her fate.

UNMOORED

KOLI

Connacht, Ireland—1883

Winter is no friendly season for voyaging across an ocean to offer yourself as a hostage to a sworn enemy.

I was resigned to it. But how tempting it was to read ill omens into gale and tempest—might be that was inevitable. As a child of the Elf King, you could rightly say that *I* was an ill omen incarnate.

Standing on the deck of the Danish mail steamer in the pelting rain, I could not beat back my resentment. I had been offered as consort to King Finvara, the lord of the Irish fairies. Our union was meant to reinforce a peace accord signed after the Battle of Ben Bulben, where my people, the Icelandic shadow elves, had fought alongside Fomorians, the ancient enemies of Ireland. Such unions were a longstanding tradition for good reason—they often worked. Yet in spite of tradition, even in spite of the wishes of his powerful cousin, Queen Isolde of Ireland, the haughty Finvara would not stoop to a union with a "goblin"—a slur his people often used against mine. And my mighty race—defeated decisively in the bloody battle for possession of Ireland—had no recourse but to agree to our enemy's revised terms.

I wish not to be misunderstood. I had no desire to wed the fairy king. But I was proud of my lineage. I could have chosen any elven lord—any Fomorian prince, even—and would have made him a formidable ally, a curse upon his enemies. In obedience to my father, I had accepted my exile to the lower isle, and yet Finvara offered only scorn in return.

Now I would enter the stronghold of our enemy, offering myself as a political prisoner. I would be despised for the dark magic in my blood, as well as my fierce appearance. My hair was black as a cloudless night, and even the light of the Irish summer sun would raise no gleam upon it. The iris of my eye was a shade of gray so near to black that it unsettled mortals. Across my cheeks and the bridge of my nose had been stamped the small, star-shaped marks of the highland elves, so ancient they remembered an Iceland with trees.

If my mixed elven-mortal ancestry had taught me anything, it was how to live among those who would only ever see my otherness.

On the morrow, I would begin my life as a hostage among the soft and bloodless descendants of the Tuatha De Danaan. I would not run a household or hold court. Nor would I produce heirs for a noble husband. But I would serve my father and lord as a spy in the house of his enemy. For my father and his Fomorian allies would never accept defeat. They would bide their time and remain bound by the accord with the Irish for only as long as they must. As their appointed agent, I would gather the information they needed to mount a new offensive.

As prisoner rather than mistress of Knock Ma, this charge would not be easily carried out. But neither would I be required to live a lie, nor bear the children of a man I could never love.

"We approach Galway Bay." Ulf, a captain in my father's army who'd served many years as my bodyguard, joined me on the foredeck. Menacing as he was—large and wolfish, with flesh both scarred and inked, and forever scowling—he was visible to no one onboard but myself. All the other passengers were mortal, and the elves were Hidden Folk. They had lived among Icelanders for many centuries—for the most part, without ever being seen by them. It was a subtle magic, requiring blending in with the surroundings. Yet, there were still seers who could perceive Hidden Folk.

I had a foot in both worlds, and my elven kin's ability to hide in plain sight was one I did not share, though I could melt into a shadow easily enough. Neither was I immortal, though time had not marked me—despite the fact I had outlived my mother, so far, by nearly sixty years.

An angry wind whipped the ends of my hair against my face, stinging my skin. Ice needles rained onto the deck and collected in my traveling cloak. As Ulf studied the waves, my gaze came to rest on the upside-down ash tree branded into his neck—the mark of the Elf King, which both symbolized and mocked our ancestors, the ancient gods of the Northmen. It was a mark we shared, though mine had been inked between my shoulder blades when I came of age, rather than burned into the flesh. The mark served as a reminder that however far I might venture from Skaddafjall, my father's stronghold on Vestrahorn Mountain, I was still his to command. Trusting me with such an important task had demonstrated his faith in me—though as an unmarried daughter, I was in a unique position to serve. And I was eager to prove myself.

My gaze followed Ulf's, settling on the Irish ironclads guarding the mouth of the port. Only three months ago these ships had destroyed the entire Fomorian fleet. It had happened in a harbor just north of here, turning the tide of the battle for Ireland. Early in the fight, the Irish goddess of war—for reasons neither mortal nor immortal would likely ever understand—had becalmed the ironclads, snuffed their steam engines, and bewitched their powder, rendering their cannons useless and forcing them onto even footing with the Fomorian longships. But King Finvara himself had raised a wind that freed the ironclads. Vain and vile though he might be, I must never let myself think of him as weak.

The fairy king, our returning warriors had told us, was mortal, or at least had once been. He was the youngest son of an Irish earl whose immortal ancestor—the King Finvara of ancient days—had taken possession of his body and mind before the battle of Ben Bulben. In fact, a number of the Irish nobles—including Queen Isolde herself—had immortal ancestors who had worked through them to assist the allied armies of Faery and Ireland.

What must it be like, I wondered, to commune with the spirits of ancient heroes within your own head? Navigating the marshland of my complicated ancestry had been challenging enough.

The steamer drew alongside Claddagh quay, and I studied the mist-shrouded waterfront, just stirring to life in the gloomy morning light. The rain had now lightened to a drizzle, and I prepared to disembark with the other passengers, but without my escort. Under the terms of the agreement, I could bring no attendant of my own kind.

I bid farewell to Ulf, who had been my constant companion since the death of my mother. As he conveyed my father's final command, the mark between my shoulder blades tingled.

"Remember where you come from."

In the court of the fairy king, I would hardly be allowed to forget.

Making my way along the quay, I watched as my fellow passengers were greeted by waiting friends. It was a snug and orderly harbor, filled with fishing boats. When I reached the end of the walkway—beyond which was the village with its neat, white cottages—I looked for a carriage from the fairy king's court.

I watched the passengers proceed into the village, friends carrying their bags or straining under the weight of their trunks. I watched as some of them climbed into carriages, while others walked along the waterfront. I watched the steamer's crew transfer bags of mail to waiting carriers.

While I had expected no fanfare, neither had I expected to be kept waiting for longer than the steamer's paper cargo. I glanced at the ship, which was already drawing away from the port. My trunks rested alone on the stones of the quay.

As the last straggling passengers moved past me, they failed to hide their curious, pitying glances, and I grew hot with anger under the confining layers of clothing that had been forced on me before I left Iceland. The fact that Irish women would tolerate such purposeless torture was a sure sign I would never fit in among them. No one could bowhunt in such clothing, or even breathe without making noise. I swatted at the mourning veil that masked my alien features—the star markings, and the curved and pointing tips of my ears. Shoving the dark net back over the top of my hat, I glanced up and down the waterfront.

Sighing heavily, I tipped back my head, welcoming the cold winter rain on my fevered cheeks.

He will answer, I vowed. I was nearly a hundred years old and had spent many of my days staring out at the ever-changing Atlantic, wandering across the lava fields and black-sand strand, watching the aurora borealis painting itself upon Iceland's sky. I knew how to bide my time.

FINVARA

The truth of it was, I forgot her entirely.

Ireland was navigating stormy seas. The doors to Faery had been thrust open at the Battle of Ben Bulben, and open they had remained.

None of our lives would ever be the same—least of all my own.

Born Duncan O'Malley, a bastard fourth son of the Earl of Mayo, I had been largely ignored by my family and allowed to come and go as I liked for the first three decades of my life. My mother, orphaned young and fostered by a pirate captain, inherited his ship and took up smuggling, which led to her meeting my father on Claddagh quay over an illicit purchase of weaponry. The sealing of the deal turned carnal, or so I am given to understand, after my mother offered him a pull from her hip flask. The earl was smitten, and soon extracted a promise that my mother would one day return and marry him. I would never have known about any of this had my mother not related the story—my father was laced too tight to ever discuss it with me. That my parents loved each other was obvious to anyone who saw them together, but still it was hard for me to imagine how my mother had abided with him the short time she did—she died of fever barely a year after their union was legitimized.

After I came of age and spent a few years on my mother's crew, I too had chosen—and enjoyed—the freewheeling and masterless life of a sea captain. Until last year, when Ireland's ancient enemies had threatened, and a fairy king of legend—one of the Tuatha De Danaan—revived his connection with his mortal descendants by invading *my* mind and body.

Early on, he and I struggled for control of this earthly vessel. In the end we joined forces to defeat our Fomorian foes, and after the battle, we formed our *own* accord.

As part of that agreement—and at the urging of my cousin, the Irish queen—I exchanged the life of a smuggler for the bonds of public service. I assumed my ancestor's title as king of fairies. His centuries-long reign lived like the memory of a dream in the depths of my mind. Yet he and I parted ways—*he* moved on to the Land of Promise and no longer spoke in my mind, as he had done in the days leading up to the Battle of Ben Bulben. He would never again overpower my intellect, but I had acquired his magic, which drew on the elements and the land itself—though perhaps I would never be as adept at wielding it as he was.

A life at sea is not without peril or adversity, but let me not understate how unprepared I was for what this transformation would entail. Until the seal between Ireland and Faery was broken at the Battle of Ben Bulben, the great king's castle, Knock Ma, had been splendidly whole in Faery while only a ruin in Ireland. After the battle, the two overlapping worlds had attempted to merge—with varying degrees of success—and Knock Ma had manifested again in Ireland in its original glory. The very forest that surrounded its walls in Faery had regenerated, radically altering the Connacht countryside, creating all manner of difficulties with the local farmers. Even within the castle walls the worlds were merged, with corridors overrun by puck and sprite.

Suffice it to say, my transition from smuggler to statesman had much occupied my time and energy. Truly, it was no wonder that I had forgotten about her—the goblin princess that had been foisted upon me, and whom I had narrowly avoided *wedding*.

I was only reminded of her when a servant was sent from the kitchens to inquire about the dietary requirements of our guest, at which point a mad scramble ensued. Knock Ma was still working to establish relationships with local tradesmen, and I had no idea how a carriage was to be hired on such short notice. In the end, we paid a farmer for the use of his cart, and my household staff did what they could to make it comfortable. I understood the lady we were expecting to be somewhat savage, and I hoped that she would not be too deeply offended.

Before Queen Isolde had returned to Dublin, she had advised me to appoint a steward to help manage my affairs. I had not liked the idea at the time, but I was beginning to see the sense in it.

"Your Majesty?"

I did not immediately glance up as a servant entered my study, where I'd been looking over an ancient map of Ireland. I had always loved maps, from the time my mother had taught me to read them. This one depicted an Ireland *so* ancient it was almost completely blanketed by forests, its contours suggesting the country had once been more mountainous—and far less boggy.

"Aye?" I said at last, turning.

The fellow was one of the servants from my family's estate. My father had sent them "so that there might be familiar folk about you," but I suspected it had more to do with keeping an eye on me. The earl had always been fond of me, but until the Battle of Ben Bulben, he had never taken me very seriously. Understandably perhaps, as I had never taken *myself* very seriously.

"Princess Koli has arrived," announced the servant. The man was ever grim-faced—I suspected he had not come to Knock Ma voluntarily—but at the moment he looked like he had swallowed a toad.

A smile twitched on my lips at the poor fellow's discomfort, but I managed to conquer it. "Very well, Keane. See that she's escorted to her chamber, and that she's made comfortable."

"Your Majesty," the man cleared his throat nervously, "the lady is insisting—"

He was interrupted by a flock of ravens sweeping in through the door, filling the study with the noise of their great flapping wings and gravel-throated cries. The servant shouted and stumbled, and I staggered back toward the open casement.

Only a spell, I realized, fanning out one hand and murmuring, "Disperse." The birds had been conjured, and it was a simple enough trick to wave them away.

Merely shadows, they flew out the window and dissipated the moment the light struck them. But the last of the birds raked my head on its way out, sharp talons scraping the edge of my ear.

"Blast," I swore, swiping at the wound with the back of my

hand. Glancing at it, I saw a smear of bright blood. There was something unfamiliar in that spell. Nothing deadly, certainly, but something *angry*.

When I turned again to the servant, I encountered a figure clad in mourning crepe, her veil obscuring her features.

"Koli Alfdóttir?" I inquired. She was straight and narrow as a reed, and nearly as tall as I.

"Your *Majesty*," she spoke sternly, in perfect modern Irish, "I understand that neither of us is pleased by these circumstances, but was I to expect *less* than common courtesy from the king of fairies?"

"Forgive me, lady," I replied, feeling truly repentant despite the stinging wound on my ear. "We're topsy-turvy here, as you can see, and I quite forgot you were arriving today."

I realized belatedly that I had perhaps been more frank than necessary. The creature snatched the veil away from her face, and her gaze burned into me.

"*Did* you," she said, a quiet rage simmering under her words.

I had little experience with elves, though I had seen them at Ben Bulben. My ancestor's impressions also resided within me, and they were tinged with both fear and scorn. Fierce though she was, the princess was more womanly than I had expected—her ears were curved and pointed, but there was no sharpness to her other features, nor were there antlers or long teeth. Her skin did not appear to be inked with designs—though it was impossible to guess what there might be beneath that ghastly dress—nor did she wear the face paint of a warrior.

"My apologies, also, for your . . . for your mode of conveyance. My court is newly established, and I had not—"

"I understand that I am despised by you, sir," she seethed. "You have made that plain enough."

How I wished she would shout, or outwardly storm. This barely suppressed violence was far more troubling. There were both light elves and shadow elves among the Hidden Folk, and my ancestor had had little use for either—he considered them all to be arrogant and untrustworthy. They were said to be descended from Loki, the Norsemen's lord of mischief, who had disguised himself and fled the wrath of Odin after causing the death of one of his sons, discovering Iceland in the process. But the shadow elves had earned the reputation of goblins, sometimes murdering mortals in their beds. An Irish fairy might play a cruel or even gruesome prank, but the fairies were answerable to *me*. This woman was not.

"I *hope*, lady, that I have done no such thing," I said in a conciliatory tone.

But I had rejected her hand outright, and her father would have told her so. The lady's pride would of course be wounded. And lady she was, I could see that now. I began to feel ashamed of the various ways I had humiliated her.

There was aught I could do but try to smooth her ruffled feathers. Fortunately, my ancestor and I both had considerable experience in managing ruffled females.

"Come now, madam," I continued. "You must be fatigued from your journey. I will escort you personally to your chamber so that you may refresh yourself."

KOLI

Something about me had surprised him, that much was clear from the way he was staring. Was my appearance such a shock to him, or was it that he had expected to find a wart on my nose and a hump on my back? Hooves, perhaps, or a tail? I, too, had been surprised by his appearance. He was not the fair and golden lord that I had anticipated based on the stories my people told about the Irish. His skin was brown, and his head was covered by tight curls that had been burnished reddish gold in places, presumably by the sun. It reached down past his shoulders, but he wore it tied back from his face. His lips, framed by his dark beard, were an ashy rose color and shapely as a woman's. His eyes, like many an Icelander, were an unclouded blue.

Though he did not *look* like my idea of an Irish king, he was every bit as arrogant as I had expected.

"No, sir, you shall not," I replied. "I prefer the company of the servant."

I turned then, not bothering to ask his permission to withdraw, and walked straight out into the corridor. I heard him mutter something to his man, who scurried after me. I eyed the servant impatiently and he ducked his head in submission, or fear, or perhaps both, and then scurried around me.

"This way, my lady," he murmured, walking ahead.

Good, I thought. *Let them be frightened of me.* If the servants kept their distance, it would make my task easier.

Had I still thought it possible that I might be regarded as a guest rather than a prisoner, I would have been disappointed when the servant escorted me not to the keep, but to the very top of the castle's nearest tower. Still, its chamber was spacious and comfortable, and its barred windows offered sweeping views of the rolling hills, which were thickly wooded, with ghostly columns of mist reaching into the low clouds.

It would be a relief to finally be alone after the long voyage. If I could arrange for my meals to be brought up, I'd never need to leave—and perhaps that was just what they had hoped for. But I would not fulfill my purpose here by hiding in my chamber. Nor did I believe I could endure such confinement for long. At home, I had spent as little time as possible inside my father's stronghold.

I noticed an unfamiliar object in one corner of the room, across from the bed. It was a tall cabinet with a clock case at the

top—a grandfather clock. This was something outside the experience of an Icelandic villager—I recognized it from books I'd been
given by my English tutors. But it differed from other grandfather
clocks I had seen in that it looked to be made of an oil-stained
metal rather than wood, and its gearworks were not contained
behind the glass door of the cabinet. Rather, it appeared to have
spilled its inner workings on the outside—toothy gears of all sizes
were affixed around the base of the clock, and their movement
produced a rhythmic chorus of clicks. There were even small
pipes that occasionally released snake hisses of steam. The clock
case contained two faces, one for displaying the time, and one for
displaying, I believed, the phases of the moon.

"I will have that removed at once, my lady," the servant assured
me, and I could hear the shudder in his voice. "Such oddities have
been popping up all over the castle."

I turned to study him. "Popping up?"

"Yes, my lady," he replied, nervously dropping his gaze. "We
don't know why. Captain O'Malley—" He broke off and cleared
his throat. "His *Majesty* believes that with recent changes—with the
ancients walking among us again—time may have become confused.
No longer knows what belongs where—or when—if you follow."
He cleared his throat again. "One can only hope it is a temporary
condition. I will have it removed at once, my lady," he repeated.

"You will do no such thing," I countered, moving to stand as a
barrier between him and the clock. It was the only thing in Knock
Ma that had captured my interest, and I felt a sort of kinship with
it. Ugly and unwanted, ominous in its mystery. Unmoored from
time and place.

The servant looked bewildered, but he bowed his head in
assent. "I will send a maid to help you unpack your things." Then
he withdrew.

I turned and grasped the small knob on the clock cabinet's

door, tugging it open. I felt a movement of warm, strangely scented air against my face—it reminded me of incense, but tinged with something bitter. Inside, the clock was empty—a shadowy recess with no workings. I supposed it made sense, as the machinery had taken up residence on the outside.

I slipped my hand inside slowly, reaching to feel the back of the cabinet.

My arm passed through all the way to my shoulder before I yanked it out and staggered backward.

CURIOSITY

KOLI

"Odin's eye!" My hand should have met the back of the clock, or at least the wall, by about my elbow. I bent and peered into the empty case.

There's some enchantment at work.

I stood, hands on hips, pondering the mystery. Sensing movement near the tower stairway, I turned to find a maid entering the room.

"My lady," she said, curtsying.

I almost ordered her away so I could continue my examination of the clock. But now that my earlier anger had faded, I realized the servants might very well be my only source of information in this place. I couldn't afford to make them hate me. My curiosity would have to wait.

Over the course of the next few hours, I suffered a series of indignities that at home I would never have tolerated. The lady's maid, who introduced herself as Sorcha, was so frightened of me that I did finally have to dismiss her. Another servant then came to ask about my dietary requirements, and based on her questions, I became convinced that they had believed I dined on toads and spiders. And after I was summoned to dinner by yet another servant, I went down and discovered a sentry had been posted at the foot of the tower's stairway. I paused to study the stern-faced woman, and after the briefest glint of surprise when our eyes met, she continued staring straight ahead as if I were not there.

The sentry's features were similar to my own. She was tall, her hair long and dark, but a glossy brown. The backward curving tips of her ears parted her hair on either side of her head, while I had twisted up my hair in a way that left my elven ears in plain view. But her complexion was woody—mottled and faintly lined in a way that reminded me of the bark on a twig.

When I started down the enclosed corridor toward the keep, the sentry followed a short distance behind me. But after a moment I halted, sighing. I didn't know where I was going.

"I've been summoned to dinner," I said without turning. "Could you help me find the way?"

"When you reach the next corridor, turn right," the sentry replied in a neutral tone. Her voice had a husky quality, like my own. "Then left at the next one. After that, you'll find the door on your left."

I was ashamed of how relieved I felt to be acknowledged by her. Why should I care? The attention of the other servants had annoyed me.

When I reached the hall, I found it empty, and I wondered if there'd been a mistake. *Or perhaps he intends to keep me waiting again.*

But I was glad to have a moment to compose myself and look around. The hall was a comfortable size, neither cramped nor cavernous, with room for a long table. I had passed a much larger hall when I first arrived, just inside the castle's main entrance, which was probably used for more formal occasions. At the head of the table was a fireplace, hearth ablaze, and at the foot was an alcove with a window looking out onto a courtyard garden. The casement was open slightly, and I was almost certain I glimpsed flowers in full bloom—in March. The scent of roses wafted in.

I moved to the window and leaned out, breathing in the aroma. The garden was enclosed in a conservatory that butted right up against the exterior of the hall. It was a modern structure, light and open, with numerous glass panes and detailed ironwork. Night had fallen, but tiny blue lights flickered among the greenery, and I wondered whether they were living creatures. It was exactly what I had imagined a fairy garden would look like. I was puzzling over how the plants kept warm in a climate that saw so little sun, when I sensed movement behind me and turned.

"Only two days ago, you could not have enjoyed such a view."

"Your Majesty," I said, cursing the breathless note in my voice. I turned and curtsied, bowing my head to cover my sudden fluster.

"I'm sorry if I startled you," he said.

He should not have been *able* to startle me.

The king wore a dinner jacket that reminded me of a naval uniform—long, with a wide lapel and folded cuffs—and a wine-colored waistcoat. His boots were tall and polished to a high sheen. His appearance was very distinguished, but now I could see that the king, too, was uncomfortable. And there was also something odd about his eyes—in the low light of the hall, they seemed to faintly glow, as if lit from behind.

"What did you mean about the view, Your Majesty?" I asked, mostly to bridge the awkwardness.

He nodded at the window. "The conservatory. Two days ago, there was no such place."

That did not seem possible. I glanced again at the garden and noticed a rose now resting on the windowsill, where my hand had been only a moment ago. The bloom was so deeply purple it was almost black. I recalled the servant's uneasiness over objects "popping up." Clocks were one thing, but structures? No wonder the staff was skittish.

"Will you join me?" asked the king.

Servants entered the hall carrying steaming bowls and covered platters. I had expected the king would take the head of the table, but our places were set across from each other on the long sides. It was gracious of him, I had to admit. Perhaps he did regret his earlier treatment of me—or at least wished me to believe so.

"I'm not sure what you're used to, lady," began Finvara, "but we're rather sad here at present. There is no court to speak of. Queen Isolde has promised a visit, but with the upheaval, I think it will be some time before she's able to leave Dublin."

I assumed he referred to the aftermath of the recent battle. Much as I had dreaded the hateful gazes of his courtiers, this was worse—we could not but make awkward dinner companions. I wished that he had not felt obligated to entertain me.

"I have no expectation of becoming a true member of your court, Your Majesty," I said, hoping to spare us both further discomfort. "There is no need for you to take pains such as these. Will it not be better for us to be honest with each other?"

His chest swelled as he took a deep breath. He gestured to the table, and we both moved to sit down.

"I quite agree," he said as a footman ladled soup into shallow bowls. The king glanced up at him. "We'll manage the rest of it. All of you may go."

I stared as the servants departed.

"You as well," the king said to the sentry, who had stationed herself just inside the door. "Wait outside."

When we were alone, we sat a moment in strained silence. It appeared that the king, at least, was not afraid of me. Much as I might have enjoyed seeing him quaking like his servants, his unfazed manner—combined with the unorganized state of his court—was far more to my advantage. I might not be monitored as closely as I had feared.

"You are not afraid of me?" I couldn't resist asking him.

His eyebrow jutted up. "Should I be?"

My gaze faltered down to my soup bowl. He was not easily unbalanced. In truth, I had known it the moment he so coolly dispatched my *furies*, as one of my English tutors had referred to the magic that seemed to burst out of me when I experienced any kind of strong emotion. Even when one of the birds had drawn his blood—a thing that had never happened before—he had hardly reacted.

"We are enemies after all," I replied finally, meeting his gaze. I had not expected him to be afraid. I had expected him to be repulsed. If he was, I had not yet seen it in his face.

He held my gaze a moment. "You have been frank, lady. May I?"

I felt a flutter of anticipation and clasped my hands in my lap. His scrutiny was unsettling. I had been examined by both suitor and would-be assassin and felt it less.

"I imagine that you were sent here against your will," he began, "just as I have agreed to foster you against mine."

Foster? My blood boiled at the notion. Like marriages, fostering was often a component of peace accords. A child of one side would be sent to the court of the other to help ensure hostilities would not be renewed. While it was true I was still answerable to my father, I was certainly no longer a *child*. Neither had I been sent here against my will, though I had loathed the idea of it.

"*Fostering* may have been how it was presented, Your Majesty," I replied tightly. I knew that I should stop. *Let* him think me a child. The more he disregarded me the better. But my anger at his arrogance ran away with my tongue. "But I am not a child, as you well know, because your queen and my father had originally intended that we would *marry*."

He shook his head. "Forgive me for the poor choice of words. I am no statesman. I only wanted to make you feel welcome. To lessen the sting of . . ."

The king hesitated, looking uncomfortable, and I glared at him. "Of your rejecting my hand and instead offering to take me as your political prisoner?"

He sat back, sighing long and loud. "Do you *wish* to marry me, princess?"

I froze, the blunt question causing my breath to catch.

"I'm not asking what your loyalty to your people and your father requires of you," he continued. "Do you, yourself, wish to marry me?"

I swallowed. "I do not."

"No, indeed," he said with exasperating smugness. "We are very different—neither of us is anything that is pleasing to the other. But I was in no position to refuse the queen's request outright, as I expect you would not wish to refuse your father, so here we are. Can we not try and make the best of it?"

That I will certainly do. I bowed my head in acceptance. "Of course, Your Majesty."

I had known that I would be as distasteful to him as he was to me, yet his confirmation of it was more than I had bargained for. In physical form, *he* was not as repugnant as I had expected.

"I know that it is Your Ladyship who has been forced to leave your home," said the king, "but we are alike in ways that may not have occurred to you."

I stared at him, dubious.

He pushed his soup bowl away and rested his forearms on the table, interlacing his fingers. "Is Irish comfortable for you?" he asked. "We can speak English if you like. I regret I speak neither Elvish nor Icelandic."

This consideration on his part was unexpected. "My English is much better," I admitted. I had learned it from childhood. Irish had only been added in recent years, in preparation for the eventual takeover of the country by my father's allies.

"I have been here—" he continued in English "—this *castle* has been here, fewer than three months. Once I left my family for the Battle of Ben Bulben, I never returned to them. Before all this, I was a sailor. A ship's captain. It was a life that pleased me."

"So I understood, Your Majesty," I said with a nod. "That is, I knew that you had not always been king."

His laughter startled me. "The farthest thing from it. The ancient O'Malleys were pirates, and so was I."

FINVARA

The angry, brooding thing almost smiled, I would wager on it.

"A pirate," she said, raising her brows into the line of dark fringe that covered her forehead. "A sea raider, Your Majesty?"

I knew that she was thinking of her father's allies, the Fomorians, a tribe of monstrous creatures—demons, goblins, wraiths, giants—that hailed from a hidden island kingdom. I also knew that I had exaggerated in calling myself a pirate.

I reached for a decanter of wine and filled our glasses. "More of a smuggler," I admitted. "My blood made it inevitable—on both sides. My father is descended from Grace O'Malley, the pirate queen of Connacht, and I inherited my first ship from my mother. *She* was born a slave on an island in the Caribbean, where she was both freed and orphaned by a rebellion. She was raised by pirates and spent most of her life at sea."

The almost-smile faded. "I see," she replied faintly. I didn't know the lady well enough to guess whether she was given pause by my mother's enslavement or by my unorthodox family. As I understood it, the princess was her father's sole heir and carried the blood of two noble lines.

"When the captain who raised my mother died," I continued, "she inherited his ship and became a smuggler."

"What did she smuggle?"

"Men, mostly." Again her brows disappeared into her hair. "Escaped slaves. She carried them from America to Europe."

"To Ireland?"

"Aye, she did have business in Westport sometimes, not far from here. That's how she met my father."

The elf maid agitated her soup spoon. Her countenance was impenetrable as Hadrian's Wall, but I could feel the gears turning behind it. She was a guarded and watchful creature, and I sensed there was little she missed.

"And you followed into your mother's profession?" she asked.

"Eventually." Squeezing the stem of my wine glass, I pulled it toward me. "She left me to be raised by my father, though she did visit us sometimes—he was a widower, and lonely. As the youngest of four boys, and a bastard to boot, I had no prospects in Ireland. So when I was old enough, I persuaded her to take me on as crew. When America's war over slavery ended, she returned to Ireland and married my father, as she had promised him she would. I struck out on my own."

"Did you continue as a smuggler of men?"

I drank from my glass, fervently wishing for stronger spirits. The girl's dark stare raised the hairs on the back of my neck. I had aimed to soften her this evening, thinking I might prevent her becoming one more problem I'd have to personally manage. I realized now that this would not be the work of one evening— and might not be possible at *all*.

But no more angry ravens had descended upon me, and I considered that to be an improvement.

"With the war over, there was no need," I replied. "While smuggling out slaves, my mother had also smuggled *in* goods to raise money for her operation. I focused exclusively on that part of the venture."

"Profit, you mean."

She was quick, and direct. I gave a short nod. "Profit."

"What goods?"

"Absinthe, mostly. They developed a taste for it in America, in Louisiana specifically, but it is heavily taxed. The same for other imported spirits. Also coffee and chocolate."

Her curiosity apparently sated, she at last raised the spoon to her mouth. The spring-green soup smeared her burgundy lips. As her tongue swept the residue away, I noticed that her lips were soft and overfull. Even with her countenance resting, she appeared to pout. It was a contrast to the sharper lines of her face, and not an unpleasing one.

She blotted her lips with her napkin and set down her spoon.

"Not to your liking?" I asked.

"It's a . . ." She hesitated. ". . . a *texture* I have not encountered before."

I couldn't help laughing, and she glanced up sharply. *Tetchy as a ginger mare.*

"Peas," I said. "I don't much care for it either. Let me help you to something else."

I slid her soup bowl aside. "I had not intended to bore you with my personal history," I said, uncovering and peering into the other crockery. "The point I wished to make is that I'm just getting my bearings here myself. We'll be finding our way together."

As soon as the words left my mouth, I knew I had overplayed my hand. She studied me curiously, and I offered a placid smile before turning my attention to serving lamb and potatoes.

The sturdier fare appeared more to her liking, and bodily

needs took the place of conversation for a while. Her manners were more ladylike than I had expected, but there was no daintiness to her appetite.

When she had cleaned her plate, she sat with her eyes lowered. "The suggestion that we might undertake *anything* together seems, to my thinking, overly optimistic, Your Majesty."

This one is going to give me a run for my money.

"Maybe so," I agreed. "I hope I have not offended you. I only wanted you not to feel completely alone."

KOLI

I could not meet his gaze. Was any of this genuine, I wondered, or was he attempting to charm me out of my enmity? It was a game that two could play.

"That is kind of you, Your Majesty," I replied.

Seconds ticked by while he watched me. I concentrated on softening my features—loosened my jaw, parted my lips, flattened my brows. He reached for the wine and refilled both our glasses, though I had drunk only a sip or two from my own.

"Is there anything I can do to make you feel more at home?" he asked. "Is your chamber comfortable? Is there anything wanting?"

Meeting his eyes, I rested my forearms on the table. "I want for nothing but some way to occupy my time." *Some occupation that will allow me to move about the castle listening at doors.* "I'm not used to being idle."

He brightened. "Of course. What are your talents, my lady?"

I stared at him. *Conjuring ravens. Poaching sheep. Lurking in shadows. Walking barefoot over glacier ice, volcanic rock, and steaming ground.*

"Talents?"

"How did you bide your time in Iceland? Ladies in Ireland

and England . . . some play musical instruments, some knit or do needlepoint, some do charitable work . . ."

His face fell slightly, and I feared that I had failed to conceal my disgust. "Were you in some manner employed by your father?" he persisted. "What was your role in his court?"

The same as in this court: I spied on his enemies. Sometimes I killed them.

"I grew up very differently than you, sire," I said, "but my parents, too, lived apart. My mother, though descended from an ancient queen, was born a simple farmer's daughter. Shortly after my birth, we moved to a cottage on the crater lands outside our village. My father sent us gold and other things of value from Skaddafjall, but what wasn't spent on essentials was used to hire tutors. My mother said the world was growing smaller, and education would broaden my prospects."

The king's expression betrayed an awakening interest. Little as I liked to speak of myself, I knew it was an easy way of gaining another's trust.

"Your mother was a wise woman," he said.

"All else I learned from my mother was to aid our survival." I rested my folded arms on the table. His bright eyes reminded me of the gemlike glacier fragments that studded Iceland's shoreline. "My homeland is a sort of hell, Your Majesty," I said. "A place where your countrymen would not thrive." *And yet I would never have chosen to leave.* "The landscape is continuously sculpted by ice, fire, and wind. One is always a heartbeat away from death, whether through cataclysm, exposure, or starvation." I leaned toward him. "In Iceland, you can bake bread by burying it in the ground. Once, a family near my home was killed when a hot spring bubbled up under their cottage."

The king stared, and I knew I had interested him in my story. But I did not share the rest of it with him.

My mother's "congress with elves"—though it had been undertaken for the benefit of her people—was blamed for this calamity. The year before I came of age, the villagers drove us over the cliff behind our cottage. My mother plummeted to her death, and I clung unseen to the rocks until Ulf found me and took me to Skaddafjall.

"I do not wonder at your self-sufficiency," said the king, a breathless note in his voice. "What of your father?"

The inked brand between my shoulder blades tingled. I felt the Elf King's distant gaze upon me.

"When my mother died, I was taken to live with him. His stronghold stands invisible to mortals among the ridges of Vestrahorn Mountain. It is a bleak outpost, overlooking the black sands and untamed ocean, yet very peaceful. My life was very different there, but easier in some ways. I was never again hungry."

I sipped from my wine glass, collecting my thoughts. The events I was recounting had occurred decades ago, but I remembered them clearly. My mother's death, brought about by the scorn of her own countrymen, was a wound that had never healed. She had predicted that the memory of her sacrifice, and the peace that came with it, would one day be swallowed up by the Icelanders' hatred of the elves.

"And how did you occupy yourself there?" asked the king, bringing us back to the original question.

"That would be difficult to explain, Your Majesty. My life has stretched over many years. When I lived with my mother, I was not permitted to travel farther than the village, though we knew my father's people were always watching." *Which had saved my life, and somehow not my mother's.* "In my father's house, I was assigned a bodyguard, and I wandered all over the country with him as my companion." *I learned to understand the ravens. I ranged with my cousins, the young shadow lords, over the Icelandic highlands. I sewed vengeful seeds among the villagers who killed my mother.* "I was taught to use a bow, and often hunted game for our table."

I watched him closely, and I did not see him flinch at the idea of a lady bowhunter. I had been warned to expect strange notions about the proper place of women in these lower islands—and needlepoint as a vocation seemed a strange notion indeed—but Finvara's mother had been captain of a sailing ship. I was about to suggest that my skills at hunting might be of use here—I had not been permitted to bring my bow, and I hoped to persuade him to give me one—when Keane burst into the hall.

"Sire, you must come!"

The king turned, looking more weary than wary. "What is it?"

"There is a *ship* in the sky above the castle."

LOST

FINVARA

A ship?

I stood up, saying to the princess, "Forgive me for cutting short our conversation."

"Of course," she replied, rising from her chair. "May I join you, Your Majesty?" I could see that she was as eager as I was to inspect the new arrival.

I hesitated. Was she my prisoner? My guest? Was it advisable to trust her? She was right that it was deuced awkward. I certainly could not arm the woman with a bow, as she had seemed about to suggest a moment ago, but I could see no harm in her accompanying me.

I nodded. "If you wish."

We followed the servant to the great hall, which was dimly lit and empty at this hour. A stairway along one wall of the two-story chamber led up to the battlements, and we climbed and emerged on the parapet. I heard my companion's intake of breath as our eyes were drawn to the beast—floating in the sky above the forest, just southwest of the castle, was a full-sized sailing ship.

Night had fallen and a waxing spring moon, the color of the inside of an oyster shell, hung above the vessel, flooding light over the landscape below. Until recently, this area had been an unremarkable stretch of farmland and grassy, low hills that gave way gradually to the rough and mountainous bog country of Connemara. Now it was thickly forested, and Knock Ma was the highest inland hill in Connacht. On a bright evening like this, my lookouts *should* have seen an airship approaching from any direction.

The deck of the vessel was illuminated by lamps, though there was no sign of a crew. It was neither like my own ship *Aesop*, a fast-sailing barque, nor quite like Captain Grace O'Malley's *Sea Queen of Connacht*, a tub-hulled and stodgy Gap galleon that had once navigated the void between Ireland and Faery. Halfway from stem to stern, a great black balloon was suspended in the rigging. There were square rigs furled on either side of it, and a set of narrower sails—in the shape of wings—affixed to the hull. The figurehead was a black bird. Near the bow was inscribed the word *Corvus*—the name of the crow constellation, which appeared next to Virgo in the southern sky.

What the devil did it mean that the Elf King's daughter, who had greeted me with an attack of ravens, and a mysterious airship styled like one had been deposited on the doorstep of Knock Ma on the same day?

"Do you know this ship?" I asked the lady.

She shook her head. "I have never seen such a vessel, Your Majesty."

Was it likely she would have told me if she had? I turned to Keane. "How did it come to be here?"

"No one knows, sire," he replied. "It just appeared, like all the other things."

All the other things. Mechanical creatures, fantastical clocks, unsolvable puzzle boxes—you could hardly walk down a corridor without tripping over something that had just *appeared*. Now airships?

I continued to study the vessel, seeking some means of boarding her for a closer inspection. She rested about fifty yards above the castle's battlements and about the same distance to the southwest. The parlor tricks I had mastered using the magical knowledge inherited from my ancestor were not powerful enough to overcome the laws of gravity.

"Is it a ghost ship, your majesty?" asked Keane.

"She looks real enough to me," I replied. "Though if you're asking about the nature of her crew, I'd say that's anyone's guess."

"Your Majesty," said the lady, the whites of her eyes bright in the moonlight, "your servant has explained to me about the recent . . ." She dropped her gaze, and her lips worked silently as she sought a word that eluded her. There was something inexplicably appealing in this fleeting display of vulnerability. "About the recent *manifestations* in your court," she said finally. "I can imagine that they would be unnerving for you and your servants. But must it follow that they are evil in nature?"

It occurred to me that the same sentiment could easily be applied to her.

And it then occurred to me that might be exactly why she uttered it.

Ach, I was neither born nor bred to courtly intrigue. This waltzing about, trying to avoid saying anything that might make you appear weak to your enemies, seemed like a colossal waste of time. Was this how my life would be from now on?

"I quite agree with you," I replied, "but I'd feel a lot easier if I understood where the damned things are coming from, and why."

"How many are there?" she asked.

I shook my head. "There's a heap of them in the prison tower. How many, at this point, I could not say."

She considered a moment, and then said, "Why not allow me to look into this for you?"

I turned to study her. What exactly was she proposing?

"I can examine and catalog the items for a start," she continued. "Maybe it will help me to learn something about their nature." She glanced again at the ship, shrugging. "Maybe it won't. But I believe we can agree I have the time, and I suspect that you do not."

While her gaze was trained aloft, I took in her profile. She was so utterly alone here, and again it struck me how vulnerable she seemed. *Vulnerable as an adder.*

Yet this exile was not of her making. I did not want to marry her, certainly—neither did I wish to confine her to the tower. It was not kind, or even humane. There had been a time when I had tried to do such a thing to another woman—or rather my ancestor had tried to do so *through* me. I had cast an enchantment on a lady I now counted as a dear friend, and it still chilled me to think about it. I might not be fencepost-straight like the lady's husband—my cousin Edward, Earl of Meath—but my mother had not schooled me to mistreat any woman, even one who was my enemy. More pragmatically, would the princess not be likelier to make mischief without some occupation?

"It would please you to do this?" I asked, my fingers curling around my mother's brass compass and sundial, which I always carried in my trouser pocket.

The lady brightened—though still no smile—and looked at me. "It would, Your Majesty. These things, they interest me."

The openness of this statement had a softening effect—both on her features and my heart. I was beginning to take an interest as well, though not in the pile of oddities in the tower.

"Well then, go to it," I said. "It *should* be properly looked into, and you're right that I don't have the time." I glanced up at the ship. "But leave this one alone for now. Keane," I called to the servant, "set a watch, day and night. Notify me of any change, no matter how small. I'll not be caught out like King Priam of Troy."

KOLI

Growing up, I had hated my English tutors. They looked down on my mother and me, and in the beginning, they seemed to believe I was not capable of learning. I had worked hard at my lessons just to spite them. The last of these prickly old gentlemen had set out to *culture* me, and I had been made to study Britain's artists and poets. I had preferred the work of my own countrymen, particularly the stories of our gods that had been preserved across centuries. But one English poem had spoken to me, and I'd remembered it over the years—"Little Boy Lost" by William Blake.

> Father, father, where are you going
> O do not walk so fast.
> Speak father, speak to your little boy
> Or else I shall be lost,
> The night was dark, no father was there,
> The child was wet with dew.
> The mire was deep, & the child did weep
> And away the vapour flew.

I had expected the king to refuse my proposal. And though he had not, it would be dangerous to believe he'd been taken in by my portrayal of a "little *girl* lost." But was it really an act? When my mother died, I had learned not to hold on too tightly to anything. In fact, I'd had nothing left *to* hold on to. My father was my king, and all he expected of me was loyalty and obedience. He offered not affection, but approval. The only thing I'd ever thought of as my own was my homeland, and now that had been taken from me. Maybe Finvara had seen the truth and agreed because he felt sorry for me. It made me burn inside to think of it, despite the fact it had worked to my advantage.

"Thank you, Your Majesty," I replied.

The king could hardly turn his gaze from the ship. While it had merely roused my curiosity, I could certainly understand why he found it troubling. Now it occurred to me there was more than one reason for his fixation—he had chosen a life at sea, after all. And that had been taken from *him*.

But that was none of my concern. What mattered was I had been given license to move about the castle—far more than I had expected to accomplish on my first day.

"Your Majesty, if you will permit, I am ready to retire."

"Of course," he said, breaking from his trance. He beckoned his man. "Help the princess find her way back to her chamber."

"Thank you, sire," I replied, curtsying and turning from him. "I know the way."

I walked on, wondering whether he'd send the servant after me anyway, but he didn't. Descending the stairs on the way back to the keep I encountered my guard, who followed me as I continued into the corridor that wound around to my tower.

To be truly effective as a spy in this court, I would have to gain the king's full trust—I began to feel that might be possible. For now, I had an occupation that would allow me to familiarize myself with the layout of the castle, as well as its routines, inhabitants, and defenses.

At the moment, however, I was looking forward to solitude. This court was not yet fully established, but it was still more bustle than I was used to. At home in Skaddafjall, I rarely held a conversation as long as the one between the king and I at dinner. And there were no nervously chattering servants. Ulf and I had sometimes talked through long winter nights, but he told me of battles he'd fought, and long-dead heroes. I knew nothing about his mother or father.

As I reached the top of the stairs and entered my chamber, my gaze fell again on the clock, looming like a dark sentry at the foot of the bed.

I moved closer, watching its workings, listening to the steady ticktock, the soft clicking of gears, and occasional hisses of steam. Did the mechanics of it have any purpose? Did the *whole* of it have any purpose, beyond the obvious? These were the questions the king and I had agreed that I would try to answer.

Feeling a pain at the back of my head, I reached around and began working my hairpins loose. As the tight twist uncoiled—the curtain of hair falling heavily about my shoulders—I sighed audibly and massaged my sore scalp. This would be the last day that I arranged my hair, or anything else, in an effort to look more like *them*. Let them think me the wild thing of nature that I most certainly was.

FINVARA

After she was gone, I continued to study *Corvus* with a mixture of wariness and longing. I did not trust this apparition. Queen Isolde would have to be notified, which might very well mean that on top of playing host to a woman who more than likely wished a plague would take me, I might soon have my overbearing and obstinate cousin on my hands. The timing of it was demoralizing.

And yet, in my seafarer's heart, I craved some means of boarding the mysterious vessel so I might sail straight away from my destiny. From the court. From the crown. From the servants.

From the problem of Koli Alfdóttir and her scheming relations.

I did not, in fairness, know for certain that any scheming was afoot. But I'd be a fool not to assume that it was. The Fomorians and their northern elven allies were centuries-old enemies of the Irish, and no one entertained the notion that they'd been subdued for good. It was the reason Queen Isolde had insisted on placing someone she trusted in this outpost—to ensure the ambivalent fairy folk remained loyal to Ireland, and to keep eyes on the remote and lightly populated western wilds, where our ancient foes had traditionally made landfall.

"Devil take them all," I muttered, clutching the edge of the parapet wall. By *all* I meant both my enemies and my royal cousin, who'd abandoned me to this fate. My relationship with Izzy had always been complicated, though I knew she enjoyed my company, and she'd even sought my advice at times. But I'd guided my own ship far too long to feel easy under the management of others.

It didn't help matters that *Corvus* was so compelling. When my mind and body had first been invaded by my ancestor, the original King Finvara, my cousin and I had journeyed on Grace O'Malley's Gap galleon to Faery. Though I'd been no more than a passenger in my own body at that time, I recalled every detail. The *Sea Queen of Connacht* had been built specifically for navigating the void between the overlapping worlds of Ireland and Faery, and its methods of propulsion were still a mystery to me. But *Corvus*—with the incorporation of the hot air balloon and wing-like sails—she was a true airship. What must she be capable of? I itched to board her and find out.

Which would be a most foolish thing to do. Bollocks.

It wasn't just the risk to my person. I was *responsible* now. Responsible for upholding the treaty between Ireland and our enemies. Responsible for nurturing the fledgling alliance between Faery and the Irish people—quite possibly the touchiest of the undertakings, as the two had been separated for centuries by the seal that was broken at Ben Bulben less than three months ago.

"Keane," I called, turning decisively from the ship. The man nearly jumped out of his skin.

"Your Majesty?"

"Ask the chamberlain to come to my study." I walked back toward the stairs, muttering, "My life needs simplifying."

MISCHIEF

FINVARA

I watched the servant sweep away the ropes of hair that had dropped onto the floor in my study. My head felt light and strange, like it might float away from my body. I ran my hand over my closely shorn scalp and beardless jaw.

"You look very distinguished, Your Majesty," said the chamberlain, raising a mirror.

It came as a shock—my hair had never been short. It aged me, I thought. Perhaps it was only that I looked more serious with the heavy lines of cheek and jaw exposed, and the dark slashes of brow that now took center stage. Perhaps that was for the best. At any rate, it would be one less thing weighing on me.

"Thank you, Reid," I replied.

The man bowed. "Will there be anything else, Your Majesty?"

"No, you may go." Before he had exited the chamber, I called, "Hold, a moment. Run down Doro if you can, and send him to me."

Doro was a fairy who was somehow attached to Knock Ma. His form was really no different from any Irish gentleman's, though his flesh was so pale it glowed in the shadows. I knew very little about him, except that he was always either underfoot or nowhere to be found. Truth be told, the fellow was odd. But I needed a steward, and he'd told me he had served in that capacity before. If I didn't make some changes, I was going to make a hash of it all.

I poured a glass of whiskey and returned to studying the map of Ireland on the wall. I supposed I should go to bed. The rest of the castle seemed to have retired, and it was clear I'd roused Reid from his sleep, though to his credit the man had not complained. I liked these quiet hours when I was alone and could think. I had always loved nights at sea in fair weather, *Aesop* gently rocking and creaking under a blanket of brilliant stars.

I couldn't help wondering about the Elf King's daughter. Was she indeed resting after her long journey? My hunch said not—she had simply had enough of my company. I suspected that she, not unlike myself, was a creature that preferred her own. The difference was that she would have that option in the days ahead, whereas I must prepare for the impending official visit by my father, the Earl of Mayo.

"*Blast*," I muttered. The peace I'd enjoyed as a thrice-redundant son was about to come to an end. The queen's appointment had thrust me up on a level with Owen, my eldest brother, if not higher. I had been installed here less than a fortnight when the telegram about my father's visit had arrived. He might have at least waited for my affairs to settle before descending upon me. No doubt he'd scorn the state of things and provide all manner of unsought advice.

"Your Majesty has made a change."

I turned, irritated to find Doro had managed to enter my study without my notice.

"There you are," I said. "Where is it you disappear to?"

He smiled graciously, though it was a ridiculous question. The only creatures in this place that did *not* disappear and reappear with regularity were the mortal servants.

"Forgive me, Your Majesty," he replied smoothly. "I do not mean to *disappear*. I am bound to this place, as you know, so I am never far away."

His manner of address was flawless, like a courtier's. "That's just it," I replied. "I *don't* really know."

The gentleman widened his heavy-lidded eyes, waiting for me to explain. He had an almost feminine beauty, with soulful light gray eyes and full lips. The bones of his face were delicate, too. But there was nothing feminine about his strongly built frame. He had told me he'd served as steward to the original Finvara's succession of queens. For myself, I never would have allowed the handsome sprite such easy and regular access to my wife.

"Never mind," I said. "I've brought you here because I need a steward—someone to save me from my poor head for details, and also to help me get on better with my subjects, who seem skittish of me. Are you up to it?"

"Of course, Your Majesty," he replied with a polite bow. "I would be honored."

I stepped toward the window and gazed out at the phantom airship. "My people from Mayo are coming in two days. My father, and my eldest brother and his wife. See that rooms are prepared, and that the larder is adequately provisioned."

"I will, sire. Have you some entertainment in mind for them?"

I glanced back at him. "We'll feed them. Let them shoot our birds. What else would you suggest?"

His lips parted, and he seemed to hesitate—possibly reconsidering his decision to assist in such a hopeless cause. "I believe balls are customary, even among mortal folk?"

I frowned. "Aye."

"A masquerade, perhaps? I understand they have become quite fashionable."

It was the very last thing I wanted to be doing. I took a deep breath. "A masquerade it is."

He nodded, seeming pleased. "What disguise will Your Majesty wear?"

Finally turning from the window, I replied, "I haven't the slightest idea. You choose for me. Nothing showy. Something that covers my face."

I have become dull overnight. The old Duncan had lived for a good revel, as had the original King Finvara. All I wanted now was to have as little notice taken of me as possible. Soon I would no longer recognize myself.

Doro gave another nod. "I will see to it. Who else shall be invited?"

Was there no end to the tedious detail? I rubbed my forehead. "We'd better have the County Galway landholders, as they are the ones most affected by our presence. We'll need to hire goods and services from their tenants and merchants."

"Very good. Might I suggest inviting gentry from all the Connacht counties? The region is King Finvara's traditional domain."

"It's best," I agreed reluctantly. "What of your people? The fairies, I mean. I hardly know what's appropriate."

"They are *your* people, sire. I hope I may be forgiven for saying so."

"Certainly, they are. But I have acquired them without understanding how to rule them. What will they expect? How am I to avoid giving offense?"

I waited while he considered the question. "You must invite them, of course."

"*All* of them?" I asked, dismayed.

"I would not advise that, no," he replied. "Each faction follows a leader of sorts, much like your Irish counties. These leaders and their families should be invited, but it would offend them were we to invite all of Faery, nor could Knock Ma hold them all. I can see to it for you, Your Majesty."

"Excellent, and that brings me to another question." I fixed my gaze on him. "Is there any way of keeping them out? I don't mean of the masquerade. Just generally."

He frowned. "Out of the castle, you mean?"

"Aye. They come and go like birds." Despite the fact the Faery version of Knock Ma had asserted itself in Ireland, the fairies appeared still able to flit between worlds—and it was maddening. "Knock Ma is a fortress, and the first line of defense should our enemies come calling. I don't know how I am to secure it when there are all manner of creatures popping in and out of Faery, tramping through corridors, tripping the guards, and pulling the servants' ears. It's like the passengers are swinging in the rigging."

"I understand," he replied. "You wish Knock Ma to be emptied of fairy folk."

"Not all. The woodland fairies—the *firglas*—they are steady, and handy to have about. Good fighters. I know they served as the castle guard in the time of my predecessor, and I intend to carry on with that tradition. I must rely on your experience with the others. If turning them out will cause trouble, we will have to find another way."

Doro studied me a moment, and I wondered what he was thinking. Where were his loyalties? Finally he said, "Depend on me, sire. I will relay your wishes to the fairies. Then I can cast a boundary spell around the castle and grounds to ensure your wishes are respected."

"Very good," I agreed, relieved.

"What of our guest?" he asked. "Do you intend for the Elf King's daughter to attend the masquerade?"

I tried to read his opinion on the matter, but his expression, as always, was respectfully neutral. "She may come if she likes," I said. "I don't see any harm in it, and I don't wish her to feel that she's a prisoner. In fact, I will speak to her about it myself."

The servant nodded. "Is there anything else I can do for you, Your Majesty?"

"That will be all for now, Doro. Thank you."

He bowed and left the study.

I wished I had consulted him earlier. I was completely out of my depth. It was a feeling I was unaccustomed to, and it didn't sit well. I had absorbed much from my ancestor, the original King Finvara, but I had not *become* him. I had his knowledge of magic, but beyond the simplest spells, wielding that magic required trial and error. I could wield a sword as he could, but I had learned that art at sea—mostly to remedy boredom, as pistols and daggers were far more practical. When it came to the history and workings of this place I now called home, the memories were there, but they came to me in unorganized fragments. Many of his memories, though mightily entertaining (truly his exploits were legendary), were completely useless.

The competence of the fairy steward was a great relief.

KOLI

Not yet ready for sleep, I spent some time putting away the rest of my things. The pile of new gowns—which I had barely glanced at before handing them over to Sorcha, my maid—were safely stowed in the wardrobe. Everything ornamental that had been given to me before the journey, including a number of glittering pieces of jewelry that had belonged to an elven relation, the maid had tucked away in a box on the vanity—and there they would stay. I took my fox-fur-lined hunting boots out of the trunk and set them next to the wardrobe, and I placed my folded archer's dress on top of the stack of gowns. Finally, I drew out a raven feather as long as my forearm, and ran my fingers along its edge before setting it on the bedside table. It had belonged to the chief of the raven family that lived at Skaddafjall—a bird that I had come to know, and that had sometimes followed me on hunting trips. Next to the feather, I placed a glittering, fist-sized hunk of white spar that my mother had found when she was a child.

After that I sat, staring into the fire. It had been a strange day, none of it anything like what I had anticipated. I had never imagined the king would insult me so brazenly as to *forget* me. Neither had I expected to find him so congenial as I had at dinner. Was it possible that both had been contrived to befuddle me? Contrived or not, I was indeed befuddled.

Sighing, I rose from my seat by the fire and wandered back to the grandfather clock, determined to understand it better—as well as to distract my mind from questions I could not yet hope to answer.

I opened the cabinet, and again I tried and failed to feel the back wall, which should have rested perhaps eight inches beyond the opening. After a moment's consideration, I lifted one foot and stepped slowly into the blackness. The opening was wide enough to admit me, but I had to duck my head.

Too late I realized what should have been obvious—if there was no back wall, there might also be no *floor*. With no place for my foot to land, I pitched forward, falling into the clock with a startled shout. I found myself flailing in a starry darkness. My body spun as I tried to catch the edges of the cabinet, but I had drifted away from it. I could still see my chamber, as if through a window in the backdrop of stars. I lunged toward it but managed only to drift further away.

"*Friend in darkness*," I murmured in my native language, and a cool flame sprouted over the palm of my hand. There was nothing in this void to illuminate, but casting the familiar spell helped to ease my panic.

"Koli Alfdóttir."

The nearby voice so startled me that my arms flailed again, spinning me around. I saw another window in the black, this one filled by the face of a stranger. He reached through the opening and said, "I've got you."

The fact he was a stranger did not stop me from grasping his hand and holding on as if my life depended on it. I felt myself hauled through the emptiness until finally I tumbled onto a hard surface. Another hand closed over my arm, and I jumped quickly to my feet, jerking away.

"Who are you?" I demanded.

He bowed. "My name is Far Dorocha."

I stared, uncomprehending. My Irish was far from perfect, but it had sounded like "dark man."

"Far . . .?"

"A mouthful, I realize. The fairy queen always called me 'Doro,' and you may do the same if you like."

"You're a fairy?" I asked, casting a wary glance around me. We were standing on the deck of a ship, surrounded on all sides by stars—except for directly above us, where the opening of a rocky cavern gaped like another window in the darkness. The cavern appeared in fact to be a tunnel, and an indistinct brightness winked at the far end of it. "Are we *in* Faery?"

"This is the Gap," replied the man. "The void between Faery and Ireland. You are on my vessel, *Black Swan*."

I noticed now that his ship was similar to the one floating in the sky over Knock Ma. Only it was much smaller, had no balloon, and its figurehead was a swan.

"How do you know who I am?" I demanded. He was a luminous creature, and more like I'd imagined Finvara before our actual meeting—fair features, silver hair, and light eyes. He was smartly dressed in a dark wool suit with silver buttons that gleamed dully in the lamplight. Were he mortal, I would have judged him to be no more than thirty, but I suspected that he was not.

"I know who you are for two reasons," he replied, switching from Irish to English. "I have always served as the personal steward of the fairy queen, and though that title is currently unclaimed, I remain in the thrall of the fairy *king*, Finvara."

I narrowed my eyes. "Then you must know that I now reside at Knock Ma. Can you help me to return?"

Something knowing and amused glinted in his gaze. "Why would you want to return to a man who has made you a prisoner?"

"It is not the *man*," I said shortly. "And I am no prisoner. There is an agreement between the man and my father. I am duty bound. If you know me, as you say you do, you would know that as well."

He folded his arms. "And so I do. Will it surprise you to hear I also know your father? The second of the two reasons that I know who you are."

I stared at him, and again felt the mark between my shoulder blades tingle. "It *would* surprise me," I replied. "In fact, I'm not sure that I would believe it."

He smiled, and something about it made me shiver. "I don't blame you," he said. "Regardless, I will certainly return you to Knock Ma—*after* I explain why I've brought you here. Will that help to allay your fears?"

"I am not frightened," I replied, glaring. "And if you *have* brought me here, you had better tell me why without delay."

"Forgive me," he said with a bow of his head. "I meant no insult. Perhaps I mistook the appearance of these dark guardians. It's a keen bit of magic, conjuring them in this place. It suggests there is more to you than meets the eye."

Turning to follow his gaze, I discovered four ravens perched on the railing behind me, watching him with their intelligent eyes. I had not *knowingly* conjured them, but there was no need for him to know that.

"What is your business with my father?" I asked.

"You, in fact," he replied.

I stiffened in wariness. "I don't understand."

"It will require some explaining." He stepped closer to me, and the hairs on the back of my neck prickled. His fair features were accompanied by a serenely confident demeanor, but there was nothing dull about him. His gaze was arch and intense. His hair was pulled back rather severely, emphasizing the angular lines of his face.

"You see, your father and I are allies."

I frowned. "Did you not say you serve King Finvara?"

"I have two masters, but only one of them do I truly serve. I have vowed to take Knock Ma—and its kingship—and join with your father in conquering Ireland."

After this outlandish statement, I could only stare at him.

"Conquering Ireland," I repeated.

He nodded. "Finvara has allied himself with the Irish—with mortals. I call it foolish."

"He is Irish himself," I reminded him. "Also, the Irish and the fairies fought side by side at Ben Bulben."

"Ireland's fairy folk are more natural allies of *your* kinsmen—the elves and the other Hidden Folk—than they are of the Irish. The present King Finvara is too thoroughly an Irishman to ever see it this way."

Could this fairy really be an ally of my father, or was it a kind of trap or test of loyalty? If the latter, who had set it? Finvara? My own father?

The air in the strange in-between world was stuffy and static. I felt a bead of sweat trickle between my shoulder blades.

"You don't know whether to trust me," he said at length. "It's understandable."

There was little I could say without committing myself one way or the other, but finally I reminded him, "You said that your business with my father related to me in some way. You haven't said how."

"In two ways," he replied, curling a hand over the railing. "First, I cannot carry out this plan alone. I am bound by ancient magic to Finvara and his queen. I cannot raise my hand against him. *You* can."

Did he mean that I was valuable because I could *kill* Finvara and he could not? My father had told me that an order to eliminate Finvara might come. It would not be the first time I had served the Elf King in this way. But hearing it spoken of so soon—especially having now spent time in the king's company—came as a shock. It was a good reminder to preserve distance between myself and Finvara.

"And what is the second way this relates to me?"

He took a step toward me, and I shivered again. "Finvara has rejected your hand."

One of the ravens on the railing gave a startled squawk. My face went hot, and I dug my fingernails dug into the palms of my hands.

"I'll not be so foolish," he continued. "Once I am the fairy king, my bond to Finvara's house will be broken, and you and I will rule Ireland together with your father's blessing. You will become the queen you were born to be. *Corvus* is my betrothal gift to you—and, I hope, enough proof for you to trust that I am in earnest."

My thoughts churned. Was it possible that my father had promised me to this creature? When? Why hadn't he told me?

There came a time in my childhood when I understood that even though my mother had no husband, most women did. She had made the choice not to marry my father, but I would not be permitted to do the same. Whether, or whom, I married was a decision that would be made by the Elf King. As for romantic love, I believed it had been created by storytellers. The histories I had read taught me that arranged marriages sometimes kindled affection. But knowing that I was likely to be offered to one of my father's allies, I had no such expectations. Even the less fierce among my Icelandic cousins, the so-called "light" elves, were cool spirits with hollow passions. In the world I grew up in, loyalty was all that mattered.

None of this had ever much worried me, nor did it now. In fact, what Far Dorocha was proposing felt right in every way—we were natural allies. His position as a bond servant to the house of Finvara was an unlooked-for advantage. He could move about freely, and he would be trusted with information that I wouldn't, even if I remained at court for years. It was a partnership blessed by the gods if ever there was one.

So appealing was the arrangement he described that I'd never have trusted it without the gift of *Corvus*. It was not unthinkable that even the ship was part of an elaborate trap of Finvara's. But having been present when the king first saw it, I knew it wasn't.

"Have you created them all, then?" I asked. "These strange objects that have confounded the king and his court?"

He shook his head. "I have only tapped into a vein of magic torn open when the seal between Faery and Ireland was broken."

"Are you a sorcerer?" I thought of my ancestress, Gunnhild, who'd been a sorceress as well as a deadly shield-maid.

Again his eyes glinted. "Of a kind. I was a druid once. The last of Ireland's most powerful druids, in fact, and a practitioner of blood magic. I am now a student of alchemy."

Blood magic. It was practiced by my father's seer. In some ways more powerful than elemental magic, it could be used to bind an oath, to strengthen a spell, or even to speak with the dead. It was also used for divining the future, though the information was only as good as the interpreter.

"What is alchemy?" I asked.

"It is a scientific pursuit concerned with transmutation."

I shook my head to convey my lack of understanding.

"Transmutation simply means changing one thing to another. To something better, or higher. Most alchemists are obsessed with creating gold from metals like tin. But it has far more interesting applications."

I still wasn't sure I understood him. But I *had* come here through a clock that had been transformed into a gateway to another world.

"Are you equal to it?" he asked suddenly, reaching for my hand. His fingers were cool and dry despite the humid atmosphere.

I took a step backward. "To the marriage or the assassination, sir?"

He laughed at my frankness, genuine mirth in his voice now. "Both."

"Of course," I said with a nod. "I have not come here to attend balls or learn lacemaking. I am my father's to command. It has only come sooner than I expected." I felt ashamed of the note of apology—and hint of reluctance—in my tone.

He released my hand, slowly turning to lean his forearms against the ship's rail. "It has not come *yet*. It doesn't make sense to behead the court until we are sure the courtiers will follow someone else. Redirecting their loyalty will be *my* task."

"Won't that be risky?"

Glancing at me, he replied, "Rest assured I will keep you out of it until we're certain. Should this treachery be traced back to me, it will not lead to *you*. They don't know what to think of their new king. There is some uneasiness among them about all of these changes, and they are unsure of their place in a world without boundaries. This will work in our favor."

He gazed out at the stars and continued, "Your father has told me that you do not shrink from spilling blood. When the time is right, you will find a weapon in your bedchamber."

I nodded, my heart beating faster. Anticipation? If so, why was I feeling uneasy?

"And until then?" I asked.

"Until then, give the king no reason to suspect you. I trust you to judge whether that will be best accomplished by becoming a courtier or by keeping quiet and out of the way. I will come to you when I can, and it will be best if you don't seek me out. I was watching for you this time, but I might not always be. You could become lost in the Gap."

"I understand."

Again he took my hands. "I may tell your father that you have approved of this plan?"

My eyebrows lifted. "It is unnecessary. He is my sovereign, and I serve him."

He smiled. "It has been my great pleasure to meet you, princess." The look in his eyes almost made me believe he was not repulsed. By my ancestry. By my gruff manner and graceless appearance.

He leaned closer, whispering beside my ear. "I suspect there are deep mysteries running behind your raven gaze. I look forward to unlocking them."

I felt a crawling sensation under my skin.

When he returned me to my chamber it was late, though still I didn't sleep.

In Skaddafjall, my bedchamber was also in a tower, but I had never been enclosed like this. My rooms there had a flagstone terrace, overlooking the mountain that sloped perilously toward the ocean, and on clear nights I would order my bed moved and sleep under the stars. The winters were bitterly cold, and I would cover up with furs and watch the aurora borealis, ribbons of purple and green rippling across the sky like waking dreams.

These were just the nights I spent inside castle walls. For I spent as many as I could outside in the open countryside.

In Knock Ma, the ceiling was far too close, and the window

only showed me the forest, which I had already begun to dread. I did not trust so many trees all in one place. Not only were they enormous living creatures—the lower portions of their bodies plumbing depths unknown, like an iceberg—I sensed that they were more aware than they appeared. When the breeze moved among their branches, the leaves made a sound like whispering. But it was a language I did not understand.

Though I did at last try, sleep wouldn't come, and in the small hours I crept down the stairs, intending to begin the task I'd been given by the king and at the same time explore the castle. I moved slowly and silently, keeping to the shadows, testing whether I could mark the sentry below before she marked me. When I rounded the final bend of the staircase I heard laughter, and I sank against the wall, listening.

"She's an ugly, scarecrow of a thing, is she not?"

The speaker's voice was shrill. I crept down four more stairs, craning my neck to see. Just beyond the erect form of the sentry were several smaller creatures lounging about on the flagstones like fox kits in the sun. They were angular and twiglike, their faces pointed and woody, their hair the dust-green of heath flora, but wild like thistledown.

"You know they intended her to marry the king!"

I froze, pressing my fingers into the wall's rough stones.

"A goblin princess!" scoffed the first speaker. "Married to Finvara!" The creature made a hissing noise.

Goblin. It was an unforgiveable slur. My father had made use of those base and vicious creatures in his ancient wars, and his enemies whispered that the blood of goblins and shadow elves had become mingled.

"What a shame that would have been," continued the little beast. "Him who's always courted the most beautiful women in Ireland."

The flesh at the back of my neck felt hot, and my breaths shortened.

"'Twas the queen, his own cousin, who ordered it. And *still* he'd have none of it! Locked her in the tower instead."

The twig people twittered with laughter. I pressed my hands to my chest, feeling like it might split the seams of the confining garment I wore. Then, with a sudden, wrenching tug, knife-shaped shadows swooped out of my chest.

"There'll be mischief, mark my—"

The speaker broke off with a frightened squeal as my furies swept to the bottom of the stairs, flapping madly, giving chase until the twig people scattered and disappeared into crevices in the stone.

I'll give you mischief.

BEARINGS

KOLI

When I reached the bottom of the stairs, heart pounding, I watched my furies dissipate into the shadows of the corridor. Something about their arrival had been different this time—I wouldn't go so far as to say I deliberately conjured them, yet there *had* been a moment when my anger seemed to make an opening for them.

I glanced at the sentry before starting down the corridor—and would have sworn she was trying not to smile.

"I have business elsewhere in the castle," I announced stiffly in Irish as I walked on. "The king has authorized it."

"Indeed, the king has notified me," replied the fairy woman, "Lady Scarecrow."

I stopped and turned, eyeing her sharply. Her smile had broken free, but I saw that it was not a mocking one. So she'd found the scare I'd given the twig people to be a good joke. These Irish fairies were not, as I had supposed, united in their scorn of me. It boded well for Doro's scheme, and it also made me feel slightly less alone.

"Can you tell me where to find the prison tower?" I asked her.

"Follow the corridor back toward the keep, lady," continued the guard, "and I will direct you."

The corridor torches blazed with spell-born flames. They put out white light with no smoke and very little heat. I trailed my fingers along the cold stones as we walked.

"What is your name?" I called to the sentry, who followed at a respectful distance.

"Treig, lady."

"Treig," I repeated. It sounded like an Elvish word—*trygg*. Loyal.

We made our way back to the corridor that ran between the great and lesser halls, and then wound around the courtyard.

"Watch for the stairs to the parapet, on your right," she directed. "The base of the tower contains a cistern, so the dungeon can only be accessed from above."

"Is anyone there?"

"There are no prisoners, lady, if that is your question. Though in Knock Ma it is never possible to say with certainty whether a chamber will be empty at any given time."

It was no wonder the king always appeared, to some degree, bewildered. This court was in a state my father would not have tolerated.

We found the stairway and climbed out of the keep and into the open air. The night was clear and cold, and *Corvus* still floated in the moon-bright sky. Had I been alone, I would have stopped to study the ship again—everything had changed since I'd first seen her.

We continued along the open parapet and then up another set of stairs to the top of the tower. Treig lifted the bar on the door, and we went inside. An empty landing provided access to a stairway that curved down around the inner tower wall, and I started descending into the windowless chamber.

"Be careful, lady," Treig advised. The stairway was narrow and had no railing.

At the bottom was a chamber containing four barred cells. The open area between these cells was littered with colorful objects. It was as if a demented inventor had worked for years, only to quit his workshop in the end, abandoning his creations in a heap. And these creations were *alive*, or seemed so. A murmur of mechanical noises rose from the clutter—clock ticks, soft hisses, metallic pinging, and chimes both tinny and resonant. Sometimes these noises accompanied physical activity—small movements that could be explained by items shifting as they settled.

"Odin's *eye*," I swore under my breath, impressed by the size of the collection.

Kneeling at the edge of the jumbled pile, I reached for a globe formed of badly tarnished silver—gleaming ridges interrupted its smooth surface, connecting the sections like puzzle pieces. I tried for a few moments to open the globe by pressing and pulling at the ridges. When this failed, I whispered a spell for unlocking, but still nothing happened.

I set the globe aside and picked up a porcelain doll, turning it over in my hands. She was a pale and gleaming thing with black hair and a green gown, and a windup mechanism at her back. The doll's internal workings clicked loudly as I turned the key. When the key would budge no further I released it, watching to see what would happen, and the doll jerked from my hands. A set of wings had emerged from the satin gown, and they propelled the doll in flight a few yards across the chamber. Then it dropped and once again lay motionless.

I stood up, sighing. Even working day and night, it could take months to study and catalog everything. This was exactly what I had asked for—an occupation to give me an excuse to leave my chamber and to keep me from going slowly mad. Yet now I found myself most interested in how these little machines had come about. Doro had referred to a "vein of magic" that had opened when the seal between fairy and Ireland had been broken. And the king's servant, Keane—he'd told me Finvara suggested that time had been confused by the merging of the ancient and modern worlds. These two ideas seemed to fit together into a reasonable enough explanation. Did the things also have some purpose, though, or were they just things?

"Unsettling, are they not, lady?" said Treig. She had come down the stairs behind me.

"Indeed," I murmured. But they didn't unsettle me at all. The noises they made were soothing, reminding me of the rhythmic, breathy sounds of sleep. Busy as they sounded, were they in fact resting? Could they be woken?

Moving in among them, I gently lifted a birdcage. I turned another windup key, and the mouse-sized yellow bird on the perch inside began to tweet, its dainty feet and head moving in a jerky fashion. The movement was mesmerizing, and when it stopped, I wound it again. Then again.

I touched the bars of the cage and whispered a spell: *Wake.* I started as the bird's wings stirred momentarily to life, as if it would take flight. Then they lowered again.

These objects might have been created by fairy magic, but a mortal and more modern magic was also at work. I wondered whether the king knew enough about mechanical workings to explain them to me. Would I have an opportunity to ask him?

Doro had said that I was free to spend more time in Finvara's company or keep to myself. The king did not appear to find my company distasteful—nor I his, to my astonishment. That being the case, I might as well proceed as I'd begun, and maybe he would start to trust me.

A yawn overtook me as I replaced the birdcage. I did not require much sleep, but the day had been taxing, and suddenly I felt ready to retire. Rising, I picked my way back toward the stairs.

I noticed another bird shape on the edge of the rubble—a raven formed of a grimy metal, like the grandfather clock. It was perched on a stand, and its parts were segmented in a way that suggested it was capable of motion.

My furies had first manifested after my mother's death, but even before that I had been drawn to ravens. Not surprisingly, perhaps. The elves were descended from Loki, a shape-changer who had taken the form of a female raven in his attempt to escape an enraged Odin. For a time, Loki managed to distract the All-Father's *male* messenger ravens—though not without consequence. Later, when Odin had captured and imprisoned him in a hidden hall beneath Iceland, Loki himself gave birth to the elves.

Tucking the mechanical bird under my arm, I continued toward the stairs, and Treig and I returned to my tower.

I set the raven on a windowsill in my bedchamber. Outside, the new day had dawned with more fog rolling in from the Atlantic. Slowly it consumed the tops of the trees in its march toward the castle and *Corvus*, which I could see clearly from my chamber. There was a commotion on the parapet below me, and I watched for a few minutes while sentries fired arrows at the hull of the ship. There were lines attached to the arrows, and I wondered whether anyone would be fool enough to test their weight on one. It seemed they wouldn't get the chance, as one by one the arrows bounced harmlessly off the hull. Could be there was a protective spell at work.

Weary to my bones, I finally turned from the window and lay down across the bed.

FINVARA

Toward dawn, I quit my study—and a half-emptied bottle of Bushmills—to sleep for a few hours.

The dull light of a misty morning had made a weak incursion

into the chamber by the time a servant brought my coffee and a two-day-old *Irish Times*. With it came sheets of proposed menus, decorations, and other arrangements that Doro had sent for my approval. I shuffled through them and handed them back to the servant, muttering, "Fine."

Opening the newspaper, my gaze fell on a photograph of my cousin. According to the accompanying article, after the seal between Ireland and Faery had been broken, the magnificent old library at Trinity College had become entangled with the Faery library. Other-worldly creatures scurried through the hallowed university halls, vines twined round its staircases, and trees jutted up like great columns, filling the high spaces with foliage. The venerable gentlemen who had dominion there were apoplectic, demanding that the queen restore order. The *Times* editor had demonstrated her wit by selecting a portrait of the queen where her countenance suggested frayed patience and forced courtesy, and it made me laugh as nothing had in weeks.

Yet there was a hollowness to it. A crisis of identity was playing out within me. The queen had a country to rule, as she always had. There was order to be restored—or at least some semblance of it. What was my place in this new Ireland? I had been tasked with watching for enemies and restoring a court that, while important to the citizens of Faery, was largely considered a nuisance by the Irish families who called this region home. My time was mostly occupied by listening to questions for which I didn't have answers, and wishing I was elsewhere.

I ran my hand over my cropped head, reminding myself that I'd vowed only hours ago that I would endeavor to make the best of it. But I began to feel that what I was doing amounted to suppressing my own nature, and I'd been doubting my impulses and actions—a thing I never did at sea.

My thoughts wandered to the chamber at the top of the tower, where there was a woman who must be feeling much of the same. She too had a led a very different life before the obligations of her birth had caught up to her. I decided that my first mission of the day would be a diplomatic one.

Setting the newspaper aside, I got up and dressed, my mood lifting at the thought of the upcoming visit. I could not deny the Elf King's daughter was a fascinating woman—something I'd always been drawn to. I found myself looking for reasons to summon her, despite my new pragmatic outlook. I'd not give over *all* my old diversions, by god.

My best hope of breaching those stalwart defenses of hers, I reasoned, was to spend more time in her company. When I encountered Keane in the corridor, I asked him to invite her to join me on the drawbridge.

Outside, the morning fog was clearing. The air was chill and damp, but breaks in the cloud cover suggested we would catch a glimpse of the sun. Today was the first day of spring—my new steward had reminded me of it, as it was an important holiday for the fairies, and Knock Ma had always staged revels. Doro had assured me that the upcoming masquerade would fit the bill.

The phantom ship remained in the sky above the castle, hull creaking as it shifted in the breeze. I detected no change in its status—no sign of captain or crew. I wondered how long before I had a reply from the queen on how best to manage the situation. The nearest telegraph office was at Tuam, an easy enough distance, and Doro had promised to send a man. The queen had of course been overrun with her own problems, and I was unsure if anything would attract her attention—outside of Fomorians on our doorstep.

"She is a beautiful ship."

I turned at the sound of the low but feminine voice, and for the space of several heartbeats, my breath stuck in my chest. What a difference a night had made. Her raven hair hung like a velvet cloak over her shoulders, and something had raised the pink in her cheeks. Thick as her hair was, it could not completely conceal the tips of her ears, higher and more delicately curved than those of the firglas. I saw now, too, that her eyes were not black, but closer to the iron gray of a winter sky. And the light of day revealed the strong contrast between her fair countenance and the freckles—they were tiny star shapes—that overlaid her nose and cheeks. What had perhaps wrought the greatest change, and called all these attributes to my attention, was the color of her dress—ruby port in place of the mourning black. A shade very close to that of her full lips.

"Beautiful, indeed," I agreed, lifting my gaze to hers before it became awkward. "I hope you slept well, lady?"

"Well enough." She drew closer, lips now curving downward. I tried like the devil to read *anything* in that blank—or rather, controlled—expression. "Your Majesty has transformed since our last meeting."

I smiled and ran a hand over my scalp. "Oh, aye. What do you think?"

I watched her study me, and it struck me that rather than offering an automatic compliment, she was seriously considering my question. "Less like a sea raider," she said at last.

I laughed. "I've not undergone the ordeal for nothing, then."

Her eyes settled again on mine, and she asked in a colorless tone, "You sent for me, Your Majesty?"

This is hopeless. I sighed inwardly, yet I refused to give up—I'd just have to find the proper lever to open this puzzle box.

"My family will be visiting Knock Ma in less than a week, and a masquerade ball will be given in their honor. I wanted to invite you to attend, if it would please you."

Something did then kindle behind her eyes. Surprise?

"A ball?" she repeated.

"Aye."

She glanced again at the ship and did not immediately reply. I wondered whether such things were outside her experience. "Maybe dancing is not to your liking," I added, "but there will be a banquet, disguises, and all manner of lively diversions. You would be welcome."

"I have nothing suitable to wear to a masquerade, Your Majesty." She looked at me. "Though perhaps your courtiers and kin would not feel that I need a disguise."

For the space of several moments my mind worked to produce a gallant reply, but though her tone had been arch, I'd observed a light twitching at the corner of her lips. *The princess is joking*, I realized with astonishment.

Relaxing into a grin, I replied, "Perhaps they would not, still I would be happy to provide one. I intend to go masked myself, the better to anonymously observe others making fools of themselves, and you, if you choose to attend, may do the same."

Still she didn't answer, and I added, "You may consider it, if you like, and give your answer at a—"

"I will attend," she said abruptly. And if I was not mistaken, the pink in her cheeks deepened. Now, this was a physical response that I could interpret. She was not so different from an Irishwoman after all. As to the *cause* of her sudden discomfiture, I could not hazard a guess.

"Very good," I replied, feeling gratified. The chances that this grand occasion would prove in any way diverting were dramatically increased by her attendance, and if she made my family uncomfortable, so much the better. "I will ask my steward to see to your disguise."

"I thank you, Your Majesty."

"Don't," I muttered, shaking my head. "At least not until you've passed an evening in the company of my relations and still feel that you can remain on speaking terms with me."

She lowered her gaze, clasping her hands in front of her. Rashly, I swore an oath to gods both old and new that I would make her laugh, even if it cost me an arrow through the chest.

"Now that's settled, I wondered whether you would care to walk out with me?"

Her dark eyes lifted.

"Onto the grounds," I added. "I go with the firglas patrols as often as I can. I'm not used to being confined indoors and crave the exercise. And these days I feel like my bearings constantly require correction. I thought we might have it in common. What do you say?"

IRON AND BONE

KOLI

"I will go with you," I replied.

His unexpected gallantry continued. He was not required to entertain me, and no doubt had many more pressing matters to attend to. Could it be that he still hoped to make an ally of me?

Doro would approve of my accepting his invitations, I felt certain, and more importantly so would my father. But I was uneasy, and not only because I doubted there was any way of avoiding the forest. I *wanted* to go with him.

"Excellent," he replied, and seemed to mean it. He was livelier today, and I wondered whether the weight lifted from his head had also lightened his mood. The sudden change in his appearance had shocked me. Without the hair, his other features were more prominent—the bones of his face, the high forehead, the musculature along the sides of his neck. And especially his glacier eyes.

"Are you dressed warmly enough?" the king inquired, eyeing the stretch of forearm left bare by my sleeves.

"I am used to cold, Your Majesty."

"Of course. And your footwear? We will cross some wet ground and slippery stones."

More amused than annoyed by his concern, I slid one booted foot forward so that it poked from beneath the hem of my tunic.

"Excellent," he repeated.

In addition to the previous day's stiff and uncomfortable shoes, I had cast aside the complicated modern clothing in favor of my favorite hunting dress—a simple ankle-length tunic fitted snugly, but not suffocatingly, at the chest and waist by a leather corset. I felt more at ease already.

The king too was less constrained by his dress this morning, wearing only shirtsleeves, black trousers, and boots. The smooth and snow-white fabric of his shirt could not conceal the lines of his body— the strength of his chest and shoulders. Whatever vices the fairy king possessed, they did not include indolence.

A company of the firglas—the same fairy race as Treig—had crossed the bailey, where the stables were, to assemble on the draw-bridge. They were armed with bows and pikes. As the king and I moved aside to let them pass, I noticed a pistol belted at his waist. I had no direct experience with this type of weapon, though muskets were often carried by Icelandic farmers and herdsmen. Such weapons needed fire and dry powder, and both could be easily interfered with by spells—as the queen of Ireland had discovered in the Battle of Ben Bulben.

We followed the patrol beyond the gatehouse and onto a forest path, which soon descended away from the castle. It was good to feel my blood moving, as well as the occasional beam of sunlight and the fresh salt breeze against my skin. As in Iceland, the landscape here was a living thing—clouds drifting, air damply swirling, light patterns changing.

These buoyant feelings melted away, however, once we were surrounded by wooden giants and could no longer see the castle. Nor, with the cloud cover, could I be sure which direction we were traveling. Dark boughs closed over our heads, forming a tunnel like the charred ribcage of some great beast.

"I understand there are few trees in Iceland," said the king, seeming to sense my discomfort. He walked abreast of me, and we broke the line of guards exactly in half, with four pairs ahead and four pairs behind. The king had ordered Treig to remain at the castle—maybe to make me feel less like a prisoner. I found myself wishing she had come.

"That is true, Your Majesty," I replied. "Few among my people have any memory of them."

"Do you find them unsettling?"

Glancing at him sidelong, I decided he wasn't mocking me. "Maybe a little."

"I confess I do," he said. "This forest has existed in Faery for centuries, but before my association with King Finvara, I had never seen this many trees together. Certainly not any so ancient. Oaks are sacred to fairies, and I believe these are no ordinary trees."

"They speak to each other," I said.

Raising his brows, he nodded. "Aye. Do you understand them?"

I shook my head.

He glanced up at the canopy of naked boughs. "Nor do I. But sometimes it sends a shiver through me."

I was silently marveling at yet another instance of sympathetic feeling between us when the king asked abruptly, "Those birds—do you control them, or . . .?"

Following his gaze, I discovered my furies moving in the branches. Unlike last night on the tower stairway, I had not been aware that they'd joined us. I often discovered them shadowing me at times of uneasiness. But when I was angry, there was nothing subtle about their arrival.

I tried to think how to answer him. I could see no harm in the truth. The birds were little threat to anyone, so there was no advantage to being secretive about them, and being as truthful as possible would make my half-truths and deceptions easier to manage.

"Mostly I do not, Your Majesty," I replied. "They come and go."

He frowned. "Do you know why?"

I shrugged. "It is said my people are descended from ravens."

He considered this as he watched their movements, and I felt oddly gratified by his curiosity.

"Others in your family have similar guardians?"

"No," I confessed. "But there are real ravens living atop Skaddafjall."

The Elf King said my ravens were a mark of the gods. Because I had a mortal mother, he believed they were meant to remind me where I come from—much like the mark on my back.

We walked on in silence, but after a few minutes he asked, "What did you mean by 'mostly'?"

I glanced at him, confused.

"You said that mostly you don't control them."

My eyes traced the fresh scratch on the outer edge of his right ear. Did he think I'd done it intentionally? *Would* I have, were it possible?

"My furies," I murmured.

He frowned. "My lady?"

"One of my tutors called them my *furies*"—I spoke up—"because they appear at times when . . . when I experience strong feelings."

"I see," he replied in a softened tone, and suddenly I knew that I'd gone too far. He was observant, and cleverer than I'd given him credit for. He would be able to read me now, at times when I would least desire it. What had made me tell him?

He's too easy to talk to. I would need to be more careful.

Again we fell into silence, and I thought about how much easier this would be had he been the haughty rake that I had been told to expect. I would have simply watched him from a distance, learning his faults and weaknesses.

"It is strangely quiet in the forest today," he said finally. "It's usually overrun with the fairy folk. Even worse than the castle."

I thought about the twig people I'd scared off the previous night. "Has it always been like that?"

"Aye, my predecessor's court was lively. I don't think it much troubled him. As a ship's captain, I find it disquieting to say the least. My steward, Doro, has served the court for centuries." I looked up sharply. "He agreed to help me restore some order by discouraging the traffic on castle grounds. We may have him to thank for this peaceful morning walk."

Doro was the king's *steward*? He had mentioned serving Finvara's queen—but of course that office was currently vacant. I couldn't help wondering if Finvara had mentioned Doro to watch my reaction—a kind of trap. I risked a glance at his profile, but his brow was deeply furrowed and I concluded that he was not thinking of me at all. The king was preoccupied. What had made him invite me to join him this morning? Could it be he was trying to take his mind off other troubles?

I had been at Knock Ma less than twenty-four hours, and the king was besieged. Doro and I had him surrounded, and he had no idea of it. This exile of his subjects from the castle, which Doro had agreed to manage for him—it could easily be made to look like a slight.

Excitement was what I should have been feeling. Instead, there was a heaviness in my chest. And the mark between my shoulder blades burned.

"Let us turn from the path here," said the king, lightening his tone. "There's a worthwhile view from the top of this hill."

He ordered the firglas to continue their patrol of the grounds and meet us again on their return to the castle. Then we started up a rough stairway embedded in the hillside. The stones were moss covered and damp, and I was glad for my sturdy boots.

When we topped the rise, a little breathless from the climb, the king led me to a rocky break in the trees. A steep cliff was before us, with more forest at the bottom of the drop.

"It's a fair prospect, is it not?" he said.

Wind whipped my hair about my shoulders as I took it in. The clouds had cleared and we could see all the way to the white-capped Atlantic. The view from my tower was similar, but it felt so exposed here—also peaceful and isolated. Between ocean and forested hills stretched a green blanket of farm and pastureland divided by stone fences, country roads, and the occasional white-washed village. There was bog land, too, the color of bread and half-shrouded in mist. A lake that reflected the ever-changing skyscape, and a line of snowcapped mountains to the northwest.

"It is, Your Majesty," I replied. A smile of contentment curled the edges of his lips, and his blue eyes danced. The heaviness of a few moments ago had lifted. The view, the fresh air, *something* had brought about a transformation.

Love of the sea.

Returning my gaze to the waves, I breathed in the cold, clean air. Iceland's elves were not a seafaring people, but our ancestors were. I had never lived landlocked, and was grateful for this reminder that the sea was in fact our close neighbor.

"On board my ship, *Aesop*," began the king, "in the waters near my mother's birthplace, I have felt the sun hot on my back, and have cooled my skin in an ocean so clear you could see all the way to the white sandy bottom."

An image of him leaping bare-chested from the deck of his ship came unbidden to my mind, and my heart jumped.

"It brings its own sort of joy," he continued. "But nothing compares to *this*." He waved at the countryside before us. These hills and valleys, the villages and farmland and ruins—they were as important to him as the landscape of Iceland was to me.

"Which is why you gave up your ship," I said. "To protect it. And you come *here* to remember that."

He turned to look at me—I could feel his sudden intensity and did not meet his gaze.

"Aye," he breathed, and there was a note of wonder in his tone. My eyes were finally drawn to him, and again my heart jumped.

I'll not be drawn in by a spell.

I sensed my furies gathering, and the rising fear had me reaching for their aid.

Wait.

I steadied myself. Magic always created a charge in the air— it felt like a tickle on the skin. I felt neither the tickle nor the fogginess that accompanied enchantment. I was very much awake and alive.

Slowly, I drew cool air deep into my lungs. The fear subsided, but my heartbeat stubbornly refused to slow. Finally the king looked away and I let out my breath in relief.

He cleared his throat. "On the other side of this hill," he said, pointing, "is another, smaller hill, with a saddle between. There is a barrow marked by a standing stone—you can see it, just there—a monument that predates this forest. The trees grew up and around, leaving bare the stone and the hilltop. If it interests you, we could take a closer look."

"I would like that, Your Majesty," I said, eager for release from the strange tension.

I followed him to the south-facing side of the hill, where we found a precarious stone stairway, steeper than the previous one. This path was also more exposed than the other, as both the saddle and adjacent hill were clear of trees. It occurred to me it would be a very simple thing to contrive my death in this environment.

Although no one would believe such an event to be an accident, and the king was no fool.

"Have you ancient burial mounds in Iceland?" asked Finvara, leading the way down—and in doing so, placing himself in a very vulnerable position. I was no fool either.

"We do, sire—Viking tombs. And many legends surrounding them. There are stone ships associated with the goddess Freyja that have stood for centuries. Not even the elves go near them."

"So it is here, as well," he replied, reaching the bottom of the stairs. Then he grinned. "Shall we go closer yet?"

I glanced at the monolith. I was curious, and the king's sense of adventure was contagious. "All right, Your Majesty."

We continued on to the saddle and then to a footpath that led us to the top of the mound. At its center stood the stone—narrow, but easily fifteen feet high. The stone's surface was uniformly gray—clear of lichen, moss, and bird droppings.

"Do you know who is entombed here?" I asked.

"No one has been able to tell me," he replied. "When the seal between Faery and Ireland began to fray, many places like this came to be used as doors between worlds. Gap gates were built into some of those doors—in fact there's a Gap gate inside a waterfall on the east side of the grounds. But neither fairy nor Irishman ever comes so close to this monument." Again he smiled at me. "Until now."

His mood was almost conspiratorial, and I got the sense he had wanted to come here for some time. Could it be that no one else was brave enough to accompany him? It was very like something I would do back home. I had always been loyal and obedient, but I never missed opportunities to defy authority in small ways.

I had no trouble imagining why this tomb was avoided—the very air here was different. Instead of the bracing wind off the Atlantic, there was a chill breeze that carried a stale smell—like it had come from the inside of a cave. Not like the caves along the coasts of my homeland, with pools of clear, cold water lined with spiny sea creatures and pebbles of every color, but the inland caves, where beasts—and sometimes rarer creatures—dwelled.

Old bones and musk.

The bright morning suddenly began to look like twilight as dark clouds crowded the sky, bringing with them a drop in temperature that caused even me to shiver.

"Sometimes it is for the best such ruins are not disturbed," I said. "I need not tell *you* that legends arise for a reason."

"No, indeed," he agreed. He studied me, and mischief glinted in his eyes as he said, "Could it be that you are frightened, Koli Alfdóttir?"

I felt a tickle low in my belly as he said my name. It was not the tickle of enchantment, but, I feared, of something far more dangerous.

"Only a fool does not feel fear."

FINVARA

I had finally done it. It was barely there, I'll grant you, but a very real smile curled the corners of those overripe lips. It acted like a ray of sunlight on her features, heightening the color in her cheeks and brightening her dark eyes. In that moment, it struck me that she was beautiful—not for a "goblin princess," or for an elf woman—by *any* measure. Her guarded nature, along with her thinly veiled fierceness, had hidden it from me.

It took me aback, but I'd not spoil the moment for anything, so I grinned at her. "Even a fool such as myself knows it. Yet I doubt that—"

I broke off, glancing down at the ground between my boots—for it had begun to *move*. "What the devil?"

The mound lurched like a ship tossed by a wave, and both

of us fell. The earth broke open, stones and dark soil pushing up through the grass. The shadow shapes of the princess's furies were bursting out of her, their coarse cries filling the air.

"The stone!" she shouted, and I glanced up to find the oblong slab *tilting* over us.

We scrambled madly over the ground, and a deep groaning of the earth and heaviness in the air made it clear the monument's fall was imminent. I hooked an arm around her and began rolling down the side of the mound toward the saddle. The massive stone struck the earth beside us with incredible force. Reflexively I clambered farther away, dragging her with me, and then collapsed.

The princess fell across my chest, panting, her heart hammering against me. She raised her head to look at me, dark eyes wild and questioning. We untangled ourselves and sat up, but before I could speak, a grating cry pierced the air. I felt a sharp pain and jerked away—the lady's furies were diving at my head, beaks and talons easily finding my scalp thanks to its reduced cover.

Cursing the beasts, I batted at them with my arms, and dread knifed through my gut. Had *she* caused this? Was it my death she was after?

I took hold of her wrist. Before I could question her, she cried, "*Draug!*" Still wild-eyed, she fought to free herself from my grasp.

"Nay, lady," I muttered, tightening my grip, though I did not understand the word she had spoken.

"We must go!" she shouted. Then she spoke another phrase of Elvish, and a spell seared my hand, forcing me to release her. She crawled toward the saddle as the mound continued to quake, and I looked back toward the wrecked ground where the stone had stood.

Something was clawing its way *out*. Skeletal fingers dug through the soft earth. Plumes of vapor hissed from the ground, fogging the air around us.

We were both on our feet again, poised for flight, and yet

frozen by the horrific spectacle. I snatched my pistol from its holster, and the princess reached over her shoulder, grabbing at empty air before spitting a curse and dropping her arm—*going for her missing bow*, I guessed, *and we sure could use it.*

"What do you know of this thing?" I barked.

"Draug!" she repeated. Her brow furrowed and she shook her head, lips moving in soundless frustration. She fixed her gaze on me and said, "A barrow-wight."

The risen dead. Truly the legends of my countrymen were legends no longer. I might have guessed as much myself, had I not fixed on the idea of the lady's treachery.

The creature's bejeweled and claw-tipped fingers, the size of saplings, braced against the ground as it fought its way out of the barrow. Huge clods of dirt rolled and bounced down what remained of the mound.

The princess turned and ran and I followed. We made it halfway across the saddle before we heard thunderous footsteps behind us—we were trapped. The only escape from where we now stood was back up the exposed stairway to the viewpoint and then down the other side. We'd never make it to the top before the creature caught up to us. It might not be able to follow us, but it was tall enough to bat us right off the hillside.

"What now?" asked the lady, breathless.

I raised and aimed the revolver at the monstrosity, waiting as each long, deliberate, stride brought it closer.

The wight wore a crown of dark, pitted metal, ornamented with a collection of antlers, bones, and tusks. The upper portion of its face was obscured by a pair of goggles, though there appeared to be only empty sockets behind them. The crown had a jaw piece, like a helm, made from an animal jawbone with a few remaining teeth. This piece, connected and hinged with rusted gears, hung slightly open, revealing thin gray lips. Some kind of flexible tubing extended down from the jaw, wrapping over both shoulders. As the wight exhaled with a loud hiss, fog rose in the air in front of its face.

Taking a long stride, the creature raised a mace, and I fired my revolver. No enchantment interfered with the firing mechanism, and I kept pulling until the piece was empty. I had a good eye, and every shot had struck either the head or the hide-covered chest—one bullet even dislodged a tooth from the jaw piece. But the wight's only reaction was to begin swinging the spiked iron ball on its chain in preparation for attack.

"It's already dead!" cried the princess, and we scrambled aside as the iron ball descended toward us and struck the earth, spraying pebbles and dark soil.

"It *breathes*, does it not?" I shouted back. "If you've a better idea, please advise me!"

There came a series of rapid swishing noises as a volley of arrows flew over our heads—the firglas patrol had found us and begun their own assault from the ridge above. I could hear the captain shouting orders. But the arrows were even less effective than the bullets, bouncing harmlessly off both helm and hide. What we needed was a crushing force, like a cannonball or catapult.

Aboard Aesop *we'd make short work of it.* We were *not* aboard *Aesop*, however, and the wight was readying the mace for another attack.

We avoided the blow again, the massive iron ball knocking loose the bottom stones of the stairway behind us. We'd not hold out like this for long, trapped on the saddle with the cursed thing.

"Keep it occupied!" called the princess, moving away.

"*What?*" I called after her. "Where are you going?"

She was off at a run, and I muttered a curse before shouting to the patrol on the ridge, "Keep up the attack! Hit it with everything!"

After bending to load up my arms with stones—because it was the only thing I could think of to do—I ran in the opposite direction of the mad elf woman, flinging stones at the giant as I went.

KOLI

Arrows and pikes sailed through the air. The king was flinging stones and yelling like he was deranged. And it was *working*—the wight paid no attention to me. I whispered a shielding spell just in time to divert a stray pike, and when the weapon bounced harmlessly to the ground, I grabbed it.

It breathes, does it not? The king's question repeated in my mind—such a creature should *not* breathe. A draug was no more than a reanimated dead thing. Maybe the fog pouring out of it was not breath at all, rather a result of some mechanical process, similar to what I'd seen in the little machines at Knock Ma. No windup keys this time, but steam power, like the ship that had brought me to Ireland.

Could it be that the steam was conducted through the smooth black hoses that curved over the wight's shoulders?

I ran across the grassy saddle, circling around behind it. The hoses were concealed beneath a rodent-gnawed animal-pelt tunic that draped down the wight's back to its knees, where a torn leg-covering revealed a joint formed of bare bone reinforced with an iron hinge. Through the rat holes I glimpsed metal workings—gears, joints, and pipes. The bristly tail of one of the pelts used to make the tunic hung down the middle of the wight's back.

Panicked and anguished cries erupted from the ridge, and glancing up I saw the giant had landed the spiked ball on top of the firglas patrol. As their leader shouted, assessing the damage, the creature yanked on the wooden baton to retrieve the ball. It did not budge. The spikes dug into the earth, making it harder to free the weapon from below the ridge than it would have been from above.

The firglas were mustering, and a handful of them scrambled, spider-like, onto the chain that connected the ball to the baton. As the giant strove to wrest his weapon free, ignoring the firglas creeping closer, a large stone flung by the king struck its helm, knocking loose one side of the jaw piece.

The wight let go of the mace and the baton slammed against the hillside, sweeping the firglas to the saddle below—and likely to their deaths. It then rounded on the king, who shouted something in his own tongue. The hairs on my neck lifted as lightning forked down from the sky, accompanied by a huge crack of thunder. The strike grounded itself in the creature of iron and bone.

It was an impressive display of magic—I'd never seen anyone but my father conjure lightning. The king would have had to call on air, fire, and water, and such a powerful spell could exhaust one or more of those resources for hours. If the wight survived the strike, there would not likely be another.

The creature stood frozen, and I held my breath. Then came a loud hiss of steam, and it raised its bony fists to the heavens, loosing a bray of fury that shook the ground and caused me to clamp my hands over my ears. It took a step toward the king.

Suddenly I remembered something—the "vein of magic" Doro had tapped into to create *Corvus*. Was it possible this was his doing? He couldn't have known that we would come here today, could he? He *was* the king's steward, and Finvara had obviously been as far as the saddle before. Was I meant to let the wight destroy him? But as the Elf King's daughter—and the descendant of a powerful sorceress—would I not be suspected of involvement in his murder?

The wight again brayed its rage as the king evaded the swinging fists. This was the only chance I was likely to get to help Finvara.

Glancing skyward I found my furies, who were making a hellish racket as they circled the scene of battle. "Make yourselves useful for once," I grumbled. I clenched my fists and shouted my command.

The birds began diving at the head of our attacker, but I did not pause to congratulate myself. The wight stood maybe ten yards away from me—it was far enough to build up speed, and I would need it, because the king's lightning had ruled out a buoyancy spell to aid my effort. A magic-wielder like my ancestress, and even my father, could draw on resources from much farther away—my own magical ability was feeble in comparison.

Gripping the pike in both hands, I ran. I struck my first target, a small stone slab that would add distance to my jump, and I pushed the tip of the weapon against the rough surface, grunting with effort and vaulting skyward.

Then I focused on my second target: the bristly tail that hung down from the giant's tunic. *One chance.*

My shoulder struck the wight's back with enough force to stop my breath, but I caught the tail in one hand and latched on, hauling myself up, hand over hand. The wight spun in surprise, flinging an arm to brush me loose. A deadly sharp talon sliced my leg and I cried out. Pushing the searing pain out of my mind, I squirmed and shimmied my way up until I could almost touch the wight's shoulder.

Still clinging to the foul tunic, I braced my feet against the wight's back. Then I launched up and out with my legs as I let go of the tunic, making a desperate grab for one of the black hoses that hung down from the helm. I caught it with my left hand, grunting as my weight came onto my arm. I reached up with my other hand and secured my grip. Then, kicking against the wight's ribs for leverage, I began to swing and tug.

The hose did not release, but my weight pulled the wight's head to one side, unbalancing it. The giant stumbled. I held on, continuing to tug and twist, arms burning from the strain.

"Look out!" came a shout from below, and on instinct I let go. The wight's hand cut through the air just above me as I fell. The impact against the hard ground knocked the breath out of me. I'd only just avoided landing on the stones.

When I glanced up, I saw that the wight's taloned hand had sliced the hose clean through—it coiled and whipped out like a serpent, spewing steam.

Then, the wight listed.

"Koli!" shouted Finvara. "Move!"

I rolled onto my stomach and kept rolling, but suddenly I slammed against the edge of the slab I'd used as a vaulting platform. I'd not escape this time—the giant was falling straight toward me. Crossing my arms over my face, I cried out and braced for the impact.

STONES

FINVARA

The barrow-wight had spun on its heel at the last, and down it crashed, right on top of the princess. For a moment I stood frozen in horror, but then I heard a muffled groan and bolted toward the colossus.

"Lady!" I cried, running along the length of its body. Could she have survived?

Not possible.

Another groan rose from somewhere beneath it, and I moved toward the sound.

"Lady?" I reached the stone slab the giant had toppled over and bent down to look. The slab had propped up the giant's torso enough to form a small cave, which had prevented her from being crushed.

"*Fires of Laki,*" she swore, turning her head to grimace at me, "the *stench.*"

Relief warmed my chest and I laughed out loud. Then I

summoned what was left of my patrol, directing them to help me. As we took up positions alongside the body, one massive leg kicked and we jumped back.

"Blast, it's survived!"

"Cut the other hose!" cried the lady, her voice strained and even more muffled. The giant's weight must have shifted.

Tugging the dagger from my belt, I rushed toward the head. The wight thrust out an arm, swiping clumsily but with enough force to knock me down.

I cried out as my shin struck a sharp rock. Then I rolled out of range and jumped up, running again at the head. Finally I reached the remaining hose and sliced it through, and the wight's flailing arm dropped to the ground with a thud.

"With me!" I called to the firglas, and we lined up along the body and shoved.

"Keep it up," I urged. "A little more."

Grunting from the strain and sweating like beasts, we managed to raise it enough for the princess to crawl out.

"All right, lads," I called, "let it go!"

The massive body slumped, and I knelt beside the princess. "Are you injured, lady?"

Raising the hem of her skirt, she inspected a long gash down one calf.

"Ach, let's get you back to the castle," I said grimly.

If not for her boot she'd have suffered worse, but as it was, blood was pooling on the ground beneath her leg, and the color had drained from her face.

"I can walk," she said, her tone low and determined.

"I think you'll have to," I replied, "but we need to stop the bleeding first."

I began unbuttoning my shirt. She watched me, wide-eyed, as I took it off and rolled it into a long strip from collar to hem.

"May I?" I asked.

She nodded, and I wrapped the shirt snugly around her leg, tying the sleeves to secure the makeshift dressing. Then I took her calf between my hands, pressing my palm against the wound to slow the flow of blood.

"Forgive me," I murmured. "I don't have the magic for something like this."

This was not entirely true. My ancestor had possessed some knowledge of blood magic, but I had walled it off from my consciousness. Blood magic exacted a price—you could not replenish one man's blood without spilling another's.

"Thank you, Your Majesty," she said, "it's much better." A bead of perspiration had collected above her lip.

I kept up the pressure for a little longer before checking the dressing. Splotches of bright red had soaked through, but it looked like the bleeding had slowed.

"I think we could try now," I said. "If it starts up again, or if it's too painful, we'll find another way."

I held out my hand and she gripped my forearm, cool fingers pressing into my skin, and pulled herself to her feet.

"Easy," I said, linking her arm through mine. "Rest most of your weight on me."

The firglas were prodding and poking at the fallen giant. They had flipped back the animal-skin coverings, revealing a strange amalgamation of mechanical and organic materials. There was a combustion chamber in the belly region, and a reservoir in the chest. Pipes for carrying steam, and pistons for operating gears and levers. Bits of gray flesh clung in various places—the lower jaw, the arms and legs.

Already dead, the princess had said. Mechanically animated, it appeared. But how?

Lingering on the field of battle, I glanced down at the woman on my arm. "How did you know what to do?"

KOLI

There was no accusation in his tone or expression, but I knew he must suspect me. *I* would suspect me. Yet I might very well have saved his life, and I was sure he knew it.

"I guessed, Your Majesty," I replied. "I spent some time examining your little machines last night, and it occurred to me this creature might be like them."

The king frowned. "First the ship, now this revenant. They are almost like . . ." His eyes moved over the exposed workings of the wight. "They're like expressions of magic that have adapted to our mechanical age. What has caused it, I wonder? The opening of Faery?"

"Perhaps, sire."

This had struck me as Doro's handiwork, and my feeling had not changed. What was he doing? He might have killed us both.

"Forgive me," said the king, squeezing my arm. "You are impressively stoic, lady. Let's get you back to the castle."

With the first step I felt a stabbing pain. I gasped and stumbled, and Finvara slipped an arm around my waist, preventing my fall. His hand pulled my hip against him, the heat of the steadying touch chasing away the pain.

"Try again," he urged, "but let me take your weight this time."

In his state of half-undress, it was impossible not to be affected by the *maleness* of him—despite the fact I was used to a rougher sort. The king was lithe and smooth-skinned, but there was nothing soft about the lines of his broad chest, the plane of his belly, and his thick upper arms. His body had been sculpted by a life at sea, while his flesh had an ageless quality. That he was pleasing to look upon I could not deny.

He released my waist and again offered his arm. I hooked mine through his and also gripped the inside of his elbow with my other hand, fingers pressing into taut muscle. Then I allowed myself to sag against him.

"That's it," he encouraged, and together we took a few steps forward.

I limped along beside him, feeling with every step like broken glass was embedded in my leg. When we reached the half-ruined stairway, we stopped.

"Bloody hell," the king swore. "Whole-bodied, I think you'd manage it—no doubt you're more sure-footed than I am."

He ordered the uninjured among the firglas to begin collecting wood for a litter, but then changed his mind.

"The hillside's intact enough to scale, I think, but it's too damn steep for a litter." He stood a moment considering, and suddenly snapped his fingers. "We need Doro. There may be a way to use Faery to get out of here." He ordered two of the firglas to return to the castle to fetch the steward.

"Bring some rope, for good measure," said the king, "and see that a servant is sent for a surgeon."

I sank onto the grass to wait. The heavy atmosphere had cleared, shafts of sunlight penetrating the lighter cloud cover. I closed my eyes, feeling the warmth spread over my face and chest. It would be awkward seeing Doro under these circumstances. I wondered when I would have an opportunity to speak with him alone—I had many questions for my new ally.

The sound of the king murmuring in Irish drew my gaze. Though he spoke too softly for me to make out the words, I could feel the pull of his magic and guessed he was trying to coax the stones of the stairway back up to their places. He was calling on earth rather than air or fire, so it had a chance of working.

But it might be a more complicated undertaking than he realized. The steps were not just stones—they were ruins. As such, they were bound to the once-living beings that had built the stairway. They might choose to return to their man-made resting places, or they might resent the king's attempt to manage them after having been disturbed for the first time in centuries.

I got up and limped over to join him. When he paused in his incantation, I began to chant in Elvish.

I did not often sing spells, and by the king's reaction, I don't believe he was accustomed to *hearing* them sung—he stared at me with his jaw hanging half open. Some kinds of spells could *only* be sung. The king was using a spell of command. To balance his effort, I sang a spell of persuasion.

I didn't know whether an Icelandic spell-song could have any effect on a pile of Irish stones, but I raised my hand, gesturing to the king to continue. He began his incantation again, and as our voices mingled, the lumps of granite began to roll, slowly and awkwardly, back up the hillside. My heart beat faster as the soil itself shifted uphill, defying nature's laws to reform the stairway's foundation. It felt satisfying, watching each step fit itself into place.

Finvara's voice trailed off, and I sang the last lines of what had become a lullaby, urging the stones to return to their rest.

"We make a good team," pronounced the king.

"Odd," I said.

He laughed, and it jolted me out of the trance that had led me to such an honest reply. "Thank you for saving my life," he said. "I hope you'll not regret it."

This was an exchange that could not help being uncomfortable. Besides being enemies, we now had Doro between us.

Shrugging, I said, "I couldn't have done it had you not provided a distraction."

"I count it among my many useless talents."

My eyebrow shot up. "Conjuring lightning is not a useless talent."

Again he laughed. "*That* was an outright miracle. I've never done it before and doubt I could do it again. It was desperation."

The king seemed to enjoy laughing at himself. It was not a common quality among my people, and I believed my father would call it a weakness. Your own vulnerabilities were to be concealed, and those of your enemies exploited. There was a lightness to the king's character that was outside my experience. I had to admit I was intrigued by it.

Turning to study the results of our combined spells, I said, "With your assistance, Your Majesty, I think I might attempt the climb now."

He frowned. "We have the other side to descend as well. Would you not rather wait for my steward? The fellow is uncommonly resourceful. I can't help but think we might make use of the Gap to abbreviate our return to the castle. I avoid it if I can, as accurate Gap navigation seems to be a combination of magic, luck, and blind faith, but I'm willing to—"

"No," I said, probably too quickly. "There's no need, Your Majesty."

Finvara eyed me doubtfully. "As you like."

He came closer, and again I took his arm. Even in the chill air, his skin was warm. I let my fingers slide half an inch so I could feel its texture, then wondered what in Freyja's name I was doing.

When we reached the steps, the king offered a smile of encouragement, though I could see the worry in his eyes. Worry about *me*.

His binding of the wound had helped to ease the pain of walking, and by leaning some of my weight on him I was able to climb all the way to the top. The descent was trickier, and by the time we made it down to the forest path I was breathing hard and sweating.

Awaiting us below were more of the king's guards, who'd marched out to meet us—and, I was grateful to see, a sturdy little dapple mare. The king gave instructions about the wounded still on the hill above, and one of the firglas led the mare over to me— her small and stocky build reminded me very much of the ponies in my homeland. No sooner had I gripped the saddle—taking a deep breath to fortify myself for the step up into the stirrup—than broad hands wrapped around my waist and lifted me to the mare's back. I landed in the saddle with a startled exhalation.

"Thank you, Your Majesty," I said as our eyes met. My heart raced, and where his hands had squeezed me, the skin tingled. I watched as he checked the girth and claimed the reins from his servant, placing them in my hands.

Resting a hand on the mare's neck, he said, "It's an easy ride back, my lady, and you'll soon have a more qualified surgeon."

My leg wound was not insignificant, but it would mend. Yet I worried over what other mischief may have been wrought this day.

FINVARA

Doro met us on the drawbridge, and before I could reproach him for ignoring my summons, he offered an apology. Despite the fact I had appointed him my steward, he was still magically bonded to the fairy queen—he could only leave the castle by her order. While the office was vacant, he was trapped here. I felt a pinprick of guilt over the discontent I'd experienced earlier, at the vantage point—separated though I might be from the life I loved, for the most part I was still my own master.

After explaining what had delayed him, Doro informed us that the surgeon from Tuam was not coming.

"What?" I demanded. "Why not?"

"I believe he is afraid of Knock Ma, Your Majesty."

"Damnation," I muttered, though perhaps it should not have come as a surprise. "What is to be done for the princess? I'll not send her six miles on horseback to *him*."

"It does not signify, sire," said Doro. "I would have saved your man the trouble had I known his errand. What we want is a fairy doctor, and that we have."

By his tone, I understood him to mean himself. Was there anything he couldn't do?

"You can treat her injury?"

"With her permission, sire."

Doro glanced at the princess, and she nodded.

"Very well," I agreed, studying her. The color had not returned to her face, and her eyelids were heavy. "I think rather than have her attempt the tower stairs, we'll open a chamber on the lower—"

"I can make it, Your Majesty," she insisted.

I was unconvinced, and when Doro excused himself to collect the supplies he needed, I accompanied her back to the tower. As we mounted the stairway, I could see that she was weaker, and the palm of her hand felt ice-cold on my arm.

"I believe you are chilled, lady."

"I am tired," she said. "That is all."

"Be that as it may, you do not look well. With your permission, I will carry you the rest of the way."

She froze, turning to study me with wide eyes.

"Have I your permission?"

She measured the remaining distance with her gaze. Then she glanced at the steps behind us. We were about halfway to the top. Her hand stretched toward the stone wall for support, but before her fingers made contact, she swayed.

I reached for her, and she let out a surprised cry as I scooped her up in my arms. Before she could protest, I had started climbing again.

"I've got you," I said in what I hoped was a reassuring voice.

She curled an arm around the back of my neck and locked her hands together, and this small, trusting gesture triggered a movement of my heart.

"This is unlike me," she assured me in a ragged voice. I could feel her trembling. "A few minutes ago I felt fine."

"It's a deep wound," I replied, and my chin brushed the top of her head. "You've lost a good deal of blood, and it's caught up to you."

"Maybe so, Your Majesty."

"Undoubtedly so," I insisted. Despite the confidence of my tone, I was impatient for Doro's return. Her head fell against the arm she'd wrapped around my neck, and she murmured something in her own tongue.

"Lady?" I said.

"Hurts," she replied faintly.

When I reached the top of the stairs, I walked to the bed and set her down on the coverlet. Her eyes were closed, and she was shivering visibly.

"Lady?" I repeated as Doro and the princess's maid joined us. She didn't reply.

"Her condition has worsened," I said to my steward. "She's badly chilled."

Doro instructed the maid to build up the fire, and he began arranging his materials on a nearby tea table.

"Is there something dangerous about this wound?" I asked him. "More so than it appears?"

"There is," he confirmed. I watched him place a handful of dried leaves and twigs with the bark removed in a mortar. Then he began crushing them. "The scratch of such a creature is bound to putrefy. I must treat the wound before necrosis sets in. If I fail to do so, it will spread."

"Necrosis?" I stared at him. I didn't know the word, but it sounded ill enough. "Do you mean to say her life is at risk?"

"Only if I delay. Let me work, sire."

I watched as he assembled a poultice from his crushed leaves and carried it to the bed. I bent over the princess and unwrapped the makeshift dressing, which was soaked with fresh blood. When

I saw the injured flesh, I swore under my breath and stepped back. The skin around the wound had gone gray, with a pattern like strange, feathery veins beneath.

Doro bent over her and applied the poultice, murmuring what sounded like a healing spell in an old form of Irish. Not blood magic, I didn't think.

I studied her face. She looked peaceful enough, though she was frightfully pale. It had not occurred to me that she might die, and I was suddenly, acutely aware that it mattered to me.

"I WILL CONQUER THIS"

KOLI

When I woke, I found that the king had gone, but I was not alone. My maid was asleep in the chair by the fire, and Doro stood at the window gazing out at the forest.

There was a water goblet on the bedside table, and I picked it up and drained it. Doro turned.

"There you are," he said, smiling.

"How long have I been asleep?" I asked hoarsely.

"Nearly twenty-four hours," he replied, and I sat straight up, groaning as pain knifed through my injured leg.

"Rest, lady," he urged. "It's the best thing for you."

My maid had begun to stir in her chair, and I called to her, "Sorcha, could you bring me something to eat?"

"Yes, lady," she said, jumping to her feet and smoothing her hair back. The poor woman was still frightened of me. "I'll fetch some soup from the kitchen."

I watched her go, and when the sound of her footsteps on the stairs faded, I said, "It was your doing, wasn't it?"

Doro lifted his eyebrows.

"The wight—it was your own creature."

"Ah, so it was."

"Did you not think that it might be dangerous?"

"Certainly, I did."

"Then why? Why produce such a thing? It might have killed us *both*."

"Might have," he said, moving closer to the bed, "but did not."

His gray eyes were round, very light, and as thickly lashed as a woman's. They offered a pleasing contrast to the strong lines of his jaw and long nose. His expression was smug and serene. At the moment, I was finding the whole luminous, mysterious package of him decidedly irksome.

"I will thank you to speak plainly, sir. What are you playing at?"

He looked surprised by my anger. "I am furthering our interests, as I have promised to do."

"By nearly *killing* me?"

"You were never in real danger. I trusted in the resourcefulness of both you and the king. You would not be defeated by one such creature. And I knew that should one of you be injured, even gravely, I could heal you."

I stared at him, aghast. "You seem to be saying that the wight's attack was planned. That it was intentional."

He smiled blandly as my ire increased. "And so it was. The king believes you saved his life, and he now trusts you. He bore you to the top of the tower himself, and he expressed genuine concern over the severity of your injury."

Most if not all of these things were true, but I was not reassured, as he had probably intended. Instead, I could not help contrasting the king's actions with *his*. Doro appeared to have saved my life, but he was also the reason it had needed saving.

If I'd understood my betrothed correctly, today's adventure had been contrived to induce the king to trust me so that I could kill him at a time of Doro and my father's choosing. It was a dangerous game. If the wight had killed the king, it could very easily have been blamed on me—a malevolent creature like that, rising out of the ground to attack the king only a day after my arrival. Was Doro confident to the point of arrogance?

I studied him like the answer would suddenly appear in his face.

His expression began to lose its smugness, and he sounded slightly wounded when he replied, "Can you not see that this is proof of my regard for you? I never doubted your actions."

I frowned. "Could you not have at least warned me?"

"I assure you, the endeavor would not have been as successful had you known in advance—according to the account of the firglas, you performed beautifully. More to the point, I had no way of knowing *when* circumstances would be right for the barrow-wight to be woken."

Sighing, I leaned against the headboard. "How was it done?"

Doro brightened—he liked to talk about his work. "Blood magic is used for reanimation of earthly creatures, but the barrow-wight was something completely new. Due to natural decay of the body, revenants are usually quite physically vulnerable. By combining blood magic with alchemy, I made him stronger."

I failed to suppress a shudder. "You told the king you are unable to leave Knock Ma. Is that true?"

He gave a grim nod. "I can slip into the Gap, as you have seen, but I cannot travel in either Ireland or Faery unless I am commanded by Finvara's queen."

I began to see how he had come to covet the crown. It was hard to fault him for wanting to change his circumstances.

"Your bond will be broken when you become king?"

He hesitated, and I could see the thoughts working behind his placid eyes. "My bond was forged by magic more powerful than mine, yet that is my hope."

And if not? To be free from the more distasteful restrictions of his bond, he would need a queen he could trust—or perhaps even control.

It struck me that I had traveled all the way to Ireland to live in an extension of my father's court—complicated relationships, shifting allegiances, constant spying, and eventually, assassinations. Why would it be any different, or why would I *want* anything different? It was a life I'd been raised to and understood. For some reason it gave me a sinking feeling.

Doro was watching me closely, making me even more uneasy. I could not afford for him to question my loyalty. Fortunately, I had been paying attention and had learned a sure way of distracting him.

"Who was the barrow-wight in life?" I asked.

"A very ancient Fomorian king, killed in battle by the Tuatha De Danaan."

"How did you use alchemy to make him stronger?"

He sat down on the edge of my bed. "Do you recall me telling you of the vein of magic that opened when the seal between Faery and Ireland was broken?"

I nodded.

"There is a Gap gate inside the barrow—inside the king's tomb. Anything that passes through it is altered and comes out an amalgamation of Faery and the modern world."

I stared at him, thinking about the inhabitants of Knock Ma's dungeon. "Expressions of magic in a mechanical age," I murmured, echoing Finvara's words. "The little machines in Knock Ma, you said they were not of your making. Did they somehow—"

He held up his hand and I paused. The sound of Sorcha's footsteps carried along the stairway.

"We must continue this discussion at a later time, lady," he continued. "Have I your forgiveness for adopting extreme measures, in light of our success?"

There was no arguing with the fact that our plans were more likely to succeed if the king trusted me. Whether or not I agreed with Doro's methods, he was holding up his end of our agreement. The question of whether I trusted him would have to wait for further evidence, and I was thankful he had not asked me. One thing I did trust in—if he caused my death and my father learned of it, he would pay with his life.

Unless he's more powerful than Father.

But that could not be.

Doro was eyeing me expectantly, and the maid had reached the top of the stairs.

"You have it," I replied.

FINVARA

With each passing hour, I felt more grateful for my new steward. Not only had he handily sorted the chaos in my court, he had prevented an international incident by saving the life of the Elf King's daughter. A trustworthy first mate was worth his weight in gold.

But as I watched him apply his arts to healing the princess, I realized I knew very little about him.

Doro was present in the memories I had acquired from my ancestor—he had long served Knock Ma's queens. I knew that under their orders he'd been involved in some shady dealings—in one memorable instance, a mortal woman the king had abducted and married had ordered Doro to steal the daughter of a nearby chieftain to serve as her maid. At the same time, the fairy servant had also been responsible for such menial tasks as fetching tea and attending the queen when she rode out with hunting parties. There was a note of disdain associated with those memories—I sensed my ancestor considered Doro beneath his notice.

As soon as the princess was deemed out of danger, I left her in the care of my steward and her maid and returned to my study with the intention of writing to my learned friend, Miss Ada Quicksilver. Miss Quicksilver was in fact Lady Meath now, the wife of my cousin Edward Donoghue, earl of Meath. She was a student of Faery, and like myself and Edward, was connected to Faery through her own ancestry. She and her banshees had helped defeat our enemies at Ben Bulben. I composed a brief message inquiring whether she had ever encountered a fairy called "Doro" in her studies. I then placed the letter in the hands of a courier, instructing him to carry it to the telegraph office in Tuam and remain there until a reply was received.

With that accomplished, and with my steward otherwise occupied, I tried to focus on preparations for my family's arrival, which was only a few days away. But I was preoccupied with the attack in the forest. Queen Isolde had, after all, left me squarely in charge of safeguarding the west of Ireland, which, in addition to being the location where the Fomorians had always histori- cally attacked, still felt so remote in comparison to Dublin that it might be another country. I doubled the number of firglas watching from the battlements and ordered additional patrols into the rolling green countryside west of Knock Ma—even to the very borders of the vast bog land beyond. I also resolved to appoint a marshal to help me manage our defenses and military affairs.

With the rending of worldly boundaries that resulted from the Battle of Ben Bulben, I imagined it would be some time before Ireland returned to anything like normal—if in fact it ever did. The aftershocks—the evolving geography, the influx of fairy folk, the mysterious objects and visitors—made it very challenging to feel that I was giving my role as guardian of the west the attention it required. I couldn't help resenting the time I'd been forced to devote to this impending family visit. Only a day ago, I had also resented my obligation to house an enemy within our walls. But now, the Elf King's daughter had somehow become the only inhabitant of the castle who made me feel like my old self.

All the more reason to leave her in Doro's care and focus my efforts where they were most needed. I gave some thought to how I might fill the marshal position, and then resolved to consult my father when he arrived. He would certainly have an opinion, and it might soften him toward me and save me the lecture I was anticipating. I also looked into the servants' preparations for my family's arrival. As I suspected, my steward had things well in hand, despite his current preoccupation with the princess's care. Knock Ma had become a hive of activity, with food and supply carts coming and going. The servants had been assigned to corridor-sweeping and rug-beating duties, and great clouds of dust—along with whole armies of spiders—were chased from the castle. Vases, cushions, and draperies appeared, festooning the great hall and brightening the chill, damp spaces—and my mood, truth be told. I was at home with this purposeful busyness.

I did not forget the princess in all this. I sent servants to inquire every few hours, and Doro assured them that she would recover. I was wrestling a strong urge to visit her and find out for myself, when the courier returned to the castle with a one-line reply from Lady Meath:

Advise caution until receipt of letter to follow.

This was troubling. Perhaps my wariness was not unfounded. But what could I do? Doro was the only one at court who knew how to care for the princess, and my father was due on the following day. My steward's aid could not be dispensed with. I resolved to keep my arrangements as they were, and hold my cards closer to the chest, until I received Lady Meath's letter.

Two days after the battle with the wraith, Doro proclaimed the princess recovered enough for him to return to his duties. He also informed me that she would likely be able to attend the masquerade on the following day. I was greatly relieved, for her recovery of course, but also because I intended to use her shamelessly as a distraction from the tediousness of entertaining my Mayo relations. The irony was not lost on me that a pleasing companionship had sprung from what I had at first considered quite a bothersome arrangement. Truth be told, our encounter in the forest had reinvigorated me. In the twenty-four hours that followed, my surliness had subsided, and I had found the yoke of responsibility easier to bear.

Later that same morning, before the arrival of my family, a letter was brought to me. It had been delivered by a rider who had arrived in haste. On the outside of the envelope, the author had neatly penned: "King Finvara (Duncan O'Malley)." That Lady Meath had felt it necessary to circumvent both telegraph office and traditional post caused me further concern, and I broke the seal immediately.

Dearest Duncan,

Let me first communicate to you the pleasure Edward and I both felt upon receiving a message from you, regardless of brevity or circumstance. I do hope that you are well, and that your life at Knock Ma has not turned out to be as tedious as you feared. I know the queen was vexed over your defiance in the matter of the elf maid, but I must say that I applaud you for standing your ground. Was it not enough to ask you to give up your life at sea?

I confess, however, that I have a great curiosity about your ward. I have begun to study Iceland's Hidden Folk and find them fascinating. Is she formidable? I do hope so; it will suit you so much better.

I laughed. How well Miss Q—Lady Meath—knew me. How it warmed my heart to hear from her. These friendly lines reminded me how isolated I had been in my new outpost.

Forgive me, I have wandered far afield of your original question. Regarding your new steward, "Doro," it is not a name I recall seeing in the lore. There is, however, a steward figure named "Far Dorocha," and it occurred to me Doro might easily be a shortened form of that name. Far Dorocha is said to be the servant of "the fairy queen," which could refer to the wife of Finvara and would explain why he appears to be attached to your household. Do you possess any ancestral memory of him?

This was it: Doro must be Far Dorocha. I had not mentioned in my message that Doro had served the fairy queens—it had not seemed an important detail. Dear Lady Meath was worth her weight in gold.

Regardless, I will again urge caution. The Far Dorocha I have studied, in addition to aiding the queen of fairy in some morally reprehensible endeavors, is also referred to as "the black druid." He may very well be the druid that collaborated with Edward's ancestor in creating the seal between Ireland and Faery. If these beings are one and the same, it would mean he is very powerful. He is said to be quite cold and apathetic, and he is known to possess great cunning. If he is truly bound to the house of Finvara, then you may at least rest easy that you will not be murdered in your bed by him. But it is the fairy queen that he serves, and as there is currently no lady filling that office, I would watch him closely and refrain from taking him into your confidence. At least until a time when you can be sure of his loyalties.

I hope this information is useful to you. Do not hesitate to send me further inquiries, and I will reply with haste. I had very much hoped to visit you at Knock Ma, but Edward . . . well, he is being very Edward, because of my "condition." He says that the fact I sit up reading until all hours is bad enough. I suppose I cannot blame him for not wanting to embark upon another journey into the unknown just now.

There, I've told you our news, but you must keep it under your hat. The queen has lost interest in us, at least for the time being, and we would like to keep it that way as long as possible.

All of my love and Edward's,
Ada

Despite the warm glow that kindled in my chest upon discovering that she and Edward were expecting a child, I couldn't help feeling this Doro matter was a great nuisance—just when I'd thought I was getting my house in order. *Was* the fellow dangerous? Should I confront him? Send him packing? Was that even possible?

He had served me well thus far, and that was putting it mildly. I was inclined to leave well enough alone. *I* had not found him cold or conniving—on the contrary, he had proved respectful, obedient, and resourceful. If it *was* within his power to assassinate me, he could have done it many times, so stealthily did he slip about the castle. He had also saved the princess's life, the most important service he'd yet to render.

In any case, no change could be made until my family's departure. I would have to keep my eye on him as best I could until then.

KOLI

Doro was giving me herbs for sleeping, and they had caused vivid dreams. The morning he left my bedside, I woke with a giddy feeling in my chest and warm fluttering in my belly that were slow to fade. Recalling that I'd been dreaming about Finvara, I covered my eyes with the heels of my hands and softly groaned. But covering my eyes did nothing to erase the images of the two of us playing in the hot-spring-fed lake at Mývatn. *Or* the memory of the feel of his bare skin sliding against mine, his hands clasping my waist. I touched my mouth, remembering with a sudden thump of my heart that I had tasted his lips in the dream. I closed my eyes, feeling the phantom kiss again.

Freyja help me.

Sitting up, I swung my legs down and eased my weight onto them. The pain in my injured leg had faded to a dull ache. I made my way slowly to a window.

It was a clear morning, and I could see all the way to the sea. The air in my chamber had become stuffy and stale, so I reached through the bars and pushed out the casement, taking the fresher air into my lungs.

I recalled that the king was expecting his visitors today.

Though I was told Finvara had inquired about my recovery, I had not seen him since he'd carried me to my chamber. It was just as well, because my mind was unsettled.

If even three days ago someone had told me how it would be

between us, I would have laughed. The Elf King's daughter would never fall into such a trap—for any sympathy of feeling between the fairy king and myself *must* be a trap. Yet somehow, inexplicably, it felt as if a kind of bond was forming.

Doro had risked my life because he wanted to be king. Finvara had bloodied his hands binding my wound. All of Doro's reassurances, despite sounding reasonable to my ear, rang hollow in my chest. My loyalty to my betrothed was an extension of my loyalty to the Elf King—I did not yet know whether I trusted or even liked him.

But in the end, it didn't matter.

I took a deep breath, gripping the windowsill. "I will conquer this."

I heard a soft metallic click and glanced down at the mechanical raven resting next to my hand. The windup mechanism must have held onto a tiny reserve of energy, because the bird's head had made a slight adjustment.

Raising my eyebrows and looking into the lifeless eye sockets, I asserted, "I *will*."

FINVARA

My family's carriage arrived in the early afternoon. The firglas had been watching for them, so the servants and I were ready and waiting to receive them in the great hall. All was tidy and bright, and a light, cold luncheon had been laid out on one end of the long banquet table. The party of travelers would be small—my father, eldest brother, and sister-in-law—and the lesser hall would have been more intimate. But the adjacent conservatory remained a fairy wilderness despite Doro's valiant efforts at restoring order. The steward himself had suggested we avoid it at least until the ball, when any remaining fairies would easily blend in with the guests. There was also a part of me that wanted to remind my father how far I had jumped in rank—presiding at the head of table in the great hall was one sure way of doing it.

Still, I fidgeted like a schoolboy as the sounds of nickering horses and jingling tack reached us from the bailey.

"The Earl of Mayo," called Doro from the great double doors, and my father entered the hall dressed in his formal military jacket, dark green with gold braid. He stopped to wait for the rest of his party, eyes moving over Doro. My steward was, as always, impeccably dressed, and had even donned a modern jacket and trousers for the occasion. But there was no masking his otherworldliness.

"Lady Mayo," said Doro, and my sister-in-law Margaret swept into the room, smiling with pleasure to see me. She too stopped just inside the entrance to wait, as her husband—my brother Owen— was announced, followed by a young woman I had never seen before.

"Miss Elinor O'Malley." A relative, apparently.

The formalities over, the party approached the head of the table, and I walked over to meet them.

"My lord," I said, reaching out and shaking hands with my father.

"Son." The earl was stern-faced as ever. The fact that his expression never changed made him impossible to read. It was easiest just to assume he was displeased. If you were mistaken, it came as a pleasant surprise.

Margaret stepped forward, enveloped in a cloud of dark-blue fabric, and leaned in for a kiss on each cheek. The earl's eyes never left me, and I was grateful for the distraction of the rest of the family.

"How good it is to see you, Duncan," said Margaret.

My father cleared his throat. With her back to him, the earl failed to see that she rolled her eyes and winked at me. "Your Majesty," she corrected.

"You too, sister," I replied, and meant it. Margaret had always been kind to me.

"And Owen," I added, reaching out a hand to my brother.

He nodded, a smile twisting up one corner of his lips—he would be finding all this a bit much. I couldn't blame him. "How are you, Duncan?" he asked, grasping my hand.

My father's frown deepened.

"Very well," I said. "It's good to see familiar faces."

Conscious that we were neglecting the spare O'Malley, I looked at her and smiled. "I'm pleased to meet you, Miss O'Malley."

Her smile broadened as color rose to her round cheeks, and she curtsied. "I am honored, Your Majesty."

"You may not remember," began Margaret, "but Elinor is a cousin of yours. It will have been some years since you've seen her. She has been living at Castlebar as my companion, and we have become thick as thieves."

I inspected the young lady again. She was fresh and lovely as an Irish country lass should be. She possessed a quantity of bouncy golden curls, the physics of which were a mystery to me as they seemed to never stop moving.

"You don't mind that we've brought her without leave, do you, Your Majesty?" asked Margaret sweetly. "She's a dear little thing and I confess I can hardly stand to part with her."

"Of course not," I replied. "The more the merrier."

Again the pretty thing blushed, and I turned my attention back to Margaret to give her an opportunity to recover. "Have you arrived with an appetite?"

"How considerate of you," replied Margaret, her eyes moving over the plates of cold meat and cheese. "I am famished."

My father grunted. "Aye, let's eat."

MASKS

KOLI

The carriage crept like a great moon snail along the steeply climbing road to Knock Ma's gatehouse. The drawbridge was just wide enough for it to pass. When it finally reached the bailey, I watched with a mix of curiosity and dread as the occupants emerged. Why I should dread them was a mystery—I would likely never meet them.

They are his people.

I turned from the window, vexed with my own mind. But a moment later I was back, wondering how the ladies—there appeared to be two of them—would manage the stairway from the bailey to the keep in those ridiculous dresses. I supposed that Irishwomen must be schooled in such things, because they ascended to the entrance without mishap.

Turning away again, I limped back to the bed. I was fidgety from too much confinement, yet my injury had left me weak.

Doro had decreed I should only attend tomorrow evening's festivities if I continued to rest until then, so when the maid came with my next meal, I asked for another of the sleeping draughts.

I had more appetite than I had since the injury, and my full belly and Doro's soothing herbs soon made the idea of rest appealing again.

Feeling sunlight on my face, I woke to discover that I had slept through the day and also through the night. The maid had already come with my breakfast, leaving the tray on the bed beside me.

I drank the cold coffee and ate a boiled egg before rising. My leg was stronger.

There came a sudden bang and I started, my head jerking toward the noise. I crossed to the window. I could see nothing through the trees, but I heard someone shout, followed by a long peal of feminine laughter. *A hunting party.* The king was entertaining his relations.

The unexpected pang of self-pity caused me to seek some other way to occupy my time, and I noticed something draped over one of the chairs by the fireplace.

I saw a note resting atop what looked like a pile of black feathers. "Enjoy the masquerade, lady," it read.

Doro. This was my costume for the ball. I would soon be getting out of this room.

I lifted the gown. It was a complicated assemblage of feathers and crepe—a raven disguise. How clever of him. There was also a feather cloak, divided into two sections to look like wings, and a beaked leather mask.

I wondered what disguise the king would wear. Would I even have an opportunity to speak with him? He would be busy playing host and entertaining his kin. I had some reservations about the evening—I had always disliked crowds. But I was curious about the guests, and my mask would make it easier to observe others without them noticing.

As the day wore on, I grew impatient. Nothing inside this chamber held my interest anymore. Finally I moved to the courtyard-facing window to watch the ball preparations. I couldn't lean out because of the bars, so I dragged a stool over and stood on top of it to get the proper angle.

Servants marched over the ground like ants carrying breadcrumbs. Occasionally I got a glimpse of my betrothed moving among them, directing their efforts, but he never glanced up at the tower. By sunset, the courtyard had been transformed—there were burning braziers, globes of colored light, flowers everywhere, and tables draped with white cloths. I could see the tiny floating lights flickering through the roof of the conservatory.

My own preparations for the ball would require the assistance of both Sorcha and the chambermaid, and they arrived at nightfall to assist me. The number of garments involved was astonishing—even worse than the gown I had worn the day I arrived at Knock Ma. Layers of petticoats, corset, bustle, stockings, not to mention the elaborate costume itself.

By the time the ladies finished, we were all a little breathless. I studied myself in the full-length mirror—and studied the servants while they observed me with thinly veiled horror. There was little chance I would go unnoticed, but at least my identity would remain concealed.

I made my way carefully down from the tower. My leg ached, but it was tolerable, and I had bound it for additional support.

Treig was waiting at the bottom of the stairs, and she smiled at me as I descended. "Very impressive, my lady."

"I agree," I said, "though the credit is not mine to take."

"Doro is a man of many talents."

I watched her through the mask's eyeholes, wondering

whether there was more to her statement than the obvious—yet her expression had not changed.

"So he is," I replied.

"I will escort you, lady," she said, "and I promise to keep out of your way. With any luck you will not notice me at all. If you tire, or find that you need anything, signal me by raising your hand and I will come."

"Thank you, Treig," I replied, and I turned down the corridor, listening to her soft footfalls behind me. I was bewildered by her change in address—she had gone out of her way to make me feel like a guest rather than a prisoner. Had Finvara spoken to her? Or Doro?

I continued out to the courtyard, which I had watched being transformed into an outdoor ballroom and salon. The braziers dotting the gleaming flagstones provided both heat and light, and the colorful globes hovered over the buffet tables, the musicians' corner, and a seating area that had been furnished with plush armchairs and couches. The first full moon of spring hung overhead like a plate in the sky, washing the revelers in its blue-white light. No one was dancing yet, although the musicians played a lively tune, and guests had begun to dip their cups into the punch fountains.

Many small beings skipped about the flagstones, and I took them at first to be children. After looking more closely, I realized they were fairies. Unlike the other guests, they wore no masks or disguises, just loose clothing made from various shades of a shimmering, diaphanous fabric. Nor did they seem much interested in communing with the larger folk, though the larger folk were frequently forced to change course to avoid tripping over or colliding with them. Their figures were silvery in the moonlight, and many of them were winged.

There were also claylike, stolid figures, with pendulous noses and generous beards. They reminded me of dwarves, the ancient metalworkers who dwelled in forges under the Icelandic highlands.

I even recognized the stick creatures that I'd frightened from the foot of the tower. They recognized me as well, or perhaps were intimidated by the costume, and erupted into sparrowlike warning cries before scurrying to the other side of the courtyard. I couldn't help feeling pleased by their panicked departure.

All of these beings, then, were Finvara's subjects. The rest would be his family and other visiting dignitaries—Irish men and women, subjects of Queen Isolde. After a while I became aware of a tension among the Irish—they seemed uncertain about the fairies skipping in their midst. The reunion of Ireland's ancient and modern peoples was only months old, after all. It was a tension I understood, growing up in the shadow of the longstanding enmity between Icelanders and elves.

"That is an enviable skill, my lady."

A figure wearing a porcelain mask and long white tunic had walked up behind me. A crown of ivy rested in his fair hair.

"Doro?"

"Pythagoras," he corrected, "a philosopher of ancient Greece. And I see that you are Raven, brightest and most mischievous of birds, and a servant of Odin."

"Indeed I am, with thanks to you," I replied, bowing my head. "But *what* is an enviable skill, sir? Frightening fairies?"

He laughed. "You stand here on the periphery of the ballroom, a most striking figure in black, and I don't believe any *but* the fairies have noticed you."

I had cast a spell to make my costume appear no more than a shadow.

"And yourself," I corrected.

"Well, I too am a fairy." Glancing out at the guests, he continued, "I must beg your leave for now, I'm afraid. I promise to find you later in the evening. Please enjoy yourself, princess."

"I shall," I replied, but my heart sank a little. I understood that I was his by agreement with my father, but must we dispense with courtship altogether? At this point I knew Finvara better than I knew my betrothed.

I was being childish, of course. He was the king's man and responsible for Finvara's guests this evening—in addition to his own intrigues. It would not further our interests for Doro to be dangling after *me*.

As he moved away, I thought to call after him, "What disguise does the king wear?"

He was already out of hearing.

My gaze moved over the costumed revelers, studying them more closely, and one in particular caught my eye. Her disguise was as striking as my own, though different in every way. She wore a gown nearly the same peachy pink as her flesh, and her mass of golden curls had been artfully extended and incorporated into the fabric, all the way to the floor. The costume created the illusion that she was nude, with modesty preserved only by her hair. She wore no mask, only her own flushed cheeks and full red lips. A strange costume, I thought, but there was a story that tugged at my memory, an English one, about a queen who rode through her city unclothed as some form of protest.

I admired the lady's boldness. The costume was having its desired effect, or so I thought, as she was surrounded by male revelers. Even a few of the half-sized, bearded fairies hovered nearby, peering over the rim of their ale tankards with openly lustful expressions. I could catch no more than snatches of the group's conversation, but by observing the lady's movements and gestures, it was clear she had a favorite—a tall man in black and white, wearing a satin jester's crown and black mask.

I continued to watch the lady, fascinated. So absorbed was I by the brazenness of her interaction with her admirers, I did not immediately notice when her gaze began to flicker in my direction. After a few sidelong glances, she fixed her eyes steadily on me, and my breath caught. My spell was not strong enough to hide me from careful observers, and it could be that my steady attention had drawn *hers*. If so, she was more perceptive than I would have given her credit for.

"Cousin," she said, audible now that she was turned in my direction, "do you see that nightmare over there? That raven *thing?*"

My jaw clenched and I stiffened. I felt a hard tug at my chest as my furies broke free without warning. The chit's eyes went wide and she took a step back, uttering a cry of alarm.

No!

This was disastrous—a kind of attention Doro would wish me to avoid. But before I could attempt to recall them, the jester stepped in front of the girl, and with a wave of his hand, the shadow birds scattered, melting into the star-studded blackness.

My stomach turned. The girl's favored suitor was King Finvara.

The other guests could see me now—I knew because of the way they stared. The music too had faltered, and the musicians started to pick their way back through the notes in an attempt to cover the disturbance. Another lady had taken the arm of the frightened young woman and was directing her toward a punch fountain.

The attention of the other guests began to drift back to their companions, but the jester—*the king*—still stared at me. Humiliation singed my cheeks and wrung my insides, and I turned and fled the courtyard. The first escape I encountered was the conservatory adjacent to the hall where I had dined with the king. I pushed open the door and walked inside, my labored breathing a harsh disruption of the tranquility of the garden, and the quiet melody of trickling water.

This was what had come of too much time spent with the king. I cared about what he thought of me. And watching him save his pretty countrywoman from my furies . . . How had I ever come to believe he and I had anything in common? We were truly as different as light and shadow.

The air in the conservatory was heavy and too warm, but the trickle of water was soothing, as was the sweet smell of flowers. I sat watching the fairy lights float around me.

Above, plinking noises sounded on the roof. Glancing up, I saw the spiderlike feet of my furies pressing against the glass as they hopped about, their feathers washed a deep, lustrous blue by the moonlight.

"Useless beasts," I muttered, "go away."

With a single cackling protest, they launched up and faded again into the night.

The door to the conservatory creaked as it opened, and I froze. I would apologize to Doro for losing my temper and promise him to better control it in the future. He would accept my apology, because I had accepted *his* for almost killing me.

"May I join you, lady?"

My heart thumped.

I had not anticipated *this* interview would come so soon. I gained a moment to compose myself by gathering my voluminous skirts so they wouldn't ensnare me as I turned.

"Your Majesty," I said, curtsying deeply, grateful for my mask. He too still wore the jester's mask.

Closing the door behind him, he took a few steps toward me. "How is your injury, if I may ask?"

I swallowed. "Much improved, I thank you."

"I am glad to hear it."

My hands brushed nervously along the feathers of my skirt as silence stretched between us.

"She meant nothing by it, I assure you," he said finally, lifting his mask to reveal a soft expression. His kindness only deepened my sense of shame at my loss of control.

"She is young," he continued, "and you are thoroughly intimidating in that disguise."

"I apologize, Your Majesty." My words came out too fast. "I had not realized she could see me, and was startled by her remark."

"I confess *I* had not noticed you there," replied the king, "or I would not have left you standing unattended."

The warmth of his tone began to work a kind of magic on me. My breaths came easier, and I lowered my stiffened shoulders.

"That is kind of you, sire. But I would not have wished you to abandon your companion. No more than I would wish you to take notice of a storm cloud while the sun was shining so warmly on you."

A smile spread over his face. "Some sailors enjoy a good squall, my lady."

Heat flooded my cheeks and chest.

Before I could think what to reply to such a statement, he continued, "The ray of sunshine is Miss Elinor O'Malley."

"A relation, then?"

"So I am told, though a distant one. I don't recall meeting her before this. I'm not entirely sure what motivated my family to bring her, except that my sister-in-law is very fond of her."

I raised an eyebrow at his apparent innocence. "You can think of no other reason, Your Majesty?"

His gaze turned curious, and he tilted his head to one side, like he was trying to better see through my mask's glass-covered eyeholes. I pushed it up and away from my face, and he smiled at me.

"Thank you," he said. "That disguise is remarkably unsettling. Doro's handiwork, I'll wager."

I nodded.

"If I'm not mistaken, that's a plague mask," he said. "A long time ago, physicians wore them when treating patients."

In addition to paying tribute to my Elf ancestry, Doro had made me a specter of death. No wonder the maids and the young lady had taken fright.

The king gestured at his own costume. "He made mine as well. I'm quite pleased with it, as it accurately reflects how I feel most of the time."

A fool. It struck me that Doro had been making a statement with his choice—and suddenly I was angry. What need was there to humiliate Finvara? It was arrogant and petty and besides that, untrue.

"Now tell me, lady, what it is that you know and I do not."

My heart raced. Had he a suspicion about Doro and I? "Your Majesty?"

"Will you tell me what insight you have into Miss Elinor's presence here?"

I quietly let out a breath.

"You really have no idea?" I asked.

For a moment he looked blank, and then he groaned and rolled his eyes. "They expect me to marry the lass."

The realization so annoyed him—and his reaction was so dramatic—that laughter bubbled up in my throat, but I managed to swallow it. "Is that such a bad thing?"

"I wondered why my father had not been lecturing me," he replied, growing more disgruntled as the new understanding took hold. "He's trying to preserve my good humor."

"She's very pretty, isn't she?" It was an honest question, as I'd had limited exposure to females like Miss O'Malley.

"Aye, she's pretty," he confirmed, raising his hand and letting it fall. "But she's a child. Another soul to look after is the very last thing I need, and the earl should see that. He wants to have the title fully under O'Malley control, and it's gotten the better of his good sense."

"Maybe he wants to leave someone behind who is more willing to be controlled by *him*." My tone had sobered. I believed both Doro and my father intended to use me in a similar way.

The king eyed me keenly. "Aye, I believe you have it. And I thank you for removing the blindfold before the trap could close over me. That's another debt I owe you."

I stared at him, dark wings fluttering against my heart.

The king stepped closer and offered his arm, the bells on the points of his drooping crown tinkling. "Are you well, lady?"

"I am, Your Majesty, thank you." I shook my head at his offer of support. A memory of the shape and firmness of his arm rose unbidden in my mind.

"Your leg is causing you pain." He stepped closer yet, the arm still offered, and not knowing how to refuse without seeming ungrateful, I took it.

"Maybe a little," I said, a strange warmth pooling in my belly as I touched him.

He led me to a nearby bench, and we both sat down. I would have released his arm then, but his hand now covered mine.

"Lady," he said, studying me, "no one here has been unkind to you, I hope?"

The question took me by surprise, and his scrutiny did nothing to improve the clarity of my thoughts, or quiet the bubbling warmth in my chest.

"No, sire."

He eyed me with such concern—I almost would have thought *tenderness*—that I dropped my eyes to the hand I had fisted in my lap.

"I'm relieved to hear it," he replied. "If such a thing should happen, I want you to come to me at once. Will you promise to do that?"

"If you wish," I said faintly.

"I do wish."

FINVARA

Her confusion tugged at my heart, and I believed I understood it. She had never expected, nor probably wanted, friendship from me. She was raised to be my enemy, and to make matters worse, I had slighted her.

Goblin princess.

How keenly I felt that now. Now that I knew her. And this golden Irish beauty—who my family was trying to serve to me like a pig on a platter—had called her a *nightmare*.

"Now that you've been with us a little while," I said, "do you find that there is anything you lack? Does your chamber suit? Do you require more attendants?"

She looked at me with an expression of bafflement. "I have everything I need, Your Majesty."

"I would like to discontinue your guard," I said. "Having been in battle with you, I know that one firglas warrior could hardly stop you should you take it into your head to kill me. But for your own safety, I believe it's best that the guard remain."

"I don't mind. Treig has been kind to me."

"Then you may consider her your personal attendant rather than your guard," I said, relieved to be able to do *anything* to make myself feel less the brute. "I will speak to her tonight."

"That is kind of you, sire," she said with hesitation in her voice. "Only ..."

I waited for her to formulate her thoughts. We still mostly spoke English between us, though I had lapsed into Irish at times. I doubted she was as comfortable even with English as I was.

"Why?" she asked finally. "I am not wanted here. You were forced to take me. Only a few minutes ago, I menaced your party guests. Do not think me ungrateful, I just don't understand why you should care for my comfort."

I took a deep breath and sighed. She was not going to let me off easy.

"Because I regret the circumstances that brought you here. Because I recognize the unfairness of it, and I'd like to make your life here more tolerable if I can."

Because it turns out you're the only person in this asylum I have anything in common with.

Her fingers squeezed my arm slightly, perhaps even involuntarily. But it fired my blood and emboldened me to add, "The fact is, I enjoy your company, lady. Truly, you're my only friend here, as strange as that must sound. You make me feel a little less lost at sea."

Again her gaze fluttered to her lap, and she replied faintly, "It is kind of you to say so."

Had I said too much? Her wall was up, and I couldn't guess at her thoughts. It was possible that she'd become more to me than I to her, and I had made her uncomfortable. I'd at least been honest, and hopefully accountable for my poor behavior early on.

"I had best return to my guests," I said, more for her sake than mine. Her hand slipped from my arm as I stood up. "Doro will scold if he discovers me hiding. Will you dance with me, lady? Unless you prefer to return to your chamber and rest, in which case I will fetch Treig."

Finally she looked up at me, and while there was no visible smile upon her lips, I sensed one in the offing. When, I wondered, had I become such a keen student of her expressions?

"One dance, I think, can do no damage, Your Majesty."

A small victory, but I flushed with pleasure. Smiling, I held out my hand to her.

KOLI

There was a lightness in my thoughts and in my step as we left the privacy of the conservatory. It was tempting to lie to myself—

to believe the buoyant feeling was the result of my successful campaign to gain Finvara's trust. The truth was that I was pleased to have his trust for its own sake.

The king had called me his friend. Where was the distasteful pride I had expected? The contempt and arrogance?

These questions were chased by less welcome ones. Was it possible he had concealed his nature in a scheme to earn *my* trust? Was he capable of such deceit?

He is the fairy king.

Outside the conservatory, he helped remove my cloak and laid it on a nearby bench. Then he led me among his guests, and the burbling stream of their conversation dried up. I looked for Doro, and our eyes met across the dancefloor. He signaled the musicians, and the strains of a waltz began.

In the court of the Elf King, we did not waltz. When the union between the Elf King's daughter and King Finvara had been first proposed, a new tutor had been brought in, and I had learned to waltz and improved my Irish.

Now the king and I faced each other. Our masks were in place again, but I could see the crinkling around his eyes and knew that he was smiling. He took my hand in his, and his other hand came to my waist. The buoyant feeling surged as he swung us into the melody, and we began to move around the floor. He led with such experienced grace that my own inexperience made no difference.

"You dance beautifully," said the king, his voice muffled behind the mask.

I raised an eyebrow at the courtly compliment. "It is kind of you to say so, Your Majesty, but I know that I do not."

"Truly, you are light on your feet," he insisted. "Did you dance in your father's court?"

"Not generally, and never like this. Though it was part of my education."

"Well I am grateful, as it has afforded me the pleasure of being your partner. But you must tell me if you tire, or if you feel any pain."

Other couples had begun to join us on the floor. At one point we glided close to Elinor, whose partner wore a white wig and a brilliantly gold jacket.

"Your lady's disguise," I said, "it's from an old story, is it not?"

"*My* lady?" said the king archly. "If I didn't know you better, I would suspect you of needling me."

I smiled inside the mask.

"Elinor is disguised as Lady Godiva," he continued. "According to the English story, the lady was unhappy about how heavily her husband taxed his subjects, and she rode through the streets unclothed to give them relief."

"I am confused as to how this would help, sire."

He laughed. "You've a lively sense of humor, lady."

"I am in earnest," I protested. "In what way could it improve the situation? Unless she intended to make them forget about the taxes altogether."

His eyes sparkled with mirth, and his hand tightened on my waist. "Indeed, you may have it!"

I found myself thinking of warm water—skin gliding over skin—and lost the thread of our conversation.

Thankfully he continued, "Her husband told her that if she rode through the streets naked, he would remit the tax. Essentially he wanted her to stop pestering him."

I shook my head. "A strange story."

"Aye. It's meant to titillate, I think. Much the same as Elinor's costume."

At that moment, we again spun in view of the lady and her partner, who had whispered something close to her ear and caused her to laugh—a sound like tinkling bells.

The king's powers of observation did him credit, despite the fact he had not suspected his family's plot. King though he might be, it did not appear that he would be permitted to determine his own fate any more than I would be.

And it is so much worse than he imagines.

The thought settled like a cold weight in my chest, dragging me back down to earth.

AN ILL WIND

KOLI

The waltz wound down, and I scanned the courtyard for Doro. While the king and I were dancing, I had noticed him moving about the banquet tables, where he made small adjustments to dishes and decorations, and spoke quietly to the fairy folk who had retired there. At the moment, he was talking with a group of stately firglas. They were dressed in regal finery that belonged to another age, and each wore a bright and bejeweled mask shaped like cat eyes. One of them glanced briefly in our direction.

It's begun already. Something sharp twisted in my belly.

"My lady."

The music had stopped, and as the king released me, I turned to find Miss O'Malley waiting nearby. Her cheeks were closer to raspberry than pink now, and she was wringing the fingers of one hand with the other. Her eyes were wide, her lips parted, and she appeared unable to speak. I pushed back my mask, and her features relaxed.

"Elinor," said the king from behind me, "this is Princess Koli from Iceland. She is the Elf King's daughter, and my guest."

"Your Highness," the young woman addressed me in a more determined tone. She stepped forward and curtsied, so surprising me that I glanced back at the king. He too had removed his mask, and he smiled and raised an eyebrow.

"I am pleased to make your acquaintance," she continued. "I hope that you will forgive my earlier rudeness." She wrung her fingers again. "Your disguise is very—" She blinked rapidly, and looked a little lost.

"Intimidating," I suggested, taking pity on the poor thing.

"Indeed," she breathed gratefully, releasing her fingers. How childlike she was. The king was right—she might be of age, but she was too young to stand beside him. He needed a queen, not a charge.

"I too must apologize," I said. "My birds frightened you. Sometimes they act before I can stop them. They offered the king the same treatment the first day I met him."

This made her smile. "Did they, cousin?"

"Aye, they did," replied the king, moving to stand beside me. "Though we're old friends now."

This familiarity verging on intimacy washed over me like a warm wave.

"Thank you, lady," said the girl, curtsying again.

"Now Elinor," began the king, "I believe you've promised me a dance."

He held out his hand, and she took it eagerly. The strains of the waltz began, and as they moved away, the king glanced back. His expression was soft and grateful, and the smile he turned on his glowing partner had first been directed at me.

There is no duplicity in him, I realized in a moment of purest anguish.

"Princess?"

My composure had collapsed, and I felt my furies mustering.

I took a full breath before slowly turning. Doro stood with his hand outstretched.

"Will you dance?"

Less than an hour ago I had wanted this. Now I wanted to tell him I was tired—I wanted to return to my chamber and make sense of what was happening to me.

Instead, I reached for his hand. He pulled me into his arms and we began our circuit of the dancefloor.

So cold, I observed. While heat radiated from the king. I could feel it anytime he was close. But Doro—if I closed my eyes, I would wonder what had let in the draft.

"Are you enjoying the ball, lady?" he asked.

"Well enough, my lord," I replied amiably.

"Your deportment has been exquisite," he said in a quieter voice. "Even the burst of violence that accompanied the O'Malley chit's rude remarks worked to your advantage in the end. I believe the king is actually *fond* of you."

My stomach churned as we spun. "I believe he is."

"I am concerned about the girl, though," he continued. "She is very like the ancient Finvara's favorite wife. The king's family has thrust her at him, and the fool has no idea."

The fool. Anger flared again.

"He has an idea now," I said crisply.

He studied me, and the eyes behind his mask narrowed as he smiled. "You told him."

I nodded. "You're right, he didn't know."

Doro laughed, and it made me feel very differently than the king's laughter had. "What did he say?"

"He was not pleased. He resents their interference, and he feels she is too young."

Doro's eyes were bright. *Hungry.* "You must encourage his thinking in that vein."

"Of course." Doro *would* fear the girl. If the king married Miss O'Malley, Doro would be bound to her, and all his plans would be finished.

His plans, and mine too. *Freyja help me, can I go through with this?* I felt a sudden pinprick between my shoulder blades, where my father's mark was inked, and I flinched.

"We cannot be too careful," he continued. "The lady's beauty will be hard for him to resist, being what he is, and the lady is far too keen for my liking. But that I have in hand."

Uneasiness caused me to grip his shoulder. "What do you mean?"

He smiled. "I shall simply frighten her away."

The thought of the last frightful thing he'd done only increased the uneasy feeling.

"It may not keep her away indefinitely," he continued, "though it won't need to. The king has already committed multiple offenses. He gave an order to expel most of his subjects from the castle. He organized this family fete in place of the equinox celebration that his subjects expected. The firglas chieftain already questions the legitimacy of his new king. Even before Duncan O'Malley arrived, they were grumbling about suddenly finding themselves under Irish rule."

"So the thing is nearly done!" I replied, shocked. How had he managed it so quickly?

"Thanks in large part to you, lady."

FINVARA

Elinor kept up a steady stream of conversation—almost entirely on her own—which freed me to keep an eye on my steward and the princess.

She is easy with him, I thought. Though it was hard to be sure with their masks. It would not be surprising if they had grown close—he had treated a grave injury and nursed her back to health. She was an intriguing woman. Perhaps not charming in the traditional sense, but she was observant—clearly more so than I—and her wits were sharp. She was endearingly plainspoken, and just this evening I had discovered her capacity for humor. She could more than hold her own in a scrape too, which was not a quality found commonly amongst gentlewomen.

At the times when our bodies had been close, I was sure that I had felt the pull of sensuality in her—a river I suspected ran quite deep, despite her often reserved exterior. I wondered whether Doro had felt it, too, and shuddered at the thought.

It struck me that all these qualities taken together made up the sort of woman I would one day hope to make my queen. The irony of it almost made me laugh aloud—the Elf King's daughter, the woman that I had spurned!

As the dance continued, I thought of Lady Meath's letter, and darker thoughts crept in. Might Doro be a danger to me? Her letter described an ambitious man. Would such a man be content passing through eternity as a servant, especially if he was indeed a druid, and a powerful wielder of magic? Was he even now living a double life? It would certainly explain why I didn't know where he was more than half the time.

Doro was giving the princess his full attention, and it occurred to me to examine whether these suspicions had more to do with *her*. Was I jealous? I had told her she was my only friend here, and so she was. Was I unwilling to share her? My predecessor and ancestor was notoriously jealous. And there had certainly been times when I had myself behaved competitively when it came to women.

All I could say for certain was the pair of them had my lines tangled, which was a condition I generally guarded against.

The waltz was ending. After bowing to Elinor and handing her to the next eager partner, I scanned the courtyard for the princess.

Doro was escorting her back toward the castle. She leaned on his arm, limping slightly. I allowed myself one moment to regret it wasn't me accompanying her to the tower.

Determined to cease wrestling these thoughts so that I might engage with my relations and attempt to make myself agreeable to my other guests, I headed for the banquet tables.

My opening salvo consisted of eliciting Lord Galway's opinion on the quality of fowl sport in this county, followed by his lady's preferences with regard to the various bakers, butchers, and grocers. Then I moved on to Lord and Lady Roscommon.

I passed *hours* in this manner, or so it seemed, making sure to speak to every dignitary in his or her turn. My own subjects proved, as ever, the most challenging. The easiest to hold actual conversation with was the chieftain of the firglas, Yarl, who spent most of his time on his estate—which was located in a region of Faery that had not, at least so far, merged with Ireland. He and his wife were aloof, however. Most of his people seemed to possess that quality, and as of yet I'd failed in my attempts to soften them. Princess Koli had apparently managed to form a connection with Treig. It occurred to me there were a number of similarities between the princess and the firglas, and I wondered if perhaps they shared ancestors.

The smaller fairy folk were hopeless pranksters, with the conversation skills of little children—except they made even less sense. They spoke a very old form of Irish, and they connected words in baffling ways. I had to content myself with observing their capers and tossing them sweetmeats and trinkets, which they were ecstatic over. I thanked my stars again for Doro—despite the doubts weighing on me—as he had ensured we were well stocked with both.

During a leaden conversation about the art of knife-sharpening with a trio of half-pint fellows who'd drunk too much ale, I noticed the princess had not in fact retired—she was secreted in the shadow of a rose arbor near the conservatory, resting on a stone bench. The sight of her lifted my spirits, and as soon as I could politely excuse myself, I sought a tankard myself—as well as a glass of punch, which I intended to deliver to her personally as a reward to myself for my valiant social toils.

I was still awaiting a servant who'd gone to fetch a tray of clean cups when a scream rent the convivial atmosphere.

KOLI

I preferred the seclusion of my bower to marching across the dance floor in every way but one—I had to forgo the company of the king. As my eyes followed him performing his tedious host duties, my mind kept returning to the things he'd told me in the conservatory, and to the heat our banter had seemed to generate in the waltz that followed. Had he felt it too?

I would banish such thoughts, only to find myself, moments later, imagining how it would be had we actually wed. Would I be by his side, acquainting myself with his subjects? Would I find the sustained chatter more bearable in his company?

Would affection have grown between us? *More* than affection? Would we have become man and wife in more than name? The waltz had suggested that possibility.

This last thought set off a not-subtle fluttering in the very lowest part of my belly. But the pleasant feeling was cut off by a searing pain between my shoulder blades, and I gasped.

I closed my eyes and cleared my mind, breathing shallowly until the pain began to subside.

I haven't forgotten, Father. I just had no idea it would be so hard.

I was about to rise and return to my chamber when Miss O'Malley and her friend—the king's sister-in-law, dressed as a shepherdess—passed by without noticing me and entered the conservatory. Once inside, what had been a whispered conversation continued in normal voices, and thanks to the thinness of the glass-paned walls, I could hear all of it.

And tedious it was. They admired the roses and the twinkling lights. They discussed the guests' various disguises. They rattled on about the music and dancing. No unmarried gentleman or lady was spared a critique of their person, their manner, or their skill on the dance floor.

I was again rising to retire, when the ladies began to speak of something that *did* interest me.

"What do you think of Duncan, Nora?" asked the king's sister.

Duncan, I knew, was Finvara's given name—the name he had used until very recently.

The girl giggled. "Oh, Margaret, he's very dashing and handsome, isn't he?"

"And so I told you he *was*," replied the other lady in a lilting, teasing tone.

"And chivalrous," continued Miss O'Malley, "the way he jumped between me and those frightful birds!"

I locked my fingers together in my lap.

"That goblin woman! The hateful thing. I wish he had not been forced to take her. To think they would have her *marry* him." Margaret made a clucking noise. "You needn't worry though. I can't think why he asked her to the ball—pity perhaps, his heart has always been more soft than sensible—but I'm sure she's kept locked in the tower most of the time."

She's an ugly, scarecrow of a thing, is she not? I closed my eyes, anger kindling inside me. My furies lined up on the bench on either side of me, their harsh voices uttering protests I could not.

"*Shush*," I hissed, and they fell silent, cocking their sleek heads from side to side as if they were listening as intently as I.

"Nay, don't speak so, Margaret," replied Miss O'Malley in a sobered voice. "I don't believe he thinks of her that way. She apologized to me and spoke very kindly. I do feel sorry for her, though, so far from home. And of course she's not pretty, though in her own country she may be considered a great beauty."

My anger dampened. Miss O'Malley might be childish, but her heart was not hard.

"Well, my dear," replied Margaret, a slight stiffness in her tone, "don't worry yourself over her. Your kindness does you credit, to be sure. The king and your lovely self will be perfectly—"

Margaret's speech was cut short when one of the two ladies let out a piercing scream.

I sprang from the bench, hurrying to the conservatory and throwing open the door. Margaret was staggering backward, eyes wide with terror, but Elinor—*something* was dragging her into the lily pool. I saw what looked like octopus tentacles—except they were smooth and black, like the steam hoses that had animated the barrow-wight—coiled tightly around the girl's ankles. The hoses ran into the pool, which was far deeper than it appeared—and in the middle of the pool I saw the sodden head of a woman half-emerged from the water, her stringy hair tangled with water weeds and shells, the whites of her wide eyes glowing in the moonlight. I might not know Irish fairies, but I knew a water hag when I saw one.

I ran to the pool, my furies sweeping in behind me. Gripping Elinor under the arms, I tried pulling her away. But another tentacle flew up from the surface of the water and coiled around my arm. The terrified girl was almost fully submerged, dark water staining the fine, pale fabric of her dress. She clung tightly to my free arm as the tentacles continued to drag us both.

My furies dove at the hag's head—this time requiring no urging from me—and they snatched out long strands of hair as she slashed at the air above her with the remaining tentacles. The hoses were tipped with copper points and one of the birds gave a squawk of pain as it was swatted right out of the air.

I cast a simple displacement spell, and the water in the pool began sloshing from side to side, as in an agitated bucket, so that with each wave, Elinor was able to catch a breath of air. I was now submerged to my waist.

My mind flailed, seeking a spell that would end the attack. If I tried something strong enough to injure or kill, I might harm Elinor. Had I my bow, I could easily dispatch the creature.

Relief swelled as Finvara joined us, slashing a tentacle with a knife and freeing one of Elinor's legs.

Then I heard an angry shout—an Irish curse—and a firglas pike flew over us, striking the naked and sagging flesh of the water hag. The point of the pike pierced her chest, and the tentacles released and flopped back into the pool. Crawling on our knees in the muck, the king and I took hold of Elinor and dragged her out of the water. She collapsed onto the flagstones, coughing.

"Can you stand, lady?" asked Treig, stooping over me.

I gripped the firglas woman's outstretched hand and she raised me to my feet. My leg felt like it was full of angry hornets.

"Thank you, Treig," I said, squeezing her hand before releasing it.

The displacement spell had faded and the pool calmed. There was no sign of the hag except for the end of a severed tentacle near the water's edge. Elinor appeared unharmed, though she was sobbing. Mud coated her from head to foot.

"The goblin woman!" cried Margaret. "She tried to drown her!"

My heart jumped to my throat and my eyes darted from Margaret to the king, whose expression was grim. Before I could speak, Treig said, "Nay, majesty. The princess was trying to save her."

The king returned his attention to the young lady, speaking to her in soothing tones. He took a dry cloak from the hands of a bystander—Doro.

I recalled my earlier conversation with my betrothed. *I shall frighten her away.*

FINVARA

"I'll see to your other guests, sire," said Doro.

"Do," I replied curtly, rising to my feet. *And a curse on you, this place, and every bloody creature in it.*

"Margaret," I called to my sister-in-law, "take Elinor to her chamber. Her injuries do not appear serious, but send a servant to find me if we need to fetch a surgeon." I'd order the firglas to drag the man here by his ears if I had to.

As Margaret moved to comply, my father joined us. There was no mistaking his mood.

"Duncan," he said gravely, "I would speak with you."

Before turning to him, I finally allowed myself to look at the princess. She stood soaking wet and hunched against her servant.

"Are you injured, lady?" I asked her.

"I am well, Your Majesty."

Hadrian's Wall. If I hoped to pry anything more from her than this stiff reply, I must wait until I was away from my relations.

"Treig," I said, "help Princess Koli back to her chamber."

The guard hooked an arm around the princess's waist, and I hesitated, ludicrously, hoping for one last glance of—what? *Anything.* Anything that would shed light on what was going on in the lady's head.

It was the second attack since her arrival, and she had been present on both occasions. I couldn't ignore that fact, yet neither could I bring myself to believe she'd had anything to do with it. Mightn't it be a new phase of the unusual events that had been happening since the seal was broken?

"*Duncan*," insisted my father.

My insides knotted as I turned to him. "Let us return to the keep."

He followed me back inside the castle, to the hall where I had dined with the princess. I conjured fire, and the candles and hearth flared to life. The effect was impressive, and I hoped it would temper the lecture I was about to receive. It was a foolish hope.

True to form, I thought as I removed the jester's crown and dropped it on the table, the jingling bells seeming to mock me.

"What is happening here?" began my father, his dark-blue eyes flashing. "Do you exercise *any* control over this place or its inhabitants?"

"Precious little," I admitted with childish ill humor. I knew my father, and there was no point in protesting. No point in explaining that I was trying, or that I had taken measures. It wouldn't be good enough. And nor could I blame him—Elinor might have been killed. Now I must consult Doro again, and become even more dependent on him.

"Three months, son," he continued. "Three *months* you've been here. There's a strange ship in the sky above your castle. Monsters roam your grounds. You even seem to be on familiar terms with that elf woman, who could very well be to blame for *all* of this. Has the queen's faith in you been misguided?"

Forgotten was the fact that Isolde had strongly urged me to *marry* "that elf woman." Also forgotten were the harsh words the earl had himself spoken about "his mad niece" on that occasion.

"Aye, perhaps it has been," I replied, my gaze finding the window—hoping, I realized, for a glimpse of the princess in the conservatory. But she and Treig had gone. The only remaining signs of the violent attack were the crumpled lilies and the stones dislodged around the edge of the pool. The creature would have to be removed and examined. Had it been a living thing, or something reanimated, like the barrow-wight? How was I *ever* to put a stop to these unpleasant surprises?

My subjects don't respect me, any more than my father does. The queen thought my connection to my ancestor would be enough, but it isn't.

I looked at the earl, who was about to speak, and continued, "I was not brought up to this, as well you know. I've lived much of my life at sea. There was never any chance of my becoming earl, even had I outlived my brothers."

These were things we didn't speak of, and color blossomed just below the sharpest points of my father's cheekbones. He rested his hand on the hilt of the ancient short sword he always wore, even when he wasn't disguised as a chieftain of old.

"Maybe not," he said in a low voice. "I never cared for you less, nor treated you as if you *were* less than your brothers. And you have always been Isolde's favorite."

I knew that my father had loved my mother, more even than he had loved my brothers' mother. I also knew it pained him that because of the illegitimacy of my birth—and for some, the color of my skin—I was viewed as less worthy, less O'Malley, than my brothers. The fact that his royal niece valued my companionship and advice made him both proud and happy.

"Be guided by *me*, son," he urged.

I straightened. "If you want to speak to me about marriage, sir, do so plainly. Don't bring me a trinket and offer it like you would to a child. If you want to advise me, *advise* me. I have criticized myself enough for both of us."

My father sighed. He turned to face the fireplace, resting his bulk against the edge of the table.

"Don't marry Elinor, if you do not wish it. She's a good girl, and you could do far worse. Though after tonight, *she* may not wish it." He looked at me. "Marry *someone*. Someone who will strengthen your position here. That reedy fairy fellow—did he not bring a daughter with him tonight?" Yarl, he meant, the firglas chieftain. The earl folded his arms and narrowed his gaze. "Anyone but that elf woman."

I opened my mouth to reply, *I have no intention of marrying "that elf woman."* Yet the words hung on my tongue. I slipped a hand into a pocket, closing my fingers around my mother's compass.

"There's an ill wind filling your sails, son," grumbled my father. "Look to it. Before it's too late."

I rubbed the back of the compass with my thumb, reflecting on tangled lines, ill winds, and Lady Meath's "black druid." Something suddenly clicked into place.

I am a fool indeed.

A FOOL AND HIS KINGDOM

KOLI

After my maid filled the tub in my chamber and helped me out of my costume, I soaked until the water was the same greenish brown as the mud from the lily pool. While I put on my nightdress she built up the fire, and then she bade me goodnight.

Sitting in a chair by the hearth while my hair dried, I listened to the wind in the trees, which seemed to mock my restless thoughts with their violent thrashing.

Real damage had been wrought by Doro. In addition to calling the king's legitimacy into question, he'd caused Finvara's first fete to be disrupted by a violent attack that was sure to be discussed far and wide. The king would be doubted now by fairy and Irishman alike.

Which is exactly to plan and so why am I fretting?

There was no longer any mystery about it—I liked and trusted the king more than I liked or trusted the man I had agreed to marry.

As I sank back in the chair, something on the floor beneath my bed glimmered in the firelight. I rose and walked over to peer underneath.

A *knife*. Gasping, I took hold of the weapon and carried it into the lamplight. I ran my thumb over the polished wooden hilt and then touched the sharp edge lightly with one finger. It had two edges, in fact—it was an Irish skean.

Your father has told me that you do not shrink from spilling blood.

Doro had visited my chamber. I went back to look under the bed again and found a slip of paper I'd missed. The only word written on it was *snart*—which in Elvish meant "soon." I shivered.

Voices drifted up the stairs and I lifted my chin toward the sound. The king was below, speaking with Treig.

"My lady has retired," she said.

"Nevertheless, I intend to speak to her," replied the king.

My heart galloped at the sound of his boots on the stairs. I shot a panicked glance around the room. The bed was turned down—I thrust the knife between the sheets.

"I'm not dressed, Your Majesty," I called out, straightening to meet him.

He didn't answer, and the footsteps drew closer. Finally he appeared at the top of the stairs.

Our gazes locked, and for a moment, neither of us moved. My heart pounded so violently I thought he must hear it. What could have moved him to burst in on me like this?

He took a few steps into the room and I closed my parted lips to calm my breathing. He no longer wore the jester's costume, but simple black trousers and boots, and an untucked, half-buttoned shirt.

His blue eyes were cold and hard.

"Are you well, Your Majesty?" I asked, speaking low so my voice would not tremble. *He knows something.*

"I am not," he said, his voice as cold and hard as his gaze. "In fact, I am thrice a fool."

I fought for composure. "How so?"

He held a fist before his chest, and it bounced with each line he spoke. "First, I trusted Doro. Third, I walked around in that disguise while my own steward sneered at me. But second . . ." The muscles of his jaw clenched. "I trusted *you*."

My stomach roiled. Perspiration trickled down my back, and the ash tree between my shoulders began to tingle. What options were open to me? He would believe no denial, for despite his assertion, he was no fool. If I could reach the knife, I might make my escape. Treig might help me.

Or, I could tell him the truth and accept the consequences.

The mere thought of exposing my involvement in Doro's scheme caused the ash tree to burn like the heated blade of that knife pressed against my spine. A cry broke from my lips and I stumbled toward the bed.

The king moved quickly toward me and I drew away from him, maneuvering so one corner of the bed was between us. My furies poured out of me like dark smoke from the fireplace, but the king banished them.

He held out one hand in a steadying motion. "I'm not going to hurt you."

I watched him warily, drawing quick breaths as I recovered from the pain. "What *will* you do, Your Majesty?"

He hesitated, his face drawn and grim. "I don't know. What I want now is answers."

I gripped the bedpost, waiting for him to continue.

"Have you and Doro deceived me?" Somehow, he managed to keep both accusation and anger from his voice—though accusation and anger would have been easier to take.

I nodded. Again, pain knifed down my back and I squeezed

my eyes closed and gritted my teeth. Perspiration wet my upper lip.

Finvara's voice was closer as he asked, "How long?"

I looked up and caught his grimace as I replied, "From the beginning."

Am I really doing this? Any thought of attempting to continue the deception had fled. I felt powerless to do anything but answer truthfully. And yet his ability to compel me was not the result of a spell.

"To what purpose?" he asked.

My mouth went dry. I wiped my damp palms on my nightdress. "Doro wishes to—"

Pain cut through my reply. I cried out and fell forward, toward the king, who caught me.

His palm came to my cheek, and he bent my head back so he could examine my face. Tears streaming down from the pain, I offered no resistance.

His brow creased in confusion. "This is no play for mercy."

"No," I croaked.

"Has your leg worsened?"

I shook my head. His arm was drawn tightly around my waist, like a lover's embrace. Without its support, I would have fallen.

"What is causing your pain, then?"

"My back," I said. "My father—"

The burning tree spilled lava down my spine and I shrieked.

Finvara held me away from his chest and turned me. I stumbled forward onto the bed and then felt his hands at the nape of my neck, quickly unfastening buttons. As he peeled back the fabric, cool air rushed in and soothed my skin.

"Good God," he uttered. "What *is* this? Some mark of your people?"

I nodded feebly and rested my cheek against the cool sheet.

Pressing my hands into the coverlet, I felt the hard outline of the knife's hilt—and froze.

Treig heard my scream. She stands at the top of the stairs. I knew it without looking up. I only need command her. I slipped my hand between the sheets. *The pain will stop. I will have fulfilled my duty.*

But my attention was drawn to the sound of the king's voice—he was repeating the words of a spell in low, soothing tones. His voice conjured images of mountain pools, cold and deep. Of icy peaks, and frothy rivers. The searing heat at my back eased.

I grasped the knife and sat up, raising it between us.

The king's eyes flashed blue fire and his lips parted. He would cast a defensive spell—I had no more than a moment. From the corner of my eye, I saw Treig raise her pike, and I knew beyond doubt that *I* was the one she intended to champion. What I did not know was if her loyalty lay with me, or Doro.

"Your Majesty," I said, my voice raw, yet forceful enough to still both Treig and the king. I turned the knife in my hands, taking the blade between my palms. "The mark is my father's. The decision to betray you was Doro's. *This* decision, to betray them both, is my own."

I bowed my head, and I held out the knife to him.

FINVARA

The princess shrieked again and her knife clattered to the floor. Her eyes were bright and wild from the pain. I eased her damp body back onto the bed.

Tattoos were common among sailors—I had one myself of the constellation Argo—yet I'd never seen anything like *this*. An upside-down tree with a root system as large as the branches, it covered more than half of her back. And all of it was inflamed.

"Clean cloths," I called to Treig, "and fresh water from the well."

The most effective treatment for powder burns, in my experience, was cool water. I could not be sure the same method would work on a magical burn. The skin had not opened, at least, so presumably there was no risk of putrefaction.

"Bring a bottle of brandy," I called as the firglas woman started down the stairs. Then something occurred to me and I amended, "no, bring absinthe—there's a bottle in my study."

Before the seal between worlds was broken, absinthe had given some people the ability to see into Faery. It had also prevented my cousin Edward from being overtaken in his sleep by his immortal ancestor. Might it protect the princess from the Elf King's violence? It was worth trying.

Anger flared hot in my chest at his barbarity—was this not his daughter?

She betrayed you, I reminded myself.

Nay, something changed her mind.

I took up the cooling spell again, though I knew it would not work indefinitely. But soon she was resting quietly. Her face was pressed into the coverlet, and the muffled moans that snuck past her lips had subsided.

Turning her head to look at me, she said in a broken voice, "Thank you, Your Majesty."

Treig and the princess's maid returned with the things I'd asked for, saving me—for the moment—from having to figure out what the devil I was going to say to her. I was rising to meet them when the princess reached out and stopped me. Her fingers felt hot against my wrist.

"There is time to put a stop to Doro's scheme," she said quietly. "And there is a way."

"We'll speak more of it later," I replied, attempting to place her hand back down.

She held fast. "We must act before he suspects. He is powerful, Your Majesty."

I saw genuine urgency in her face, and I recalled Lady Meath's
warning. I needed to gain a better understanding of what had been
plotted, yet talking about it was causing her excruciating pain.

Glancing up at the servants, who were awaiting my direction,
I said, "Leave those things and wait downstairs."

When they'd gone, I asked, "Act how, lady?"

"He is bound to your queen. He must do as *she* commands.
You only need fill that office."

I stared at her. "You are suggesting I *marry?*"

"You—or she—will be able to stop his mischief in an instant."

I shook my head. "I'm not prepared for . . . I haven't even a
candidate."

"Do you not, sire?"

For the space of a startled heartbeat, I believed she was thinking of herself. She was of course referring to Elinor.

Of the two unmarried ladies, there was only one that I would
even consider marrying.

"I do not wish to cause you more pain," I replied, "but I think before
I consider such extreme measures, I must have more information."

Leaving her bedside, I fetched the absinthe bottle and a glass
from a tray Treig had brought. The anise fumes rose to my nostrils
as I poured half an inch and held out the glass to the princess. "It
may provide some protection. It may not."

When she had swallowed the pale green spirit, grimacing at
the strong flavor, I wet one of the towels the maid had brought,
wrung it out, and laid it across her back.

"Thank you, Your Majesty," she murmured.

Returning to her, I asked, "Can you tell me Doro's purpose?"

She took a deep breath, bracing herself. "To turn your people
against you. To take your place as king." A good old-fashioned

mutiny, it would seem. "He has been working against you since I met him. Perhaps even before. He needed *me* because . . ."

At first I feared the pain was returning, but then I realized she had simply hesitated. "Because?"

"Because of his bond to your family." Again, she hesitated. Then finally: "He cannot kill you."

The knife—of course. "*You* can."

The princess sank deeper into the coverlet, replying, "Except I find that I cannot."

I knelt beside the bed to better see her face. "And why is that, lady?"

She closed her eyes, and a quiet sigh escaped her lips. "You have been kind to me. You have been my friend while others have sought to use me."

Others. Her father, and Doro. It pinched at my heart, as did seeing such a stout-hearted lady reduced to this state.

"There is more," she continued, opening her eyes. "Doro formed an alliance with my father. As the fairy king, Doro would join forces with the Elf King to take Ireland. I was promised to Doro, as his queen, to seal their agreement."

Her dark eyes held mine, and I saw the moment the Elf King's punishment returned. Her cry was feeble this time—either she was exhausted or our methods were providing some relief.

Another tear slipped onto her cheek and I thought about all she had just given up for me. Merely because I had been kind to her for a handful of days.

"I will do as you have advised me," I said, bending closer to her, "if you agree to become *my* queen instead."

KOLI

"Your Majesty! Have you not heard a word I've said?"

"On the contrary," he replied, and there was a smile in his eyes that had not yet touched his lips. "I've heard *all* of your words, and I can think of no better way to foil the plans of my enemies."

I stared at him, incredulous. "I had intended to *assassinate* you."

He raised his eyebrows. "And were not equal to it, and warned me of the plot, *and* pointed out a way to prevent it. I can't think of a single other creature in this godforsaken place who has done more to earn my trust or been more genuinely helpful."

I rolled onto my side to better see him, careful to move slowly and not dislodge the wet dressing. My heart was beating wildly.

"I think you must be in jest, Your Majesty."

"I know you have no high opinion of me, lady, but even I would never jest about a marriage proposal."

I let my gaze drift to the window, my thoughts racing. I had made a choice—a very dangerous one—to take no more part in Doro and my father's schemes. And there was no point in denying I had come to respect and admire Finvara—I was beginning to suspect it could be more than that, Freyja help me. But *marry* him?

"Please don't be alarmed," said the king. "It need only be a marriage in name. You can think of it as a political alliance, if you like, to protect Ireland's treaty with your father, as was originally proposed. Can you not see how much better a solution it is than for me to marry Elinor? Doro would have her eating out of his hand in a matter of minutes, magical bond or no."

He was right. About all of it. Except— "What of *yggdrasil*?"

He frowned—I'd used an Elvish word.

"The ash tree mark," I said.

The hopeful light in his eyes dimmed. "Aye. That is an obstacle. Has anything we've done made it more tolerable?"

I nodded. "The cold cloths. The drink you gave me—it does seem to have dulled the effects. And your spells." I couldn't help recalling the gentleness of his voice—only moments after I'd admitted to betraying him.

"We will simply have to continue with all of it," he said with characteristic optimism. "And when we are wed, you will order Doro to discover a way to counter it."

Doro, *of course*. I had only thought to neutralize the fairy steward. I realized now, under my control, he could become a powerful ally.

"Only *you* may say, lady, whether you can bear it," said the king. "Both your father's punishment, and a lifetime of my company."

I studied the gentle upward curve of his full lips.

The king might not be in love, but he was certainly in earnest. And there was only one answer I could sensibly give.

THE ALCHEMIST

KOLI

"Very well," I said at last.

His smile broadened. "Is this an answer?"

"Yes, Your Majesty," I said more decisively, and felt a giddiness in my chest that overcame the pain in my back. "I hope you've no idea of a prolonged engagement, or another fete."

"Indeed not," he replied.

He went to the stairs and called the servants back up. Then he took out his watch. "Ach, it's not long until sunrise. Do we dare sleep a few hours?"

"We risk our plan being discovered."

He nodded. "Find Keane," he said to Sorcha. "Tell him we need the parish priest as soon as he can get here. The man is to be brought directly up. No one else is to know."

"Yes, Your Majesty," she said, and left us.

"Will you stand up with the princess?" he asked Treig. "As soon as the priest arrives, we intend to marry."

The firglas woman's gaze moved between us and then came to rest on me. She and I recognized this question as a test of her loyalty, even if the king did not. Eyebrows raised, she replied, "If she wishes it."

"I would be honored," I replied, "and grateful."

She nodded briskly and let the butt of her pike rest against the flagstones.

"Keane will have to stand up with me, I suppose," said the king. "We don't want word to get out until the thing is done."

I could not imagine how Finvara's father was going to react to his son marrying against his wishes, almost right under his nose. From what little I'd observed of the O'Malley chief, he was a proud and stern Irishman. Still, it was a shame for the king to stand up with a servant when both his father and brother were currently sharing the same roof.

The pain in my back had faded to a hot throbbing. I pushed myself up to a sitting position and swung my legs over the side of the bed.

"Take care, lady," said the king, reaching out to steady me. "Hadn't you better remain where you are?"

"If I'm to be wed," I replied, "let it not be from my bed, or in my nightdress."

He squeezed my fingers, and I stood up.

"If you'll leave us a moment, Your Majesty, I will dress." Would this be the last time I'd have privacy for my toilet? The idea of sharing a bedchamber with the king occurred to me now for the first time, causing a not-unpleasant sensation in the triangle of soft flesh below my belly.

But then I recalled his words: *It need only be a marriage in name.*

The king turned to comply with my request. "I'll wait for the priest below. Call out if you need me."

When he had gone, Treig took my direction about what I wanted from the wardrobe and helped me to dress, speaking only the few words required to do so—and for that I was grateful. I passed over the modern gowns in favor of my archer's dress, which had been cleaned and repaired since our encounter in the forest. It was by far the most comfortable item of clothing I'd brought. Moreover, as I had been wearing it when the king and I faced our first common enemy, I hoped it might bring us luck.

As I stood before the mirror trying to digest this drastic change to my circumstances, Treig came up behind me, picked up my brush from the dressing table, and began pulling it through my hair. The spontaneous kindness of this gesture drew my attention to her face, and I wondered again about the similarities between us.

"Do you know anything about your ancestry?" I asked her. "Perhaps you too have noticed how alike we are."

Our eyes met in the mirror, and she smiled. "It is said that long ago there was a migration of Tuatha De Danaan to northern lands, and that there they intermixed with other immortals. They and their descendants were eventually driven out."

"Northern lands" could very well refer to Iceland, and if it did, it would help explain the enmity between the fairy and elven peoples. It would also confirm the distant relation that I had suspected.

"Could be that we are cousins," I replied.

Treig nodded. "Could be. I confess from the time I first saw you, I have thought there was something familiar about you."

She returned the brush and reached down to unclasp a delicate silver chain from around her waist. After doubling the chain to form a smaller circlet, she raised it and secured it in my hair. The silver links gleamed in the firelight as I turned my head from side to side.

"Thank you," I said.

"It's not every day a lady is married," she replied. "You deserve better than this rushed ceremony, though I believe I understand the reason for it."

"It makes no difference to me," I assured her, but I couldn't help wondering what our wedding might have been like if it had happened as originally planned.

It was better this way. We would not begin as enemies.

Yggdrasil began to burn, and I reached out and gripped the back of the dressing table chair. The pain was tolerable now—would it continue to be? I hoped the king was right, and that Doro might discover a way of severing this connection between my father and me. I would have an opportunity to ask him soon enough. Had I more of my father in me, I might be looking forward to our first meeting as mistress and servant—the Elf King relished any opportunity to turn the tables. But I was dreading it.

"Lady?" said Treig.

I looked at her.

"*Black druid! Torturer!*"

The tinny, grating exclamation drew both of our gazes toward the source—the west-facing window. Yet there was nothing to see on the other side of the bars, save the moonlit tops of the trees. On the sill rested the mechanical raven. The bird's formerly dead eyes now glowed with a fiery light. Suddenly its neck rotated and the gleaming metal head cocked to one side.

I stepped toward it, and the light in its eyes went out.

"Before you take this fateful step, Koli Alfdóttir—" I spun at the sound of this second unexpected voice "—I would speak with you."

Doro stood in front of the grandfather clock. Treig raised her pike, but the fairy steward hissed a spell and the weapon burst into flames. She shouted, dropping it, and Doro rushed toward me and locked arms around my waist. Then he dragged me into the clock cabinet.

I fought him as we plunged into darkness, but a moment later we tumbled onto the deck of his ship. I scrambled away as he got to his feet.

"It seems my faith in you was misplaced." His irises were bright as a lightning strike.

I forced myself to stand up slowly, smoothing my skirt. "The situation is more complicated than it might appear, sir."

In fact, it was not. I had betrayed him, just as I had tried to do to the king. But unlike the king, I found it easy enough to lie to Doro.

"I hardly blame *you*," he replied, condescension in his tone. "You are not the first woman to be dazzled by Finvara. His enchantments are legendary. I did, however, believe that your mind would be stronger."

"There has been no enchantment," I said, matching his tone. "After his cousin was attacked, the king made a guess about our alliance. I had to do something."

Let him chew on that.

Doro studied me, and a host of dark wings whipped the inside of my ribcage. *Not yet*, I pleaded.

He folded his arms. "You suggest your acceptance of his proposal was subterfuge?"

My thoughts fired like arrows. He didn't know everything—seemed not to know the marriage was first proposed by me. So he had not somehow eavesdropped on our conversation—he'd perhaps overheard Sorcha sending for the priest.

"He suggested I might prove his allegation false by accepting him," I replied. "What else should I have done, my lord?"

Doro was a master at guarding his expressions, but I could see the calculation in his eyes as he considered my explanation.

"What of the skean I left for you?"

The damned knife! "I discovered it. I knew the timing of its use was critical, and I hid it when he came to accuse me."

He nodded, seeming to accept this, and I let out a breath. "It's unfortunate that we've been discovered. There was always a risk of it. While I have never before crossed Finvara or his queen, aspersions have been cast on me in the Faery histories, and he may have somehow learned of it."

Or maybe you were overconfident and got careless. "What shall we do?"

"There is a way to repair the damage. If your loyalty is unchanged, you will have no objection to marrying me instead of the king."

My hand came to press against my chest in what I hoped would be interpreted as a gesture of earnestness rather than what it really was—an attempt to hold back my furies.

"I do not, my lord. Have I not pledged myself to it?"

"Indeed you have. It will have to be done *now*."

I pressed my chest harder, swallowing loudly.

He took a step toward me. "If *we* marry secretly, before you return, your marriage to him will be invalid. It will buy us time."

"But I must return immediately," I countered, "The king only stepped away long enough for me to prepare."

Doro waved his hand, dismissing this concern. "You will tell him that I came for you, but that you escaped—even better, that you've killed me. We only need a little more time. Everything is in motion."

He waited for my reply, and I nodded. Turning his head to one side, he called, "Bran?"

My gaze flitted to the rocky tunnel above us—I had wondered about it the first time I boarded *Black Swan*. I noticed that a ladder ran up the ship's mast and then climbed a few meters in open air before reaching a stone stairway inside the tunnel. I didn't know where the tunnel led, but Doro had mysterious ways of moving around Knock Ma.

I'll never make it. Doro had hardly taken his eyes off me. Yet it seemed like my only chance.

I heard a whirring noise, and a series of clicks, and my gaze was drawn to a mechanical creature approaching us. It was child-like in size, tin face gleaming in the lamplight, eye sockets empty. The mouth was no more than a slit—a roughly cut opening in the tin. A rust-red cap sat upon the creature's head, and I noticed that the pointy tops of fleshy ears protruded on either side of it.

Part flesh, part machine, like the barrow-wight.

"Another of your creations?" I asked, shivering.

"Indeed," Doro replied, smiling fondly at the thing. "A crude and incomplete transmutation, but he signifies an important breakthrough. Bran was the first to emerge truly animate, and from that I learned of the importance of iron." He looked at me, fervor animating his expression. "Fairy creatures are light-bodied and mercurial. Our blood contains no iron, no earthly grounding. But Bran was a vicious breed of fairy called a redcap, and for centuries they have drunk and washed themselves in mortal blood."

I thought about the mechanical raven. A real raven's body contained red blood—and the mechanical one had most certainly come to life, if only for a moment.

Doro had made it sound like he was not involved in creating the little machines at Knock Ma—like they were once-living crea-tures that had passed through the Gap gate unwittingly. But Doro created Bran, and he also created the wight.

I recalled the raven's shrill warning—*torturer*. Had the raven, along with the others in the dungeon at Knock Ma, been failed experiments?

"You told me you use the Gap gate for transmutation," I said. "How does that work?"

He smiled. "I confess I'm not exactly sure. I believe when we met I told you I was Ireland's last druid?"

Last and most powerful. "You did."

"I was once called on by an immortal to create a seal between

Faery and Ireland. Centuries later, another immortal asked me to create gates that would allow the seal to be circumvented, *and* that would allow navigation inside the Gap. The gate in the wight's tomb was the first and most experimental of those gates. After the seal was broken at Ben Bulben, Faery and Ireland tried to merge, and it eventually broke every gate but the first. That one, altered by the collapse of boundaries between the ancient and modern worlds, began to function in a strange and fascinating way. I have been conducting experiments ever since in an attempt to understand it."

Goosebumps ran over my skin, despite the balmy climate of the Gap.

"Why do you . . ." I hesitated, and began again carefully. "What is it you hope to achieve with these experiments?"

His eyebrows lifted, as if he was surprised by the question. "Elegant, complete transmutation. Preternatural evolution."

I stared at him blankly. My English tutors had not spent much time on the sciences, and my interest was never more than tepid. I was struggling to keep up with Doro's explanations. Had he said that he wanted to improve upon nature itself?

I couldn't help wondering how well my father knew his new ally; the Elf King had always been violently opposed to any introduction of new technologies in Iceland. Machines that did make it onto the island were ever in danger of being tampered with by the Hidden Folk. The homes of all but the poorest Icelanders tended to have small junk heaps of contraptions that had been disabled by magic. Elves delighted in stealing them for trade with the dwarves. I'd traded a typewriter that had once played musical notes with each keystroke for a pair of custom-forged steel braces. The Elf King himself had disrupted the construction of a railway that would have operated between the capital city of Reykjavik and the town of Keflavík. The project had been abandoned—and the sinkhole my father created was declared sacred to the Hidden Folk.

"Bran," said Doro, addressing his creation, "fetch my apprentice from the lab." Turning to me, he said, "We'll hold a druidic ceremony."

It's time to go. But go *where*? How?

"Do we not require witnesses, my lord?" I asked.

He dismissed this with a shake of his head. "Handfastings were conducted long before priests or bureaucrats ever set foot on this isle. The druidic vows and the consummation will ensure the marriage's validity." He fixed his gaze on me, smiling coolly. "I regret that haste is required. It is not what I had hoped for."

The full import of his explanation sank in, and I went from cold to uncomfortably hot. My hand moved again to my chest, even as a voice inside me urged, *Let go.*

Doro turned to look after his servants, and I took a deep breath and held it. All the energy and emotion I'd been holding—the panic over Finvara and Doro's accusations, the king's unexpected marriage proposal, and the threat of an eternity bound to Doro—all of it now built inside my chest like a storm surge.

When Doro faced me again, I let all of it go. This time it was not six. It was not a dozen. My furies were legion, pouring forth in a great inky cloud, snuffing the lamps, entangling themselves in the rigging, raking beaks and talons against my enemy. Doro's voice barely rose above the raucous cries and beating wings as he shouted his protective spell.

Covering my head with my arms, I ran for the ladder. I took hold of the rails and stepped onto the first rung, moving quickly but deliberately. As I climbed, I kept an eye on the *hrafnathing*. The nightmare flock continued to swarm over the deck and around the masts and sails like angry hornets. Those that drifted beyond the rigging disappeared into the starry black of the Gap.

Doro was protecting himself with dispersion spells, like the one Finvara had used against my furies—there were just so many of them. Still somehow he remained calm, and his eyes followed me. I felt his stare like needles of frozen rain. Yet he did not attempt to pursue me. Perhaps he knew, as I did, that such a powerful spell—the most powerful I had ever cast—could not last. Perhaps he was only waiting for it to fade.

Already the rending cries were lessening, the vivid, glossy bodies of the birds dulling to shadow. I was more than halfway up the ladder—almost to the top of the mast—and I began to climb faster.

As I passed the top of the mast, my boot slipped and I yelped, sliding down several rungs, until my sweat-slicked hands managed to catch at an intersection of rail and rung. When I'd again found my footing, I continued the frantic pace to the top.

I crawled onto the first of the stone steps and flung the ladder away from the edge. Then I ran up the steps, deeper into the cavern, two at a time.

The cavern was warm and damp, and ferns and moss sprouted from pockets in the rock. The moss glowed faintly, and weak light filtered down from an opening above. Did the passage lead to Knock Ma's grounds?

At the top of the steps, I could see that magic was at work here. There was a round opening that appeared to be covered with water—though it did not run or even drip into the space below. Was there no way out? Was this why Doro had not pursued me? Raising my hand, I touched the surface of the water with one finger—it was very cold.

What *now*?

I attempted to draw my hand away, but instead felt myself pulled upward until I was kicking my feet at empty air. I struggled wildly, but soon my other arm was ensnared and I'd been drawn in past my elbows and then to my shoulders. I had just a moment to suck in a deep breath as my head too was submerged.

Gritting my teeth against the bone-deep cold, I kicked furiously toward what I hoped was the way out—though *something* was already pulling me that direction. As I swam toward the light, the water grew warmer and panic seized me—there were thermal pools in Iceland that could boil you alive. I stopped kicking, though my need to breathe was becoming desperate. I knew a spell that might create a pocket of air—but it had to be spoken. The only spell I had ever cast without opening my lips was the one that released my furies, and they were of little use to me now.

I had ceased all my struggling, and still I was being pulled into water that was growing truly hot. It was becoming difficult to think, let alone reason. I let the current take me. Then I stopped holding my breath. As water entered my nose and throat, three words bubbled gently to the surface of my thoughts.

The Gap gate.

THE RAVEN LADY

KOLI

I woke with a start and then froze, listening. Water dripping onto stone. Small, scurrying movements of birds or mice. My own breath passing in and out of my mouth.

Cold air nipped at my wet skin—nose, cheeks, fingers—but much of my body was numb.

Pushing my shoulders and head up from the rocky ground, I surveyed my surroundings. Another sort of cavern, this one partly filled with stones and loose earth. Directly overhead I saw the sky, suffused with the faintly yellow light of dawn.

Had I returned to Knock Ma after all? Would Doro follow me?

I tried to sit up, and a hot pain exploded between my shoulder blades. My hands lost their purchase, and my knuckles scraped across rough stones as I caught myself. In leaving the castle, I had also left the king's protective spells—and I had freshly defied my father's ally. There was something different about this pain, though—it was a pulsing heat, like repeated wasp stings. In the spaces between the stings, my flesh tickled and itched, like there were indeed insects crawling around inside me.

Moaning feebly, I sat up again, noticing my legs were resting in a shallow pool. I still couldn't feel them. The itching between my shoulders, however, was becoming unbearable. I reached behind my back to scratch the irritated skin. My fingers bumped against something unexpectedly silky, and I recoiled.

Dragging myself free of the pool, I looked around for the creature I'd touched—I saw nothing. The feeling was coming back into my legs, and I slowly stood up.

A wave of vertigo swept over me and I swayed.

Something feels very wrong.

The itching grew worse, and again I reached to scratch. The silky thing was still there! I twisted my other arm around to my back, feeling with both hands. The thing had a rigid form—and it protruded *from my own flesh.*

I jerked my head to one side, twisting my neck to look over my shoulder.

"Wings!" The gasp I uttered was near bottomless. I fell to my knees, chest heaving, coughing.

It's a trick of the light. But I knew it wasn't. I had passed through Doro's Gap gate. I had undergone transmutation. I was lucky to be alive.

Or was I?

Frantic, I scanned the inside of the cavern. I had to get out of here. I needed light and a mirror—and a fire. I was lost and disoriented, soaked through with no way to get dry, and Freyja help me, *what had happened to my body?*

This place appeared to be no more than a hole in the ground. To one side there was a larger pile of rubble that I thought I might be able to climb, and I made my way over to it. My wet dress hung on me like a curtain of iron, dragging at my every step. It had also split down the back, and I curled my fingers over the neckline to hold it up. My new appendages—they were no better than dead weights against my back.

I stopped in front of the rock pile. Under normal circumstances, it would be no real obstacle. In my current state I wasn't sure. Even if I did manage to scale it, where would I go? Assuming I was anywhere near Knock Ma, did I dare return? I was in no condition to oppose Doro were he to come for me again. And what of the king? He would presumably be searching for me. What would he say when he found me?

I closed my eyes, still gripping the front of my dress, shivering.

The king would be relieved to see me. He would be kind to me, and would offer what help he could. But I was certain he would never make such a misshapen creature his queen.

FINVARA

"The princess has been found in the forest, sire!"

Treig had all but burst in on me as I was leaving my chamber, where I'd gone to finish dressing and arm myself—the initial search for the princess within the castle having proved fruitless.

"In what state?" I demanded. *Is she alive?*

"I'm not certain, sire," Treig replied, frowning. "I know that she lives, though . . ."

"What is it?"

She shook her head. "I don't know. The ones who found her are whispering of dark magic and won't say more."

Why did I not heed Lady Meath's warning?

"Let us go," I said brusquely.

I didn't have the patience for superstitious dread and therefore did not stop to interview the guards who had returned. Instead I went directly to the stables to saddle a horse. Morning had broken, yet the sun was no more than an indistinct orb behind a veil of gray. Treig and I set out briskly, our mounts snorting in the chill air. When the path became too rocky, we slowed and picked our way until we met with the patrol at the base of the steep climb to the vantage point.

"Why haven't you brought her back to the castle?" I demanded of the captain on duty.

He did not shrink at my impatience. "We thought it best to consult you, sire."

"Why, in God's name?"

"Please, sire, I'll take you to her."

Muttering a curse, I swung down from my saddle and followed him up the stone path—Treig in my wake. We climbed to the top of the hill and then made our way down the stairs on the other side to the destroyed barrow. I had ordered my men to burn the wight's remains before my family's arrival, but the inorganic elements of its physique still littered the scorched ground. The toe of my boot struck one of the saucer-sized goggle lenses, and a pile of assorted gears rested a few yards away. Beyond the debris was a depression in the ground—a crater that had once been the tomb. I saw a feminine figure standing near the rim of it, and relief swelled.

Hunched between two of my soldiers, one of their cloaks draped about her, the princess had never looked so fragile. Our eyes met, and she set her jaw and straightened. In the movement, I caught a glint of pale flesh and realized that beneath the cloak she was naked.

That devil will answer for this. And he wasn't the only one.

"Why do you fools stand there?" I barked at her guards, who also straightened at the sound of my voice. "If she dies of exposure, *all* of you will pay for it."

"Sire—" began one of the men.

"We turned the castle inside-out looking for you, lady," I said, ignoring the guard. "I'm greatly relieved to find you alive and well."

She didn't answer, and watched me approach with what seemed to me a look of dread. Her face was drawn, her lips blue with cold, and there were dark smudges beneath her eyes. When I reached her, I unbuttoned my overcoat and waved Treig over. "Use the cloak to give her what privacy you can so she can put this on."

"Your Majesty, I cannot," said the princess.

"We'll help you," I replied, handing my coat to Treig. "Come, you must be chilled to the bone."

She backed two steps away from me. Her hands were gripping the cloak in the front, holding it closed, but suddenly she let it fall.

At first all I saw was *her*. I confess my imagination had undressed her before this—most recently last night, while holding her close in the waltz and telling her the story of Lady Godiva. Then, the unusual events in her bedchamber had required a measure of physical intimacy—and ended in a marriage proposal. It did not matter that my suspicion about her and Doro had proved correct. At some point over the last few days, the woman had gotten into my blood, and even had she tried to cut out my heart, I doubt it would have changed anything.

What I saw now did not exactly match my imagination. Her manner of dress had not emphasized her feminine assets. I had believed her to be reedy and strong like the firglas, and strong she was, yet here were curves where I had expected angles. Softness where I had expected steel. Her breasts were a lovely teardrop shape, with large nipples the same wine color as her lips. Her torso was too strongly muscled to pinch in deeply at the waist, but below, the lines of her hips opened out generously. I couldn't stop staring at her.

Noting the goosebumps on her skin, I did finally return to my senses. I took my coat from Treig and stepped forward—then froze as two black shapes rose, one on each side of her body.

I faltered back, hand moving to my pistol. Then I saw that it was only the cloak she had worn to the masquerade. Looking closer, I realized that it was *not*.

They were actual wings.

"I am uninjured," said the princess, offering a stiff smile, "but not unaltered."

"What happened?" I demanded, circling around behind her, trying to understand. "Has Doro done this?"

"There is a Gap gate within the barrow," she said. "Doro has been using it to transform beings into monsters. When I escaped through it, it transformed *me*."

Breath hissed between my teeth when I saw the wings had sprouted right out of her back, obliterating the tree tattoo. Hardened tissue protruded from the skin, and at the base of each wing a gear was set. As the wings lowered slightly, the gears turned. My gaze followed the graceful movement of the feathered shapes until they closed over the rounded flesh just below her waist. My rage at the violence done to her body softened to a sense of wonder and awe. She had become a goddess.

But the woman was probably in shock, and tired of standing in the cold.

"Does it hurt?" I asked, gently touching the skin between her wings.

"Not much now," she replied.

I knelt and raised the cloak again, draping it around her shoulders. Her fingers brushed my wrists as she took hold of it, and even the spare contact tugged at both my heart and my groin.

"We'll take her back down to the horses," I said to Treig.

KOLI

When we reached the bottom of the hill, the king took Treig aside and spoke with her in private before returning to lift me to his horse. I squirmed in the saddle until my wings had tucked in on either side of my hips. Then Finvara climbed up behind me. At another time the secrecy might have worried me, but I was numb and exhausted and happy to let them manage things.

Finvara, though he had been kind as I'd predicted, had also been stunned—I had seen it in his eyes. There was a part of me that felt like a damaged creature—another of Doro's broken things—and I was afraid the king would see me that way too. That he would finally be truly repulsed by me.

I bitterly regretted that the planned marriage had been spoiled. I wondered how the king would counter Doro's schemes now. Would he resign himself to the marriage with his cousin?

I knew my state of shock must be deeper than I realized when I discovered we'd been riding for some time in the wrong direction. Seated sidesaddle before the king, one shoulder resting against his chest, I tipped my face up to his.

"Where are we going, Your Majesty?"

"There's a huntsman's lodge on the edge of Knock Ma woods," he replied. "The owner abandoned it when the earth spit up these hills and trees, after the seal was broken. Doro appears unable to leave the castle, so you should be safe there."

Lowering my chin, I rested my cheek against his chest.

He dipped his head, and his chin brushed the top of my head, sending a cascade of shivers down my back. "I've sent Treig to the castle for your things, was that all right?"

"Of course, Your Majesty. Thank you."

I was being expelled from the castle. It was the best thing for all concerned. Given the opportunity, Doro would seek his vengeance. And the king would want to shield his family, especially after what had happened to Elinor. This was likely a temporary measure, though, and I wondered what would come next.

Sufficient unto the day is the evil thereof. It had been decades since I'd seen the inside of a church, but how well I remembered the clear and commanding voice of Pastor Jón. His sermons had frightened me, yet he had been kind to me when the village children had not. He had urged me to be vigilant against the darkness I had inherited from my father. It was many years after his death before I understood what that meant.

"How is Miss O'Malley?" I asked.

"Well enough, I believe. I did not have time to look in on her before I left the castle. She is in capable hands with my sister-in-law." When the king's speech was low and gentle like this, it flooded my body with warmth, like the mineral pools beneath Skaddafjall.

I recalled how Finvara's sister had accused me of trying to drown her young friend, and how I'd hoped the king would know that it couldn't be true. She had not been wrong—I'd known that Doro was planning to frighten the girl, and I was familiar with his methods.

I closed my eyes, feeling the warmth of Finvara's chest through his shirt. "Doro knows that we had planned to marry," I said. "I managed to convince him it was only a trick, but he insisted I marry him in haste so that any future marriage to you would not be legitimate." I felt the king tense, and his chest rose in preparation to reply. I continued, "I escaped him and the marriage with the help of my furies. I only mention this as a caution to you, Your Majesty, because I fear that in his desperation he may—"

"Be easy, lady," said the king, snugging his arms against me as he adjusted the reins. "You have done all you could. You must now allow me to do what I can for *you*." He clucked softly, urging the horse to a trot. "We're almost there."

I tried to doze against his chest, but the ride was bumpy, and I was growing anxious about the fact he would be leaving me soon. I told myself I would not be *completely* alone. I would be guarded, certainly, and perhaps he would allow Treig to stay. I had always been happy enough in my own company, though I had allowed myself to imagine what life would be like after we married, and the prospect of solitude had lost some of its appeal.

The clouds thickened as we rode, and a soft spring shower was soon falling. Pressed against the king, I no longer felt chilled and I welcomed its cool caress. Soon I caught a glimpse of the huntsman's lodge through the oaks—a stone and thatch cottage built on the bank of a stream.

We rode up to the small gate and the king dismounted. He held out his arms to catch me as I slid down so that I could hold onto the cloak. I felt his warm breath against my temple for the space of three heartbeats before we were joined by the small party of guards that had followed us. The king ordered the firglas to set a patrol and watch schedule, and then he led me inside.

The rustic interior was neat and clean, though the air was stale from disuse. The place had likely been owned by someone of means, as the floors were planked and the interior walls had been plastered. It was a single rectangular room containing a small cookstove, dining table and four chairs, a fireplace, and an iron-frame bed. The bed was not made, but the mattress was covered with sheepskins. It reminded me very much of the cottage I'd shared with my mother.

I watched the king circle the room—making an inspection for vermin, I supposed. When he was satisfied, he glanced at me. "Take your rest, now, lady. There's a shed outside and I'll go see if any wood or turf has been put by."

When he left, I crossed the room to the tiny kitchen and opened a casement. Just outside, the stream whispered and burbled, and a breeze carried fresh air into the cottage.

I glanced around, looking for a mirror, but found none.

Without planning to do it, I flexed the muscles around my shoulder blades, and my wings lifted slightly beneath the cloak. *I'm not broken.* I felt a swell of excitement. Raising them as I had at the tomb required a great effort, yet I couldn't help wondering if I would eventually be able to fly.

I had begun to notice sensation too. Not only at the point where the wings joined my back, but in the wings themselves—I had felt the king's arm brush against the feathers as we rode. I had also noticed *lack* of sensation: *yggdrasil* no longer burned. Could it be that the transmutation had broken my connection to my father?

Were it not for the loss of Finvara, I could think of few reasons to regret passing through the Gap gate. It had saved me from being bound body and soul to a man I had begun to hate. Though it was a bitter piece of irony that now I was free to make my own choice, I no longer had one.

I went to the bed and crawled onto it, lying down on my belly. The wool covering the mattress was pungent but soft, and I sank into it gratefully.

When I woke, the light in the cottage had shifted, and a fire was blazing in the hearth. A salty, savory aroma filled my nostrils and my stomach growled.

"My lady?"

I sat up abruptly and found Treig standing at the foot of the bed.

"Is it late?" I asked, my voice cracking. I realized I'd spoken Elvish and repeated the question in Irish.

"No, lady. A little past midday."

I looked around. The king had gone, and some creature—a hare, I thought—was roasting on a spit over the fire.

"Lady . . ."

Treig held out a folded sheet of paper. Her expression was blank, but her eyes were bright. Whatever was in the note worried her. A farewell from the king, most likely.

My mouth went dry as I took the paper with one hand, holding the cloak closed with the other. I waved it open and saw only a handful of words had been written.

He won't have you now. But I will.

—D

Something hot and acrid rose in my throat.

"How did you come by this?" I asked her.

"It was left on your dressing table, my lady."

I laid the paper on the bed. "Will you help me dress?" I asked, standing. "Though I can't think what I have that will fit me now. I suppose there'll be no more corsets in my future at least."

Treig was staring at me and I glanced up to find her smiling.

"What is it?" I asked.

"I've never heard you laugh before, lady," she said.

Could that be true? Likely it was. Even in the company of Finvara, who seemed to be amused by everything, I didn't believe I had ever laughed. I'd never thought of myself as a mirthless person, but there were few I trusted enough to let my guard down in that way. Ulf had always been able to make me laugh.

Treig brought me a bag she'd left by the door, and I smiled to find the mechanical raven had been lashed to the outside. I couldn't think what had made her bring it. Perhaps she knew, as I did, that I wouldn't be going back to Knock Ma and thought I might like to have it.

Sorting through the bag, I found that there was not a dress among them that would not have to be altered in order for me to wear it. Anticipating this, Treig had also packed the chambermaid's sewing implements, and we slit the back of an off-the-shoulder gown of light gray brocade. It had belonged to an elven relation and was at least three hundred years out of fashion in Ireland—and therefore designed before corsets. I had worn it at the Elf King's court only when he entertained visiting dignitaries—or potential suitors. It had been a favorite of my father's. I had no memory of packing it, or of seeing it after I arrived here. It must have been tucked between the modern dresses. I couldn't help wondering if he had planned for me to wear it when Doro and I wed. Which would mean he'd made the decision, without telling me, before I'd even left.

Sighing, I took up the needle and thread, folding under the fabric flaps left by our butchery and stitching the edges so they wouldn't fray. I handed the gown to Treig, and she helped me to put it on.

Smoothing the fabric with my hands, I said, "An odd costume for the occasion, but I am decent again."

"You look like a queen, my lady," replied Treig, and again I laughed, though it pricked at my heart.

"She's right, you do."

My heart stopped. I turned to find the king standing in the doorway.

"Forgive me," he said, "I should have knocked. I didn't want to wake you."

"I thought that you had . . ." My heart was in motion again. "I thought that you'd gone."

He raised an eyebrow. "Should I have? You wouldn't be the first lady to say so, though I'd thank you not to punctuate your answer by flinging anything at my head."

I pursed my lips, suppressing a smile. "No, Your Majesty."

He stepped into the room, and I saw he was holding a bow and quiver of arrows—it was even a *húnbogi*, a recurve bow. More compact than a traditional longbow, but just as powerful.

"I found this in the shed," said the king. "I thought you might like to have it. I don't know if it's all right—I confess I know nothing about archery. It's past time you had some means of defending yourself."

A smile now spread broadly over my face, and I saw it reflected in his answering grin. "That smile is answer enough," he said. "I've worked hard for it, heaven knows." He set the weapon against the wall and closed the door behind him. "Perhaps it will do for a wedding present, since it's all I've got."

"I DEFY FAERY"

KOLI

I stared at him. "Wedding present, Your Majesty?"

"Aye, did you not agree to marry me?"

"I—" I closed my mouth. My back muscles flinched, causing my wings to lift slightly. "I thought—"

"Thought to renege, did you?" he asked, though I could hear the teasing note in his voice.

Again I felt pressure in my throat, and my eyes stung. I turned from him and walked toward the hearth, where the roasting hare was dripping and sizzling.

Treig made a small noise, like clearing her throat, and said, "I saw a patch of watercress near the stream, lady. I thought I would collect some, if you like."

"Yes, thank you," I replied.

I reached for the spit and raised the hare higher on the rack, so it wouldn't burn. Then I faced him.

"I have not changed my mind," I said in a clear voice. "I only thought that you would have. And I would understand it, Your Majesty. I'm sure we can agree that things are not as they were."

"Aye," he said, with a soft laugh and glinting eye. "There was a time when it was nearly impossible to get you to speak, let alone smile. I never knew whether you were actually listening to me prattle or casting spells in your head, hoping I'd combust."

I tilted my head, eyeing him dubiously. "I believe you know what I mean."

He sobered and took a step toward me. "I do, lady, and I am sorry for all you've endured since coming here. Regarding your most recent trial, as far as I can tell you've not changed in essentials. The priest waits outside, and I mean to go through with it, if you'll have me." He held out his hand. "I defy Faery or Ireland to produce a more beautiful bride."

My hand trembled as I reached out and grasped his. The strength and heat that flowed through his deliberate touch was like nothing I had ever experienced. I felt it in every part of my body, the energy of it even raising the tips of my wings.

"I must tell you, Your Majesty," I began in a voice that wavered, "from my conversation with Doro, I came to understand that a ceremony alone is not likely to provide the relief from his interference that we are seeking."

He frowned. "The marriage will not make him answerable to you, as you believed it would?"

"Only if it is a *true* marriage." I swallowed and waited, but the king only stared at me blankly.

After a moment, his brow cleared and his lips parted. His fingers, still wrapped around mine, squeezed slightly. "I see."

I looked down, feeling hot and unwell. He squeezed my hand again, and he dipped his head to catch my eye.

Smiling, he said, "If that's meant to frighten me away, I'm

afraid you've taken the wrong tack. Might I suggest, if it is not a sticking point as far as *you're* concerned, that we take such questions . . . as they come?"

I was not, and had never been, squeamish about the sharing of bodies. None of my father's people were. I had been of age for many years, though it was only after my mother died that I ever acted on such urges. While I was still living with her, she had grown more and more devout. Our otherness became a source of suffering for her, and I was unwilling to do anything that might deepen the divide between us and Pastor Jón's other parishioners. Once I joined my father's court, I enjoyed my newfound freedom. On long winter nights the bleak landscapes called to me, and there were other solitary souls that ranged as I did.

What the king and I now spoke of was something different. We were neither countrymen nor strangers, but enemies who'd somehow found ourselves on common ground. The ways my body responded to him—they had stolen upon me. I had never before encountered a man whose mind I respected, whose companionship I enjoyed, *and* whose touch I craved more than I had ever craved anything.

He was waiting for me to answer. I picked over the words that he had used and replied, "No, not a sticking point, Your Majesty."

He smiled, and it occurred to me that soon I would have license to touch the lines that formed at the corners of his eyes, like bird prints in the sand. I would have license—would I have nerve?

"Let us join the priest and have done with the formalities," he said. "Afterward we can break our fast."

FINVARA

The parish priest, like the surgeon, had refused to call at Knock Ma. But a second messenger, leveraging the O'Malley name, had better luck persuading the holy man to attend us at the lodge that morning.

It was an easy matter to press Treig and the priest's driver into service as witnesses. The holy man, though not warm, was civil, and at least outwardly demonstrated the respect due a son of the Earl of Mayo, if not a king of fairies.

The princess's appearance did give him pause—when first his eyes came to rest on her, he crossed himself and murmured a prayer. I had to bite back an angry retort, though I recalled that my own first reaction to her had not been much different, and that was *before* she had wings. At least this meeting had involved no furies.

I introduced her as the daughter of a powerful Icelandic ally, and a new member of my court. I also told him the marriage had been sanctioned by my cousin, Queen Isolde, but that for reasons I could not disclose, must be kept secret. Whether he bought any of this, I had no idea. It was a time of transition in Ireland, and not an easy one. Some members of the clergy—particularly those imported from continental Europe—viewed the sudden influx of fairies as a threat to Catholic beliefs and teachings. This fellow was thoroughly Irish, was rumored to have secretly married his housekeeper, and, thankfully, was inclined to mind his own business. He accepted my explanation, and the whole affair was conducted with unsettling efficiency.

No longer sure whom we could trust, the ceremony—a brief exchange of Catholic vows—was conducted in the privacy of the cottage. We had a moment of difficulty over the bride's vows— her eyebrows rose half an inch higher for each of the words "obey" and "serve"—and I directed the priest to replace her vows with the ones I had spoken.

When he had gone, I sent Treig outside to watch, and I bade my bride—my wife and queen, though it had not really sunk in— sit at the table while I served up our wedding feast. I split the rabbit and placed it, along with the watercress, on two plates. I found two tankards, blew out the dust, and poured into each a healthy measure of whiskey, which I'd found in a trunk at the foot of the bed.

"Thank you, Your Majesty," she said.

"I think you had better stop calling me that," I replied, "or no one is going to believe we are married."

A smile tugged at her lips as she began pulling the rabbit apart with her fingers. "What *shall* I call you?"

"Finvara, if you like," I said, going to work on my own dinner. "Or if you prefer, the name I've answered to my whole life."

Glancing up from her meal, she said, "Duncan."

I smiled, enjoying the intimacy of my name on her lips. "That's right."

Chewing a bite of rabbit, she closed her eyes and sighed. If she'd not eaten since before the ball, she must have been famished, and I felt a pang of guilt for making her wait. But I was relieved to have the ceremony behind us.

"No," she said, shaking her head. "You are a king. Your subjects, your family, your neighbors, even your servants—they are struggling to accept this. You are Finvara, whether they like it or not." She pointed her fork at me. "Whether *you* like it or not."

It was gratifying to have my choice of queen so promptly validated. "Finvara it is, then."

She smiled her approval. "And you will use my given name?"

"Aye, if you permit me." I drank from my tankard, feeling the whiskey burn its way down to my stomach. "Koli. Does it mean something?"

"It's Elvish," she replied, "or what the English call Old Norse. My mother chose it. It means 'little dark one.'"

It was a name that carried a mother's affection. "You were close to your mother?"

A shadow passed over her face, and she stopped eating. She nodded.

I hesitated, not wanting to cause her pain. Yet she was my wife now, and I still knew so little about her. "May I ask what happened to her?"

Her gaze lowered, she rubbed at the edge of her plate with her thumb. "My father let her die."

I froze. Then I set my fork down. "How?"

When she looked at me I could see the pain and anger in her eyes. "The villagers hated us. They blamed us for anything bad that happened—illness, accidents, even soured milk. When a house collapsed and killed a whole family, they came for revenge. They drove us off a cliff."

I stared at her in horror as she lifted her tankard and sipped the whiskey before continuing. "I was always meant to live at my father's court eventually. She kept putting him off. He did not care for her influence over me. His men—they were *always* watching us. The warrior who later became my protector, Ulf, arrived in time to save me that day . . . but not her. It's not Ulf I blame."

Her relationship with her father was even more complicated than I realized.

I reached across the table and touched her hand. "What was her name?"

She offered a soft, sad smile that wrung my heart. "Njála."

We finished our meal in silence, and I got up to add turf to the fire. She rose too, walking to the bed, and after a moment returned and handed me a sheet of paper.

After reading the brief missive, I said, "From Doro?"

She nodded. "He left it in my chamber. Treig brought it to me."

"He has not accepted defeat," I said, crumpling the paper and tossing it into the fire. "But he is nearly defeated."

The page flared yellow, and then suddenly the fire burst to life, roaring like the ocean in a storm, flames licking the chimney stones and reaching out for us. I jumped back, shielding my bride, just as the flames took the form of a rearing horse, hooves tearing at the air as it screamed.

Koli's furies swept into the inferno, attacking the beast and themselves bursting into flame. I'd filled a bucket from the stream when we first arrived, and I ran to grab it from beside the door. As I flung the water, I shouted a spell of amplification. The airborne wave crashed against the fire beast, dousing it with a hiss and flooding the fireplace. Steam rose and fogged the room.

Koli coughed and waved a hand in front of her face. "You were saying, Your Majesty?"

A laugh burst from my belly, and without thinking I spun around and caught her up in my arms.

She let out a yelp, and her hands came to my shoulders. For the first time, I heard her laugh—it was a sensual sound, sweet and thick like molasses. I wanted to swim in that sound. To breathe it in and let it drown me.

Our laughter died away all too soon, but I stood frozen, smiling into her bright eyes, feeling her body pressing against mine.

"You had agreed to call me Finvara," I reminded her. My voice had gone to gravel.

She dipped her head slightly, and her full lips parted. "Finvara."

While I was studying the ruby curves of her mouth, my arms crushing her waist against my abdomen, she pressed her lips to mine.

Suddenly the fire horse was racing in my veins—or at least I felt like it was. I held her tighter, hoping the right amount of pressure might soothe the throbbing at my groin—at the same time knowing it would only make matters worse.

Her tongue glided along my bottom lip. A hard groan rumbled out of me, vibrating to the core, and I moved my hand down to stroke the curve of her backside.

She released my mouth, and the tips of our noses touched. "I have done this before, husband," she said.

I hoisted her higher, and she had to bend her head down over me to hold my gaze. "By choice, I hope," I said, searching her eyes. She nodded. "By choice. Should I have told you earlier?"

Letting her slip partway down, I pressed my cheek to hers and whispered in her ear, "I'm sure it was none of my business, but I'm desperately hoping that you will tell me *more* about it later."

She laughed, and her mouth came again to mine, greedy and insistent. I carried her toward the table. Recalling the recent changes to her body, instead of pushing her back onto it, I shoved our dishes out of the way and pulled her on top of me. Her wings drooped forward over her arms, covering our bodies like a feathery bower.

She started working at the buttons of my shirt, and I reached down to grip the skirt of her dress.

Then the door to the cottage banged open.

KOLI

Before a single thought came into my head I snatched Finvara's knife from where it rested on the table, rose to a crouch, and threw it at whatever had just ducked through the doorway. The blade struck with a satisfying *thunk*—and only afterward did my focus broaden enough to realize I had nearly assassinated a friend.

"Ulf!" I shouted. My knife had lodged in his leather chest armor.

He was a great hulking beast of an elf with a wolfish glower, a mass of coarse, plaited hair hanging from both head and chin, and dark paint masking the top half of his face, making his light-amber eyes glitter in the dim light of the cottage. Both ears were pierced with iron rings all the way from lobe to pointed tip.

"What are you doing here?" I demanded.

His gaze shifted from me to the king, who'd sat up but was

still positioned behind me. The elf warrior stepped to one side and raised a bow with an arrow already knocked.

I flexed my back muscles hard, lifting my wings and blocking his aim. "Ulf, *no*."

"You'll hide behind a woman, then?" my father's man shouted in English.

"Gladly," replied Finvara, "as it appears you don't mean to assassinate *her*."

"Ulf!" I snapped, and continued in English, "Lower your weapon. This man is my husband."

He turned his glare on me without lowering the bow. "Husband!" he barked.

"Who is this, Koli?" asked the king.

"My guardian," I answered without taking my eyes off Ulf. "My *former* guardian. He is my father's captain. What I don't understand is what he is doing *here*."

"You mean to tell me that you've married this *argr* Irishman against your father's will?"

"I have married him, and that's the last question I'll answer until you answer mine."

His eyes rolled back toward the king. "I've been sent to dispatch him."

"Sent by who?"

"By your king," he growled. "Your *father*."

"He sent you all the way from Iceland to assassinate Finvara? Is that not what he sent *me* to do?"

"He knows that you've refused. And he is *here*."

He is here. My blood went cold, and my heart flapped against my ribs like a small bird trying to escape. I glanced over my shoulder at Finvara.

"The tree mark?" muttered the king.

Of course. I had long suspected that if I acted in a way that betrayed my father's interests, not only would *yggdrasil* punish me, but the king would know it.

"He's too late, Ulf," I said, and I felt the king's steadying hand at the small of my back. "And he's broken the treaty by coming here. His ally has lost his power. If my father has business, he can bring it to me, but it's better that he goes home."

It was the first time I had ever dared to speak against my father, and I caught a flicker of alarm in Ulf's gaze.

What I was attempting was risky. If Doro was correct about the nature of the old magic that bound him, he was still a threat to us—though we had been on the brink of addressing that concern before Ulf burst in.

"If I kill this man, *hrafn*," began Ulf, "you will be queen. Your father would forgive much were you to come to him now in possession of an Irish crown, and Faery lords be damned."

"I am queen already, my friend," I said, standing and fully extending my wings. "If you try to kill my husband, I will kill *you*."

Ulf's amber eyes went wide. Then he lowered the bow a few inches and grumbled, "Loki's sack."

Digging my wings hard against the air, I leapt from the table. My feet met the floor softly, like bird feet. I reached out and pushed Ulf's nocked arrow to one side.

"What has happened to you, *hrafn*?" he asked. *Raven*, his pet name for me, had never been more fitting.

His wolf eyes had softened, and I allowed an old affection to creep into my tone as I replied, "A new kind of magic. Something called alchemy."

His eyes moved over my body, and he replied, "Impressive as that is, it's not what I'm asking." He glared over my shoulder at the king, who stood watching us with folded arms.

"Do you remember when you found me?" I asked Ulf.

"Of course I do."

"Then you remember that you had to save my life. And that when you took me from my mother's home I had nothing. At court, you were my only friend."

His mouth set in a firm line. "*Já*."

"The bond between us wasn't about fear, or duty. It had nothing to do with my father, or the loyalty we owed him. It was about trust."

Ulf frowned deeply, but he gave a blunt nod.

"That's the kind of bond I have with Finvara, and you have a choice to make, my friend."

He eyed me sternly. "Don't ask me. Not that, *hrafn*. You know I won't betray your father."

I reached up and took hold of his chin.

"Return to him, then. Tell him I have married Finvara, and that we are allies. Invite him to Knock Ma to speak to us."

Ulf shot the king a dark look before replying, "He is there already. He has seized the castle."

OLD MAGIC

FINVARA

"*What?*" I stepped forward to stand beside Koli. I glanced between the two of them and noted a distinct lack of shock in my bride's expression—but behind her eyes I saw fear.

"You and I had hardly left Iceland when your father's seer put it into his head that you were going to betray him," Ulf said to Koli. "I told *Alfakonung* that the woman had made a mistake—that you would *never* betray him." Ulf narrowed his eyes. "An hour ago we arrived at Knock Ma and discovered that it was true."

"How did you find us?" I demanded, a sinking feeling in my chest.

Ulf shrugged. "Your own people. The druid has kept to *his* promise and turned them against you."

Grinding my teeth together, I recalled how I had felt *grateful* for Doro's hand on the helm.

Koli was looking at me, eyes wide with alarm. "Your family, Finvara."

I shook my head. At least in this one aspect, I had managed my affairs better. "After you vanished, I advised them to pack up and go, for their own safety. They didn't even wait for first light." When I told my father I'd betrothed myself to Koli, I'd been pretty sure he was ready to wash his hands of me.

Koli returned her attention to Ulf. In watching their inter-action—their ease and familiarity with each other, despite the argument—a suspicion had taken hold of me: that the large and menacing elven male was at least partly responsible for the statement *I have done this before, husband.* While I had not been disturbed by her confession, it had not occurred to me I would ever meet one of my predecessors. *Bollocks*, I was not even yet among their numbers.

"Tell Father we will come to him at Knock Ma," said Koli. "Tell him we want to talk."

I caught movement in the doorway behind Ulf—the slightest shifting of shadows—as he scowled at her and replied, "I think you had better come with me *now, hrafn.*"

"I think you had better do as the queen says, Northman."

Treig now stood behind the warrior. Before he could turn, she jabbed the tip of her pike against the back of his neck—and he *vanished.*

"Hold your position, Treig!" Koli ordered. "He's still there."

Koli reached out and plucked at the air, and the knife she'd flung at him—which had remained stuck in his armor—appeared in her hand. Then she reached again, and I heard a low growl. Ulf became visible, and I saw she'd taken hold of his bow. His gaze was bright and angry

"I'll return it to you," Koli said, raising the tip of the knife to his throat. "You have my word."

The warrior finally let it go.

"Leave now," ordered Koli. "Take my message. We won't be far behind you."

With one final half-stricken glare, Ulf turned to go. Treig stepped out of his way, and we watched him stride off into the trees.

"How is it he was able to burst in on us?" I asked Treig. She had a thick, blood-smeared lump on one side of her forehead

"The rest of the escort slipped away, sire," she said. "When I went looking for them, he surprised me."

Shaking my head, I said, "I'm grateful for your loyalty. This has unraveled with devilish efficiency."

"Doro is cunning," said Koli. "You couldn't have known."

"I did know," I said, "because someone I *should* have listened to tried to warn me. But I . . ." Looking up at her, I took a deep breath and sighed, and I reached for her hand. "I had other things on my mind."

She tugged my hand. "Come husband, we don't have much time."

I nodded. "Aye. I must notify the queen. She never responded to my message about *Corvus*, and I suspect it was never sent. We'll have to—"

"Finvara."

The warm molasses in her voice drew my gaze to her. "Aye?"

"Ulf will reach Knock Ma, and he will return with reinforcements. I have only bought us a little time." She hesitated, lifting her chin before continuing, "Doro's fealty could solve many problems."

While I had not forgotten what the elf warrior had interrupted, I had *entirely* forgotten how it related to the situation at hand.

KOLI

The king's eyes burned bright with understanding, and an answering flame kindled low in my belly. I saw his hands clench and release at his sides.

"Treig," he said, "are you well enough to watch?"

"Yes, Your Majesty."

"If Ulf comes back with reinforcements, they will make noise. I want plenty of warning this time. Make sure our horses are saddled and ready."

Treig glanced at me, and I nodded. She left us again, closing the door behind her.

"Thank you," he said. His voice was low and sincere, but the flicker of heat had given it an edge.

"For what?" I asked.

He came closer. "This visit was unexpected. You must have known him for a very long time, and defying him, and your father, can't have been easy."

I nodded and looked away. "He has been a good friend." *My only friend, until now.*

"It must have been hard to leave him behind."

Something in his tone drew my eyes back to his face, and I could see that Finvara had read something in my friendship with Ulf that I had not told him. He was not mistaken.

"It's difficult to lose someone you trust with your life. But Ulf was my father's man centuries before I was born. There has never been anything he'd cross him for. Not even me."

Narrowing his eyes, the king moved still closer. His hands landed gently on my hips, sending a warm shiver through me.

"I'm not sure that's true," he said. "He didn't kill me."

I studied the smooth, brown skin between the edges of shirt that I had unbuttoned earlier. Then I touched it with my finger. *I am allowed this now.*

"That was not about me," I replied. "My news surprised him, and he would want to confer with my father before carrying out an order that could not be reversed."

The king pulled my hips forward so our bodies touched, and the muscles between my legs fluttered.

"Trust me," he said, his voice soft, "it was *mostly* about you. And I should be grateful, but I saw enough to make me resent him." He raised a hand to my cheek, fingers slipping into my hair and tilting my head back. My heart leapt to the base of my throat. "It's a weakness of mine."

As he spoke the last words, he bent over me, touching his parted lips to mine. Despite years of sun and sea air, they were silky and smooth. His tongue moistened my bottom lip. I coiled my arms around him and pressed my breasts against his chest. His hands glided down over the fabric of my dress to my backside and squeezed. I gave a murmur of pleasure and took his top lip between my teeth.

As I nipped his pliant flesh, he gasped. His hands slid around the base of my wings and up to my shoulders, and before I realized what he was doing, my dress was sliding down my arms, hardening my nipples and triggering a delicious aching.

I had not bothered with underclothing, and my naked skin brushed against the cool white of his shirt, the rough wool of his trousers. His hands tried to be everywhere at once, leaving hot trails over my back and hips.

"I haven't been able to get this out of my mind since last night, when I saw you before the tomb."

His hand glided up my ribs and he cupped it over one breast—tickling, lightly squeezing, and finally rolling the hardened nipple until I thought I would fall to my knees.

"Husband," I hissed, clutching his arms. I had known lust and urgency, but this swirling, liquifying heat was a shocking revelation.

He bent suddenly, scooping me up in his arms, and carried me to the bed. He set me down, crouching beside me with one knee on the mattress, as he began tearing at the bottom buttons of his shirt. I lay on my side, propping my head in one hand, and reached for the button of his trousers. He tossed his shirt onto the floor.

I froze for a moment, taking in the litheness of his form. His upper body was sculpted, like drawings of statues I'd seen in a book on ancient Greece. I reached out and splayed a palm across his chest, letting it slide down to his belly, appreciating the contrast of smooth skin and hard muscle. He had a body that only a few days ago I would have considered weak compared to my rough and rugged kinsmen. He was indeed a work of art.

He took hold of my hand, kissing the palm, and I found myself captivated by the sensual lines and complicated musculature of his arms. A mark had been inked on one forearm—a constellation, I thought. Before I could touch it, he unfolded my legs like a clamshell, settling between them.

I steadied myself against the bed so my weight wouldn't fall onto my back. As soon as I had stilled, that full bottom lip of his connected gently but directly with the overripe nub at the top of the cleft between my legs. I arched my back and gasped.

He began lightly circling the nub with his tongue, teasing me to the point of madness. I writhed and offered murmured protests, which he ignored, until finally I took hold of his head and pulled his mouth against me. He laughed, vibrating the delicate tissue, and he slipped a finger inside me. My muscles closed hard around him and I let out a cry of pure desperation.

He raised his head then, my body quivering violently in protest, and crawled up next to me. "Now wife," he murmured, "I do hate to see your suffering. Is there anything I can do to ease it?"

For an answer, I pushed him onto his back and crawled on top of him. He smiled wickedly as I reached down between us, thrusting my hand into his trousers, molding it around the hard, hot flesh there. Eyes wide and bright, he eased his trousers down over his hips. The breath hissed between his teeth as I guided him and eased just his silken tip inside me.

We both took long, shuddering breaths, and I spread and lifted my wings, letting my weight draw me down over him. He exhaled and took hold of my backside, pulling our bodies snug against each other.

Then he begun to thrust, and sensation erupted through me—a sudden fountain of heat that made my muscles quiver.

I closed my eyes, murmuring, "Freyja help me, it feels *so* good."

I expected him to joke or tease. *Don't sound so surprised.* But his hand came to my cheek, and I opened my eyes. "Better than good," he said. "It feels *right.*"

Flexing my hips, I began to rock my body against his. His eyes closed and he moaned, fingers digging into my hips.

Pressing my palms against his stomach, my upper arms squeezing my breasts and deepening the cleft between them, I rocked harder against him. My head fell back and I let out a moan.

"You warned against delay," he said breathlessly, hands moving up to cup and roll my breasts. "At this rate, you needn't worry."

I smiled, rising as high on my knees as I could without losing him, and I ground down hard, gratified by his sudden shout. He grabbed my hips and took control of our rhythm, using my body as a pleasure thing, driving into me and forcing the friction he so desperately needed. My vision swam, and the hot pulsing inside me suddenly released with shattering violence. Liquid sensation burst in my abdomen, splashing over my hips and buttocks and up my belly to my breasts. He froze, and I clenched my muscles around him for the space of two heartbeats. His body tensed and he let out a long, shuddering groan.

I fell across his chest, and his arms wrapped around me. Through the open window drifted the gentle noises of the stream outside, and I could almost forget these moments of peace were stolen and could not last. I raised the tip of a finger, circling one of Finvara's flat, brown nipples. He made a sleepy, contented sound and tightened his embrace.

Less than a week ago, I had wanted him dead.

The reason for what we had just done, beyond the obvious, recalled itself to my attention like a strike of summer lightning.

Doro.

The fairy steward's face came into my thoughts, and along with it came a feathery voice: *So you've betrayed us all.*

I sat straight up.

"Koli?" said Finvara, alarmed.

I held out my hand to stay him.

Far Dorocha? I addressed the voice in my head.

I hear you, Your Majesty.

Come to me at once!

I'm afraid that's impossible.

My heart sank. Had we left something unfinished? I had worried the Christian ritual would not be respected by such an old spell, yet Doro had said the vows and the consummation were all that mattered.

What do you mean? I demanded.

I have vowed never again to answer to the whims of either queen or goddess.

I didn't understand this. Was he bound, or was he not? And what did he mean by "goddess"?

After Queen Eithne escaped Faery and married another, he continued, *I knew that one day the rake would take another wife. How I have worked since then to undo the magic, but it's not in my power. So I conceived a plan to circumvent it by other means.*

And that plan has failed, I pointed out, *so how is it you are free?*

His light laughter brushed across my thoughts. *In the end it was the simplest of spells. I owe thanks to the rake himself for giving me the idea.*

Tell me, I demanded, growing impatient. Ulf would certainly be coming soon, and I began to suspect Doro of stalling.

Finvara sometimes enchanted women and locked them in towers, he continued. *He would cast spells on their prison to prevent any other magic but the enchantment from penetrating. So here I am, safe from you, in your own chamber.*

I froze. I could feel Finvara's worried gaze on me. "Koli?" he repeated.

You mean you've sealed yourself in my tower with magic? I asked. *It never occurred to me such an ancient spell might be defeated by simple fairy magic.*

What will happen now?

I counted heartbeats waiting, but no answer came.

Doro!

"Koli!"

My attention had been focused intensely inward, and it took me a moment to order my thoughts and form speech.

"Doro has figured out a way to avoid our control," I told Finvara. "He won't help us."

The king muttered a curse. "How do you know this?"

"I can reach him with my thoughts." I stood up and found my dress, and he helped me to put it on. I repeated what Doro had told me.

Finvara listened, his frown deepening. "I know the spell he means—I have used it."

I couldn't help wondering what he meant by this. I knew his ancestor's reputation, but had my new husband also trapped women in towers? He had certainly put me in one, though as far as I knew he had never tried to control me with magic.

"The spell may have freed him from us," he continued, "but I assume the spell's limitations apply even to him."

"It will fade?"

Finvara shook his head. "It's more like a magic block than a spell. It will work until he removes it. He won't be able to leave the tower without losing its protection, though. And he won't be able to cast spells that affect anything outside the chamber."

This was good news, yet . . ."The grandfather clock in my

chamber leads to his ship in the Gap," I said. "It's how he took me. Will he be able to escape that way?"

"Aye, Treig told me about the clock. He can leave, but I don't imagine his spell will continue to protect him."

I nodded, and I issued another command, though I had no idea whether it could have any effect. *Should you leave my chamber by any means, you must come to me at once.*

After a moment, his reply came. *You will change your mind about Finvara, and when you do, I will be waiting. Kill him, and I will come to you. Everything between us will be as before.*

"Koli?" said Finvara, ducking his head to catch my attention.

"I've commanded him to come to me if he leaves the tower."

"What did he say?"

"He said if I killed you he would come now."

For a moment the king just stared at me. A smirk tugged up one corner of my lips, and Finvara gave a hearty laugh. It pleased me to a ridiculous degree when I did something that amused him—it always seemed to catch him completely off guard.

"Doro said something I didn't understand," I continued. "He said that he would 'never again answer to the whims of queen or goddess.' Is there a goddess he serves?"

The king rubbed his lips together as he thought about this, and it had a strange effect on me—I wanted to taste his mouth again.

"Lady Meath," he replied, "the wife of my cousin Edward, once told me the Gap gates were created by the Morrigan's alchemists. That must be who he means."

I recalled what Doro had told me about the immortals who had asked him to create and eventually circumvent the seal between Faery and Ireland. "The Morrigan? She is your goddess of war?"

"And a nasty piece of work. The Battle of Ben Bulben would have ended much quicker—with less loss of life—had she not interfered." He shook his head. "Though she also helped us, so it's not straightforward. Lady Meath understands it far better than I."

The Morrigan sounded a lot like Loki. I had no direct experience with gods. Odin, Freyja, Thor—our Icelandic gods had been stranded after the giants destroyed the Bifrost, the rainbow bridge between Earth and Asgard, their home. Loki, as far as anyone knew, remained imprisoned beneath Iceland, and was blamed for our frequent tremors. Many of the Hidden Folk—and many Icelanders, truth be told—still prayed to the old gods, and made offerings, but no oracle had heard their voices for centuries.

If Finvara was right about Doro and the Morrigan, had the fairy steward somehow escaped *her* control as well? Would she be blocked by the simple spell he had used against us?

SHE MOST CERTAINLY WOULD NOT.

I cried out and clamped my hands over my ears. Yet the loud and powerful voice had come from inside my own head. My whole body shook from the shock of it, and I felt like snow was sliding down my back.

The king reached out to steady me. "What is it?" he demanded.

Was this some new attack of Doro's? Could it be a distraction, intended to keep us here?

I looked at the king. "We must go before Ulf comes."

AND WHERE WILL YOU GO, LITTLE LOST ELF MAID?

"Who are you?" I cried, my hands coming again to the sides of my head.

"*Blast*, Koli, what is happening?" demanded the king.

LET HIM COME, CHILD—YOUR WOLF LOVER. LET HIM TAKE YOU TO YOUR DEMON OF A FATHER. KNOCK MA IS EXACTLY WHERE YOU NEED TO GO.

They'll kill Finvara!

NOT IF YOU LET ME HELP YOU.

What do you mean?

COME TO ME AND I'LL SHOW YOU. IT WOULD BE A MISTAKE TO TELL YOUR HUSBAND. HE WILL PREVENT IT, AND THEN HE WILL CERTAINLY DIE.

But how can I—

Pain stabbed across my temples, and I thought my head would split open. The new voice was much stronger than Doro's. And it kept changing, sounding like a child one moment, then a woman, then a crone. I wasn't even sure it was all the same speaker. Strangely, an image of the ship in the sky over Knock Ma came into my mind, but then dissolved as a crackling energy raced down my spine.

The voice was too much for me, its owner too powerful. I would agree to almost anything to stop it.

Do you swear to me that you can save him?

TOGETHER WE CAN.

A sharp knock at the door pulled me out of the painful exchange. Treig burst into the room. "There are warriors approaching, sire."

Yes! I finally agreed. *I'll do what you want!*

Finvara slipped an arm around my waist. "Let's go."

"Wait!" I said, resisting him.

"Koli, what—?" His eyes were wild with urgency.

I knew that a dark power had been at work in my head, and I even had a guess at the source. Such power was dangerous—but it could be channeled and used.

But Finvara—*my* Finvara, Duncan O'Malley—he was a ship's captain, youngest son of an earl, and a hero of the Battle of Ben Bulben. It was true that if he knew what had been proposed—and especially by whom—he would never agree.

I gripped his arms. "Do you trust me?"

"Aye, but you're scaring me! Who have you been with in your head? Doro again?"

He was trying hard to believe in me, I could see it in his eyes. "Someone who can help us," I said. "We have no choice, husband.

My father will find us anywhere we go." It was no more than the truth. He would hunt us down like animals.

"Tell me!" Panicking, the king began to be angry, and his voice boomed.

"They're upon us, sire!" cried Treig. She turned, raising her pike and blocking the doorway. I heard the whoops of my father's warriors approaching.

I looked at my husband, but I couldn't bring myself to answer him aloud.

The Morrigan.

LEAP OF FAITH

FINVARA

"Treig, lower your weapon," I ordered. "Don't give them an excuse to kill you."

I could hear the elves calling to each other in their own tongue. Koli stepped away from me, retrieving the bow I had given her from its resting place beside the door. Ulf's weapon lay on the floor beside it.

"Do you think that's wise?" I asked her. There was no point shouting at her again—it was clear she'd made some kind of decision. Besides that I had agreed to trust her—I was doing my level best.

"It's necessary, husband." She nocked an arrow, pulled back the string, and swung the bow so it pointed at *me*.

She was not the first woman to do such a thing to me after a truce that involved lovemaking, though she was unquestionably the most lethal. She was also the first to sink my heart by doing it.

Ulf strode through the door, taking stock of the situation. He spoke to Koli in Elvish, she replied, and they began an animated dialogue. Elves moved to seize Treig, but Koli gave an order and they let her go. Then Koli and Ulf resumed their heated exchange.

I hoped, and almost believed, that it was a trick to get Ulf to trust her. Yet why had she refused to tell me who had offered to help her? I couldn't help feeling it had to be Doro. What could have induced her to trust him again?

If I die, the throne is hers.

I squeezed my eyes closed against the unwelcome doubts, and when the warriors came to bind my wrists, I threw one punch to live up to my hot-headed reputation before I let them take me. They used a fragile looking chain to bind me, but I could feel its magic—forged into the metal itself. I would have bet my ship that its purpose was to block its captive from using magic. I tested it anyway.

Wisp's light, burn bright, elfin charm against the night. Nothing happened.

Ulf and Koli had finished their conversation, and the elf warrior came over to me. He looked me up and down, smirked, and then swung his massive fist. My bride's velvety voice was the last thing I heard.

I woke shivering, and everything hurt. Not just my jaw, which had a lump the size of a lemon, but my back, my neck, and most of my joints. Surveying the hard lines and shadows of my surroundings, I surmised that I'd been dragged down the stairs to the dungeon and left for dead.

But they haven't killed me, and I likely have Koli to thank for that.

Groaning, I pushed myself up with my bound hands and took inventory. I'd been locked in a cell, and in the open area out front, I could see the pile of "little machines."

I closed my eyes, and the specters of doubt rose again in my mind. Somewhere close by, there was a steady *drip, drip, drip*, and I realized I was parched. I looked around to see if water had been left for me. Suddenly the door to the tower swung open and I heard feet descending the stairs. Whoever it was carried a wisp light—a green flame danced above an open palm—and I couldn't make out a face until the visitor reached the bottom of the stairs.

Koli.

She smiled at me, which caused a wave of relief to wash through me—but it was not a smile I had seen before. It was cool and brittle.

"Husband," she said, and I didn't like her tone any more than her smile.

"Are you all right?" I asked, moving closer to the bars of my cage.

Her dark eyes moved over my face, lingering on my swollen jaw. I noticed that she was freshly washed and finely dressed. She wore a wine-colored backless gown with bell sleeves—the laces at the neck of the bodice were loose, and I found my gaze settling on the curves of her breasts. Her hair had been elaborately plaited and wound atop her head. With her glossy wings and other finery, she looked like a dark angel. *My* dark angel.

"I am well," she said.

"You are *exquisite*," I corrected.

Her expression didn't change as she came a few steps closer. I noticed that she carried the mechanical raven under one arm. Stopping beside the heap of oddities, she set it on top.

"I'm sorry," she continued, her gaze resting on the bird, "I know this place is not comfortable."

At first I wasn't sure she was speaking to me. I glanced again at the stairs, checking whether anyone had followed her down. It looked like we were alone.

"What is happening?" I asked in a low voice. "Does your father—"

She faced me, her wisp light throwing a green cast over her features. "You will be allowed to live."

This was delivered in a dry and even tone, like a pronounce-
ment, and I searched her face for any accompanying emotion.

"That is good news," I said tentatively.

"I persuaded Alfakonung that you are far more valuable alive."

Alfakonung. Her father. Something unpleasant rolled in my
belly. "Aye?"

She nodded. "I will rule in your place. Alfakonung need not
grant any terms or honor any alliance. He may simply command
me, and I will command Doro."

"The druid has come out of hiding, then?" My voice had gone
flat. They had let me live, yet I had begun to feel that stones were
being piled on my grave.

She offered another glacial smile. "He knows he can't stay in
the tower forever. We'll coax him out soon enough."

I began to fret in earnest. If this *was* an act, could she not give
me some sign? Show some hint of emotion?

It's not her nature, I reminded myself. *She has always been
guarded.*

And yet my heart sank further. She was among her own
people again. She had fresh reminders of age-old bonds and loyalties. What was I to her in that long history but the fascination of a
few moments? A fool who laughed and trusted too easily.

I looked to the top of the stairs, where the door stood open.
Night had fallen, but I was pretty sure no one else was waiting there.

Koli turned then and walked back toward the stairway. Either
she was playing her part to perfection, or she had checkmated both
Doro and me in one fell swoop. I had scorned her, and he had tried
to use her. *She* had been brought up in the court of the Elf King,
and *we* were but a pair of Irishmen with a few tricks up our sleeves.

She raised her foot to the first step and hesitated. "I wanted
you to know that you won't be harmed. Although you will have
to remain here for the time being."

She continued up the stairs, and I called to her softly. "Koli."
She stopped at the sound of my voice.

"I'm relieved that you are safe," I said.

I held my breath—she did not turn. I watched her continue to climb, and when she reached the top, an immense silhouette moved into the light.

Ulf, the hairy bastard. He said something in Elvish, and there was no mistaking the affection in his tone. She replied in a voice so different from the one she'd just used—so similar to the one I had been graced with perhaps only hours ago—that I felt seasick, and had I anything in my stomach, it would have come up.

She stepped out of the doorway without once looking back. The door swung closed with a heavy thud.

KOLI

"Are you ready, *hrafn*?" asked Ulf.

My heart pounded as we made our way toward the keep, where my father waited. He and his attendants were conducting their business from the smaller of the two halls.

"Does it matter?" I replied.

Ulf didn't answer. Both of us knew there was no point.

We reached the closed door and stopped for a moment outside. It was a trick worthy of Loki that I would face my judgment in the same chamber where I had first dined with the king.

I had convinced Ulf that I'd turned on Finvara, and he had made my father believe it too. I'd told Ulf it had been my plan all along—to outmaneuver Doro and take the crown for myself. Moreover, my apparent affection for Finvara had been a ruse, one that I'd dropped as soon as I'd ensured the legitimacy of our marriage could not be questioned. I was not proud of myself for taking advantage of the fact Ulf *wanted* to believe all of this to be true.

My friend fixed his eyes on me. "I cannot say what he will do. Only that you need not fear for your life. You're strong, remember that."

The fact that he had to assure me that my father would not kill me only painted in stark contrast the difference between my new relation and the old ones.

I had never before defied my father. The mark on my back was intended to prevent me from doing so, yet its effectiveness had never been tested until I came to Ireland. After my mother was driven to her death—and before I suspected my father of letting it happen—I was grateful that the Elf King had sent Ulf to keep me safe. I was grateful to be given a home and shielded from the fear and hatred of the people in my village. I had determined to embrace my immortal relations, and I was relieved to finally learn how to use the gifts I had inherited from them—to grow strong, so that I'd never need fear my enemies. Obedience had seemed a small price to pay. I had given nearly two decades of obedience to the church, and its attempts to protect me from its flock had, in the end, proved feeble.

But my mother—she at least had loved me, despite the fact that my birth had taken everything from her. In my father's house, I had been taught that she was weak. Had she been stronger, she could have survived. Why had she accepted the mantle of shame the villagers bestowed? She should have taught them to fear her, or let my father do it for her. Instead, she became a martyr.

My father possessed not a single tender feeling for her. He did not even pity her. If he knew the truth about Finvara and me, he would despise me for such weakness, and I would face worse than punishment. A crime of defiance was small in comparison.

I nodded at Ulf, and I raised my fist and rapped once on the door. It swung inward, and he stationed himself beside it as I went inside.

The room was lit by the blazing fire and the large, round bracket of candles that hung over the table, throwing long shadows along the walls. Incense smoked from the mantle and filled the room with the familiar scent of thyme, which I associated with the court of the Elf King—it had always made me feel safe.

My father stood at the casement that opened onto the conservatory. As the door swung closed behind me, he turned.

He was even larger than Ulf, the distance between his shoulders twice that of mine—he would not have easily passed through the door, or any door in this castle. He wore his dark hair close cropped, but his beard was long and thick and elaborately plaited. The top half of his face was masked by alternating stripes of black and rust-colored paint, which gave his eyes a feral glimmer. His most striking feature, however, was the set of great, black horns that curved up from either side of his head.

"Father," I said, bowing deeply.

Though he made no sound, I felt him moving closer.

"Daughter." His voice rumbled like thunder and I shuddered. The spells he uttered could rend the very ground and roil the surface of the ocean, crack boulders and the ice on frozen lakes.

"You've been to see him?" he asked.

"I have, my lord," I replied. "The dwarf metal holds. He is no threat to us."

My father gave a low grunt, and I glanced up. He motioned to someone behind me, and two attendants, silver masks covering their faces, moved forward out of the deep shadows of the room. My stomach knotted, and a chill rose along the back of my neck.

"I commend both your strategy and execution," he said. "You have served me faithfully for most of your life. I'm gratified that you have avoided your mother's weakness, and that Gunnhild's ambition runs thicker in your blood than it did in hers. One day

you may be strong enough to cross me—even to displace me—
but that day has not yet come. And I'm afraid I cannot allow
disobedience to go unanswered."

"I understand, Father, and I submit."

My eyes darted right and left as the attendants moved toward
me. Two took hold of my arms, and another loosened the strings
of my bodice, slipping my gown off my shoulders.

My father came closer. My heart thundered and my breaths
shortened as he bent to examine my back. It was the closest scrutiny I'd received from him since the day my mother died, when I
was brought to his court for the first time.

I jumped as I felt the hot pads of his fingers tracing around
the base of my wings. "*Yggdrasill* no longer troubles you?"

"No, my lord," I admitted, and I cursed the tremor in my voice.

He moved away again and I let the breath fill my lungs. A
moment later he muttered a fire spell, and a searing lash whipped
against the small of my back. The pain was equal to the worst of
the punishment inflicted by *yggdrasill* in my chamber, and I cried
out and doubled over—only the tight grip of the king's attendants
keeping me on my feet.

I was better prepared for the second lash and determined to
make no noise, but it caught the sensitive flesh just above my hip
and I uttered an even higher-pitched cry.

When the third lash landed above the other hip, I gritted my
teeth and swallowed a moan. Tears squeezed from under both of
my eyelids.

"Shall we say one for each decade you've served me?"

Five more, Freyja help me.

The attendants released me and I straightened, pulling my gown back
over my shoulders and tightening the bodice strings. As I squared my
shoulders and turned, the tender flesh of my lower back burned.

"You are forgiven," said my father as I faced him. "We won't speak of it again."

He waved his hand, dismissing me, and turned his back before I'd made it out of the room.

I found Ulf waiting outside.

Searching my eyes, he glowered and said, "I'm sorry, *hrafn*. You've done well. They didn't have to carry you out, and he won't forget it."

He offered his arm, and I shook my head. "I need air."

"The stairs in the great hall go up to the roof of the keep," he said. "Shall I take you?"

"I know the way," I replied, laying a hand on his arm. "I'll see you at dinner."

He nodded and left me.

The great hall was dark and quiet, but tomorrow evening my father intended to show the subjects of Finvara who their new liege lord was. There would be a feast, and entertainment into the small hours. Had I intended to remain here that long, I would sit at my father's right hand as Knock Ma's new queen—though everyone in attendance would know that I too served Alfakonung.

I approached the stairway that provided access to the upper floors of the keep and the battlements—the same one I had climbed with Finvara on my first evening in the castle.

So many stairs. I took a deep breath and began ascending before I could change my mind.

By the time I reached the top, sweat had soaked my gown and my back was aflame. My breaths came so hard and heavy I had to grasp the stone wall for support.

When I'd recovered, I found another stairway that climbed to the top of the turret extending from the north side of my tower. It was an even higher vantage point, and unlike the towers themselves, it was not topped with battlements.

Here, I found no guards—they all watched from the parapet and towers below. *Corvus* still slumbered over the castle grounds, washed in moonlight. With the breeze, I could hear the occasional creaking of the rigging.

HAVE YOU BROUGHT ALL YOUR COURAGE? The goddess's voice, light with amusement, still hit me like a battering ram, knocking me against the low wall around the turret's perimeter.

"All that I have left," I muttered, panting.

Brushing tears from my cheeks, I straightened and gripped the edge of the stone wall. I raised one foot and placed it on the narrow ledge—it was about half the width of my foot. Closing my eyes, I whispered a prayer to Freyja, and I shifted my weight onto the foot resting on top of the wall, slowly lifting the other foot away from safety. If the Morrigan was wrong, I would fall probably a hundred feet to the moat below.

Before I could rise from my crouching position, I teetered, and I raised my wings on instinct to correct my balance. With my wings unfurled, I could feel the cool breeze against my back even through the fabric of my dress. I hovered there, letting it soothe my scored flesh while fear wrung my insides.

It was not the first time I had risked a fatal fall, but I had never before done so while in terrible physical pain, or while running away from my father. And I had certainly never done so while another's fate rested in my hands.

Slowly I let go of the wall and stood up, raising my wings higher.

The breeze stiffened suddenly against my feathers, unbalancing me, and I half jumped, half fell, from the turret.

NEW MAGIC

FINVARA

No one else came, not even to bring water, and I began to wonder whether they'd forget about me. Surely *she* wouldn't.

But "sure" was the last thing I was—about anything, except the fact I'd made a hash of it, just as I'd feared. Queen Isolde had put her faith in me. In my arrogance and naivete, I had banished my ancestor, unwilling to live out the rest of my life with an immortal sharing my head. A few short months later, and the fledgling kingship that I'd never wanted was lost. The enemy I was ordered to guard against was literally within the castle walls. And all I had to show for it was a queen who was strong enough to rule without me.

As a smuggler I had been in scrapes—had been boarded by both English and American naval officers, as well as more thoroughgoing pirates, and had survived to smuggle another day. An easy laugh and a friendly demeanor had carried me far in life, and

I had generally escaped with no worse damage than a dent in my profits. Until the Elf King and his daughter.

It wounded me more than I liked to admit. Letting the queen down, certainly—for Izzy and I had grown close in the years since her mother died. She had come to depend on me for information from abroad, and she was wholly unconcerned with my illegitimate birth. But also I'd failed my cousin Edward and his new wife—with all they had suffered in the Battle of Ben Bulben, and well on their way to starting a family. Not to mention my father, my brothers, and *their* families, and my mother, whom I often imagined might be watching me from the stars.

Yet the most painful wound was Koli. My instincts had always been good—they had kept me alive during those years at sea. And I had a gift for reading people. All of that had failed me with Koli and Doro.

Had she felt nothing? Thoughts of our time together in the cottage kept returning, despite my attempts to banish them. She was my wife now, by any estimation. I had held her and touched her, and she had responded beyond my wildest imaginings. Was it possible I'd been deceived even in that?

I closed my eyes—the *drip, drip, drip* was driving me mad with thirst. There was a cistern below the tower, but no way of accessing it from my cell.

Water, water, everywhere, nor any drop to drink . . .

Something caused me to open my eyes and look at the pile of little machines in front of my cell. They might not be living, but neither were they quite dead. There was a low murmur of continuous noise—creaks and clicks, ticks and tocks, even the occasional pop. What had drawn my attention there? It had been a noise that contrasted with the others, like the squeal of a rusted hinge. I noticed the mechanical raven resting on top of the pile. Had its head turned slightly toward me?

I stood up, groaning at the stiffness in my back and shoulders, the pain in my jaw, and I picked up a wooden spoon I'd found while inspecting my cell. Holding it between my bound hands, I worked my wrists and then my arms between two bars. I swung the spoon experimentally several times, both overhand and underhand, gauging the distance. Finally I let it go. It sailed toward the pile in an arc, then struck the bird's back with a *thunk*. The raven slid down a few inches and came to rest. Sighing, I looked around for something else to throw.

Suddenly a shrill voice shattered the silence. "*Brisingr, slepp bandingjann.*"

My head snapped up and I saw that the raven's eyes were burning bright.

I jumped as the links of the chain around my wrists widened, causing the chain to slacken and then drop to the stone floor.

"Fly, fly, fly!" cried the raven before its eyes again went dark.

I stood with my mouth agape, staring at the thing—what had just happened?

Your bride is trying to save you, idiot.

But how was I to get out of this bloody cell? Reaching through the bars for the dozent time, I got a better purchase on the bolt with my newly freed hands and yanked it hard—the lock still wouldn't give.

The elves had emptied my pockets—I'd noticed the missing weight of my mother's compass—but I dug my hands into them anyway. My fingers grazed something thin and hard at the bottom of my left pocket—a key!

I curled a hand around to the front of the cell door and carefully inserted it. It wouldn't turn, no matter how I jiggled it. I pulled it out to try inserting it again—before I could, it slid from my sweaty hands.

"Bollocks!"

The key struck the flagstones and bounced. I knelt and thrust both hands through the bars. The light in the dungeon was low, but the brass of the key had accumulated vibrant verdigris, and I could see it less than a yard away. I lay down on my stomach and reached one arm between the bars, all the way to my shoulder. I stretched, holding my breath, and my fingertip just touched the edge of the handle. I reached farther, feeling the rusted bars biting into my shoulder, and managed to press my fingertip just into the hole in the key's handle. I dragged it a couple of inches toward me and then, with a better grip, snatched it up.

I rubbed the key between my palms, hoping it would pick up some oil along with sweat and move easier inside the lock. I reached through the bars again, and the key clicked home this time. I turned it, drew the bolt, and kicked open the door.

Then I ran for the stairs.

KOLI

I had not truly been ready for the shock of the fall. I'd told myself that even if my wings could not be made to fly, they would likely at least make it possible to land safely. But even *that* required that I keep them extended. Once I was plummeting toward the ground, I lost all control—they went limp and folded around my body, and I panicked.

ARE YOU BEATEN?

The taunt came from the goddess while in midair, and it was just the countershock I needed. Her booming voice focused my attention on uncurling my wings, flinging first one, and then the other as far out from my body as I could. The pressure of the air against my expanded surface flipped me over, and I stopped falling, instead gliding gradually down toward the forested hills below the castle. The wind whipped against my face as the treetops rushed closer.

Experimentally I raised and lowered my wings, and the wobble this caused was terrifying.

YOU'RE NOT A BELLOWS, ELF MAID!

Suddenly I found myself engulfed by an inky black cloud—my furies filled the air around me, keeping pace with my progress, gliding then flapping, their necks twisting occasionally to watch me. I noted their wing movement, and it struck me that it was more like rowing. I tried again, pushing forward before digging down and back. My feet were all but dragging the highest branches of the oaks, but I kept this up, making small adjustments to my movements as I got a feel for it. Soon I was rising again.

Despite the assistance of the gears near the base of my wings, the amount of exertion this required was incredible. Sweat soaked me, and my shoulder blades burned. I wouldn't be able to keep it up for long.

Fortunately I didn't have far to go.

Corvus's position was higher than the turret I'd leapt from, but I had now glided west of the ship. To reach her, I had only to regain altitude and turn back the way I'd come.

Easy. Right.

After pumping my wings a few more times, I lifted one slightly, until my flight path began to curve. Soon I was pointed roughly in the direction of the ship. I was flying into the wind now, and I began to rise faster than before—the wind was giving me lift. I was dizzy and nauseous with fatigue—*just a little farther.*

I pinned my gaze on the balloon suspended between the floating square rigs, ignoring the panicked messages my body was sending, and as soon as I could see deck beneath my feet, I relaxed my wings.

Again I was falling instead of flying, and I struck the deck hard despite the short distance. Pain shot through one hip and elbow, and I scrambled to my feet.

"What now?" I cried.

LIGHT MY BURNER AND I WILL WAKE.

FINVARA

I reached the top of the dungeon stairs and yanked on the door handle—it was bolted from the outside. While fairy magic was useless against an iron lock, the door itself was made of wood. A wisp's light wasn't going to do the job and I was reluctant to cast a more powerful spell now, not knowing what I'd face on the other side. I raised a foot and kicked the door, but it held fast.

So be it.

Rather than stand pondering a subtler approach, I had spoken the first words for *Beltane fire* when the door swung inward.

A wide-eyed guard shoved the tip of a spear at me and shouted something in Elvish. I sidestepped, grabbed the weapon, and used the guard's own momentum to drag him into the dungeon. Then I darted around him and out the door, slamming and bolting it behind me.

"Finvara!"

The familiar voice drew my eyes skyward—the airship had at last *moved* and was positioned directly over the prison tower.

"Koli?" I called.

Guards shouted the alarm from tower to tower, and the arrows they fired at the ship arced over my head. Koli's face appeared above the rail, and she flung a rope ladder down over the hull. It wasn't long enough for me to reach from where I was standing, but there was a turret on the north side of the tower. I hurried around to the stairway and started up—I could hear a guard coming down. Before he came into view, I flattened myself against the wall and murmured a shielding spell—an earth spell to help me blend into the stones. He came thundering down, and when he was close, I threw out a leg and toppled him, sending him tumbling down the stairs.

At the top of the turret, the rope ladder was waiting. Guards raced along the parapet toward the tower from opposite directions. "Climb!" cried Koli. "I'll manage the arrows."

Grabbing the ladder, I climbed four rungs and then stopped, locking my fingers around the rope rails as the lines furling the *Corvus*'s square sails began to unwind themselves. The sails dropped, and the clewlines, buntlines, and sheets were manipulated as if by an invisible crew. The sails unfurled with miraculous efficiency, and the ship lurched into motion. A guard who'd taken hold of the bottom rung of the ladder was jerked over the turret wall—he lost his grip and fell with a shout.

An arrow zinged past my cheek and I glanced down—three guards on the parapet below held nocked bows. The guards let more arrows fly just as Koli called out a spell, and a rogue gust of wind blew the arrows off course and caused the ship to lurch again.

More bowmen were lining up on the parapet. Koli's wind spell had been effective, but only a powerful magic wielder would be able to call on the air element again without a recovery period. *Beltane fire* was on the tip of my tongue already, so I shouted the spell and hurled the resulting fireball at the bowmen. It wasn't as hot as real fire, yet it had a tendency to explode on impact. Despite the swaying rope ladder my aim was true, and the fireball slammed into the chest of the middle bowman, raining flames and sparks over his companions. No sooner had I cast my spell than a nearby elven guard conjured his own bright orange ball and took aim.

I heard Koli cast her wind spell again, but nothing happened, and I tried to sway the ladder as the guard hurled the fireball. In the same instant, I heard a roaring sound from *Corvus*, and she jerked upward, causing the fireball to strike the ladder two rungs below my feet. Instead of exploding, it splattered, and the brilliantly colored fire oozed and adhered like honey to the rope. Then the rope began to burn.

Arrows continued to reach us, but the stiffening wind had managed to put some distance between the ship and the castle. The arrows that did make it bounced harmlessly off the hull. I imagined an arrow would still go through *me* easily enough—I tried not to think about it as I climbed the swinging rope ladder while flames licked at my heels.

"Hurry!" shouted Koli.

Finally I reached the rail and hauled myself aboard. Koli drew a knife and cut the ladder free from the ship, and the flaming ropes dropped away.

We both looked back at the castle, holding our breath as it shrank in the distance. *Corvus* was sailing at a good clip now. Though we could still hear the elven guards shouting to each other, we could no longer see them.

"Are we safe?" I asked her. We had been casting both fire and wind spells, increasing the likelihood any new spells would fail. But sorcerers and necromancers—beings like the Elf King—could draw on the elements across a greater distance. They could cast spells lesser magic wielders would never attempt.

"With luck," Koli replied. I could hear the worry in her voice, and her eyes were still fixed on the castle. "They will not have been expecting it."

No sooner had she spoken than the skin on the back of my neck began to tingle. On instinct, I flung my arms around her, bracing as lightning forked across the sky accompanied by a deafening crack of thunder. The stark white lines reached for us like a skeletal hand but fell short.

"That was close," I breathed into her hair.

"It was a warning," she replied.

As I drew back to look at her, I heard a roaring noise and looked up to see the burner for the balloon flaring. The ship began to rise.

"Who is captaining her?" I asked.

There were a couple beats of silence before Koli answered. "The Morrigan."

Alarmed, I looked to the helm. "She's on the ship?"

"She *is* the ship."

My eyes came slowly back to my bride. *I've misunderstood.*

"She was betrayed by Doro too," Koli said.

I shook my head, even more confused. "I've seen the Morrigan," I said. "At Ben Bulben. She's a shape-changer, but she appears as an old woman or a crow."

Corvus the crow.

It couldn't be.

"It's Doro's doing," said Koli. "The Morrigan used him for his power for centuries. First as a druid, later as an alchemist. After he helped one of the Tuatha de Danaan to create the seal between Faery and Ireland, the Morrigan decided that no one save gods and goddesses should wield such power. She bound him to his queen—to the fairy queen—so he could be controlled."

This story fit together with some of the things I had been told by Queen Isolde and Lady Meath both before and after the Battle of Ben Bulben. Yet I still couldn't puzzle out how Doro, the Morrigan, and the ship were connected.

"How has he betrayed her?" I asked.

"The Gap gate that changed me," she replied, "he tricked her into going through it too."

I gave a low whistle. I hadn't misunderstood her at all— *Corvus* was the Morrigan. "Why would he do such a thing? She might have destroyed him for it."

"He had experimented on fairies first," she said, shrugging, "and most of them didn't survive. I think his bondage had become intolerable. And she would have certainly interfered with his plans to steal your crown to escape his bond."

"So he decided it was worth the risk." My eyes followed the ghostly movement of lines and sheets as *Corvus* prepared to come about. She was tacking east. "Why *didn't* she destroy him?"

"After her transformation, she was—" Koli stopped, and I recognized her expression—she was searching for a word. After murmuring a few words in her own language, she said, "She was dormant. I used a spell to light her burner, but her mind and her power—they're both trapped in the ship."

I studied the wing-shaped sails on the hull, and the dark avian figurehead. Taking a deep breath, I reached for Koli's hand and pressed it between mine. "How did you learn all of this?"

KOLI

I wanted to feel the elation of our escape. I wanted to dwell on the heat in his gaze, and the way his strong hands warmed mine. But there was more to tell, and it wouldn't be easy.

"The Morrigan is not just in the ship," I said carefully. "She's in my head."

His brow darkened, and his voice deepened. "What?"

"I can hear her, like Doro."

He gave his head a vigorous shake. "I don't like that at all, *acushla*. Doro was bad enough." Still holding my hand, he drew me closer. The word he had used, *acushla*, was not one I had learned in my study of the language, though the sound of it on his lips caused a warm flutter in my chest.

"I know." I bit my lip as his troubled gaze moved over my face. "Yet we could not have escaped without her." The goddess had seemed to move in and out of my thoughts since our first conversation. If she was listening, I hoped my gratitude would help make up for my husband's disrespect.

He raised his hand, his thumb tracing my cheekbone. Memories of our afternoon in the cottage—the hunger, the press of warm flesh—flooded my mind.

"And how *did* we escape?" he asked.

I could feel how uneasy this made him, and the rest of the story was not likely to change that. His closeness made a jumbled mess of my thoughts. I did my best to recount how the Morrigan had first spoken to me and persuaded me to accept her help.

"Do you know why she's come to *you* for help?"

There was no point in hiding it from him. "She knew I would need help to get you out of the castle. She needs *our* help to get revenge on her enemy."

"Doro."

Blowing out a breath, he ran a hand over his close-cropped hair. "The accomplishments of this fellow, the *arrogance*—it's stupefying. He gained the consent of the Elf King to marry his daughter. He tricked and imprisoned the goddess of war. He turned my subjects against me." Finvara looked at me. "Was the mechanical raven one of Doro's experiments?"

"I believe so."

"You gave it the words to free me?"

I nodded. "I wasn't sure it would work, but I didn't think you'd be able to retrieve and use the key with your hands bound. I had to try."

His hands came to cup my face, and then he bent and kissed me gently, moving his lips slowly over mine, nuzzling my cheek at the end.

"It was brilliant," he murmured. "Thank you for freeing me. Thank you for coming for me."

I splayed my hands against his broad chest, smiling as I studied his face. "Did you think I would leave you behind?"

He laughed. "You were so convincing in the dungeon I thought you might." He pulled me closer, coiling his arms around me. I concealed my discomfort as his hands brushed the fresh wounds on my back. "And they believed you about your double cross? Your father, and your *friend* Ulf?"

"They did."

"I'm glad for that. When they took us, I was afraid of what they might do to you."

I ran my hands up his arms, feeling the hard muscle under his warm skin, not yet over my amazement that I was permitted to do such things now.

"I think I surprised them both," I replied. "I have never crossed him before. My father was angry, but I believe he was also impressed."

"Well *I* certainly was. Now he will be angrier."

Angry doesn't even come close.

"So where are we going, *acushla*?"

I frowned. "I don't know this word—*acushla*. What does it mean?"

He smiled. "Something like 'heartbeat.'"

This did little to clear up my confusion, and I raised my eyebrows.

"It means someone important to you." His thumb brushed my jaw. "Do you mind?"

Feeling a pleasant shiver, I shook my head.

"Good. Now tell me, where is this vengeful goddess taking us?"

"To your queen."

Pressing his lips together, he nodded. "I hate that it's come to this, but I need her help."

"You also must warn her," I said. "There's more danger than you know."

ACUSHLA

FINVARA

Koli let her embrace fall away and turned from me—it made my stomach sink. Folding her hands in front of her, she took a few steps and then faced me.

"I have not told you all," she said, squeezing her hands together. "I had not intentionally kept it from you, but everything has happened so fast." She looked a little lost, and I had to stop myself from closing the space she'd opened between us.

"I know," I said as gently as I could. "Tell me."

She dropped her hands by her sides. "Taking your throne from you was only the first part of Doro's plan. When my father is sure of his dominion over your subjects, he will summon his allies, the Fomorians. They intend to try again to take Ireland for themselves—this time with the help of your fairy folk. It threatens not just your court, but everyone you know. Everyone you care for."

It should not have come as a shock—Doro had already allied with one enemy of Ireland. The scope of my failure as guardian of the west sickened me.

"How much time do we have to prepare?" I asked.

"My father is not one to act in haste," she replied. "He strategizes and arranges his pieces on the board until success is a sure thing. With our escape, he will have guessed we are going to the queen. He will be forced to act quickly."

"Is Doro still hiding from us in the tower?"

She nodded. "Ulf said my father tried to go up to him, but Doro has sealed off the chamber."

"Now that he must answer to you, he probably doesn't trust anyone. Is there any chance that without Doro's power to aid him, your father will reconsider his plans?"

"It will have been a setback."

"Your betrayal will also have been a setback."

"Yes." Her expression was flat, yet I knew she had to be weighing it all. Did she regret casting her lot with me? Her whole world had been upended by our marriage.

Finally she said, "The treaty has been broken. He will go to war before he repents of it, because repentance would show his enemies—and his allies—that he is weak."

Conflict was inevitable, then. So soon after the Battle of Ben Bulben.

"What do you think he'll do next?" I asked. "Were you still loyal to him, what would you advise him to do?"

She took a deep breath, and she pursed her lips together. Her eyes lifted to study the bright, barely waning moon hanging in the sky above the stern.

"Take prisoners," she said in a hardened tone. "Use them as a shield until reinforcements arrive."

I closed my eyes. "Aye." Almost all of my family lived in

Connacht, within striking distance of Knock Ma. My father, my brothers and their wives and children.

Resting my hand on the rail, I studied the moonlit countryside slowly passing beneath the ship. The night was clear, though there were dark clouds on our horizon. Yet I could not help feeling my spirits lifted by the creaking of the deck, the fair wind against my skin, and the beauty of the sky overhead.

"How long will it take us to reach the queen?" Koli asked.

Sighing, I reached into my pocket for my compass, forgetting it was gone. On a night like this I didn't need it anyway. I let my eyes move over the rigging, then beyond to the stars. Finding Orion on the starboard side and the Plough to port, I followed the lines of the Plough to the North Star. We were tacking the right direction, but then I would expect the Morrigan to know her way.

Eight knots, maybe less. *Aesop* could cruise at twice the speed. That great balloon, while necessary for an airship, must create incredible drag. There would be some compensation in the additional sails fixed to the hull, which moved through the air like oars, and in the aft propeller. I wasn't sure what powered them, but possibly steam, with the balloon's burner and other sources of combustion controlled by the ship itself—the Morrigan.

"Tomorrow," I replied. "Hopefully by midday. We should try to get some sleep." Now that the excitement of our escape had worn off, a clouding fatigue was settling behind my eyes.

Turning her gaze from the stars, Koli nodded. I walked over and offered my arm.

"This is a galleon," I said. "Normally there would be officers' accommodations in the quarter gallery—let us go and see."

We walked aft in silence, the lamps along the rail lighting our way. My bride seemed distracted, and I continued to worry about the fact we'd had to accept help from the Morrigan. If her powers were confined to this ship, that at least was something.

But it was a matter of grave concern to me that the goddess of war had gotten inside Koli's *head*. I remembered what it was like having my intellect overtaken by an immortal. Not only that, in the Battle of Ben Bulben the Morrigan had helped both sides, in the interest of drawing out the conflict as long as possible. She was anything but trustworthy.

Though, if the goddess could not enact her vengeance without us, we would at least have some means of controlling her. And heaven knew we needed all the help we could get.

"Are you talking to her *now*?" I asked when I could take the quiet no longer.

Koli shook her head. "I don't speak with her often. Her voice is—" She broke off, shuddering before she continued, "It's very hard for me to listen to for long."

Swallowing my anger, I curled my fingers over hers. "I would that I could carry that burden for you." My words came out stiffer than I intended. I didn't like feeling so powerless.

We reached the door to what would be captain's quarters on an ordinary sailing ship, and I bade her stay outside while I made a quick inspection. Koli clearly had no need of my protection—yet that had not stopped me from developing fiercely protective impulses.

The luxury of the accommodations exceeded anything I'd seen even among the wealthiest of smugglers. There was a vast quantity of red—velvet-upholstered lounges and chairs, rugs and wall hangings, cushions and lamp shades. The chamber ran the length of the gallery, with a set of narrow windows across the stern. The floors and walls were dark wood, polished and gleaming, and the ceiling was made of large squares of riveted copper that reflected the lamplight. There were also *clocks*—resting on every horizontal surface, so many of them that their ticking, gear clicking, and occasional chiming created a busy sort of musical background, more lively even than the pile of little machines on the floor of the dungeon. A glowing stove stationed in the stern had gauges, gears, and pipes that ran down through holes in the floor. Presumably the complicated apparatus was powering the steam engine as well as heating the chamber.

Koli stepped in behind me, murmuring something in Elvish.

I gave her a questioning look, and she said, "We have found her heart."

Here was a poetic turn I had not observed in her before. It reminded me of something my cousin Izzy would say—the Irish queen had inured me to whimsical tendencies.

"It doesn't make you uneasy?" I asked.

Koli laughed and shook her head, eyes still moving over the room and its furnishings—a long dining table under an antique chandelier, and a roll-top desk against one wall.

I reached back and closed the door behind us. "Why do you think that is?" I asked in as light a tone as I could manage.

She gave me a teasing smile, and it lifted my heart that I had finally earned enough smiles to be able to tell them apart. "Maybe because I'm a descendant of Loki."

I frowned. "Comfortable with chaos, then."

She laughed and moved closer. "Comfortable with chaos."

Reaching suddenly into the front of her gown, she said, "I had forgotten." She drew out a chain that was hanging around her neck.

I grinned when I saw my compass at the end of it. She lifted the chain over her head and placed it over mine.

"I used the excuse of emptying your pockets to give you a cell key," she said.

I pulled her into my arms. "That was a clever bit of jailbreaking, my lady."

Koli studied me, smiling shyly. "She was someone important to you?"

I frowned, puzzled, and she added, "Angel."

She had tried to read the inscription—I had nearly rubbed it off by now, so it would have taken good eyes and considerable effort. "Aye, the compass was my mother's—Angelique."

"Angelique," she repeated slowly.

I smiled. "You have it."

She rested her head against me, and I let my hands slide from her waist to her hips. She flinched, and I loosened my arms.

"Are the wings causing you pain?"

Her smile faded and she shook her head.

With a finger I tipped her chin back, so she'd meet my gaze. "There are consequences for disobeying Alfakonung."

I felt my expression harden. "What kind of consequences?"

She pulled her chin free. "I am far from the first to be punished in this way, though it was the first time for *me*. It is nothing, husband. And I will heal."

I took hold of her shoulder. "Let me see."

She hugged her arms around her middle, glancing warily around the chamber, and this display of childlike vulnerability caused me to burn with rage at the devil that had caused it.

"If you like," she said, "but not here."

I was not about to remind her that we had no real privacy anywhere on the ship.

Her gaze came to rest on the sleeping loft. Shallow stairways ran up the walls both starboard and port, giving access to a loft on either side of the captain's quarters—one contained a bed, and the other was lined with bookshelves.

She walked toward the stairs and I followed.

There was just enough room in the loft for me to stand without brushing my head on the ceiling. The princess moved to the foot of the bed and stood facing it. She loosened her bodice strings and then waited silently. I went to her and eased the gown down past her waist. She wore nothing underneath, and I felt a tightness in my groin that was not welcome at this moment.

In the lamplight I could see narrow, silvery marks in the flesh around her hips, like the marks of a whip, except for the color—more like burns than lashes. Neither birching nor flogging were allowed on *Aesop*, but I had seen such marks on sailors, as well as on my mother's passengers.

"What did this?" I asked grimly.

"A fire whip," she replied. "It's an elven spell."

"Will it scar?"

"It is intended to."

I ground my teeth. *I will kill him. If it's the last thing I do.*

"It must be painful," I said, straining to keep the anger from my voice.

"More so now," she admitted, "in the calm and quiet."

"What about Ulf?" I asked, my anger finding a new object. "What did *he* say about this?"

She raised her gown, pushing her hands back through the sleeves before she turned. "It was not his business to say anything."

I stared at her in disbelief. "He knew of it, and he let it happen? I thought he was your bodyguard."

"He serves my father," she said. "As you know."

"Has he not been your friend?" I argued. "Has he not been your *lover*?"

Instead of reacting to my fit of temper, she replied simply, "That changes nothing."

My blood boiled. *I'll kill him too.*

"By god, it *ought* to."

She raised an eyebrow, and she straightened her shoulders. "If it had, perhaps I would have married *him* against my father's wishes."

I sighed out my anger and offered her a wry smile. She smiled too, and I moved closer and wrapped my arms around her. "Forgive me, *acushla*. It's not you I'm angry with."

"I know."

"Men are fools, though I will claim the dubious honor of being a lesser one than your bodyguard. Would you really have married him?"

She frowned. "It was never a possibility. Neither of us would have crossed my father. If we had, he would have hunted us down."

Her hand came up and she began to trace my bottom lip with her thumb. A firebolt shot from the point of contact right through my core, and the front of my trousers went taut. The last time she'd touched me like this, we were driven by circumstances to seal our marriage vows. There was nothing compelling us now.

"I had always expected to make a political marriage," she said, her attention still focused on my lips.

"And so you have." As her fingers continued their gentle exploration, I dropped a hand to her buttocks, avoiding the injured flesh directly above, and pulled her against me. The breath hissed between her teeth. "How does it feel to be married to the enemy?"

Her lips curved impishly. "I thought that you would be unbearably ugly."

I laughed. "Are you implying that I'm not?"

She narrowed her eyes, considering. "I expected you to look more like Doro."

I lifted my eyebrows. "Is *he* unbearably ugly, then?" I'd have guessed most lasses would consider Doro to be the very picture of genteel masculine beauty. But my new wife was no lass.

"No," she admitted. "He is softer in form and feature than the men I know, yet he emanates power, and in the beginning I found his ambition compelling. When he told me I was to be his queen, the idea did not repulse me."

"*Not repulsive*," I replied. "High praise, indeed. And what about me?"

Her fingers moved to the buttons of my shirt. "I was not at all repulsed by you. It was very inconvenient."

I grinned, tightening my grip on her backside as her fingers proceeded down my chest. "I found you inconveniently *not repulsive* as well."

She gave a short nod. "You expected me to be an ogre."

"Aye, it's true."

"It was not difficult to exceed your expectations."

When she had unfastened all the buttons she could reach, I pulled her sleeves down off her shoulders, baring her breasts.

"Perhaps not," I agreed, cupping one breast, rubbing its bright nub with my thumb. "But when it comes to women, I know what I like. I leaned close to her, raising a hand to rub the other nipple. I could feel the quick rhythm of her breath as she pressed into my hands.

I whispered in her ear, "Spirit. Courage. Fire."

"Fire?" she murmured, hands coming to my arms as she leaned further into me.

I slid one hand into the front of her dress, over her strong belly muscles and into the soft, dark curls between her legs. I pressed a finger into the hot wetness awaiting me. "Fire," I repeated, and she moaned.

"Now that I have met one of your lovers," I said, my fingers stroking around her opening, "I find that I am curious as well as brutishly jealous. Tell me about him?"

She drew back to look at me, a puzzled smile on her face. "What do you want to know?"

I cupped her with my hand, inserting a finger, and she shuddered, muscles clenching around me. "How did it happen?"

She rocked into my palm, making soft sounds in her throat. Her hands came to my hips, and my finger slipped out of her as she pulled my hardened cock against her belly.

"We had been hunting in the highlands," she said breathlessly. "It was winter and there had been no game for days, but then we took three rabbits. We were so hungry we roasted and ate them all, and drank a good deal of *landi* besides."

"I don't know what *landi* is," I said with an appreciative chortle, "but I think I can guess."

I stepped back far enough to unfasten my trousers and lower her gown. Moving close again, I wrapped my hands underneath her buttocks. "Will this hurt you?"

Her hand came to my cheek. "Let's find out."

I lifted her gently, and I slowly lowered her onto my cock. She did cry out—though not in pain—and folded her legs around me. I closed my eyes, half-drunk myself on the sensation of being inside her.

"Where was I?" she said in a voice low and heavy with arousal. "*Landi.*"

She braced a hand on each of my shoulders, rocking her hips against me. "Ulf was telling bawdy stories and I was laughing," she continued, "though I only understood about half of them."

Her dark wings stroked the air around us. I dug my fingers into her buttocks, moving her back and forth over my cock, a low moan rumbling out of me.

"Once, when he peeped through a window—most Icelanders have no idea how often we watch them—he saw a dairy maid and a shepherd. When he told me what they were doing, I started asking questions. Finally I asked him to *show* me."

"You did no such thing," I choked out, thrusting hard inside her.

She leaned close to my ear and whispered, "I did."

I groaned and carried her to the bed, easing her off my cock. She lay down on her stomach, spread her legs and her wings, and looked over her shoulder at me—the challenge in her gaze was almost enough to end me. Bending over her, I pressed my palm between her legs, rubbing and kneading as she raised her backside against me.

"What did he do then?" I demanded.

She laughed at me. "He just stared with his mouth hanging open, like you are. I started unlacing my shirt. I took it off and sat there half naked in the firelight, watching him try to devour me with his eyes. Then I reached up and began touching my breasts."

"You're killing me, wife," I growled as I lowered my hips and entered her.

She gasped and pushed her hips back, shifting her knees underneath her while she braced herself with her arms. Then she began battering my belly with her backside, wringing her pleasure from me. Finally she pressed hard against me and froze. I could feel the spasms of the muscles inside her as the waves of sensation took her.

I watched her body slacken and listened to her breath. When the tension in her muscles had wound down, I bent close to her ear and asked, "What happened next?"

She drew her hips forward until I slipped out of her, cock throbbing desperately.

She rose to her knees, and she turned and unbuttoned my shirt the rest of the way. She pushed her hands inside the edges of my shirt and ran them down my chest and stomach. And then she took me between her cool hands.

The breath hissed between my teeth—her stroking fingers both soothed and stoked.

Watching me closely, she squeezed my cock and said, "He came around the fire to stand in front of me, and he opened the front of his trousers."

I let out a whimper. A *whimper*! If she'd had Doro's knife, she could have carved out my heart and I wouldn't have cared.

"He showed me how hard he was, and then I did this."

She bent over me and very slowly, very deliberately licked the bead of moisture from the tip of my cock. I cried out from the delicious shock of it.

Her tongue snaked over me and I took her head between my hands. The silky wet heat of her caress was *almost* too much. I knew I would end quickly, like a beast in the field, if I watched her face while she licked me.

When at last her mouth closed over me, I could no longer resist. At that same moment, she lifted her eyes to meet mine, and she drew back until just the tip remained in her mouth. A wave of dizziness washed over me as she swept her tongue once around it, and then she slowly glided forward until I felt myself molding into the curve of her throat.

"For the love of—"

Her lips moved back and forth over my length until I thought I would explode. My fingers dug into her plaits, and I held my breath. I could no longer stop myself from moving, but I tried to keep my thrusts as gentle as possible so as not to choke her. God—I had never felt *anything* like the tight, wet heat of her.

"Koli," I croaked, "I'm going to—"

She took hold of my hips, preventing me from drawing out, and she glided down my shaft until I was sure I felt her lips on my belly.

Stars exploded behind my eyelids and I let go.

KOLI

There was magic in that salty warm fluid, or so the ancients believed. My ancestress Gunnhild had bound men to her—warlords, necromancers, would-be kings. It was said that by her magic she lived to be one hundred and twelve, and even as a white-haired matron, men worshiped her as a goddess. Her bed was never empty unless she chose it. And when she needed men to raise a sword in her name, she was never left wanting.

I was no sorceress, but the way my husband was looking at me made me feel just as powerful.

"God in heaven, wife," he croaked. I lay on the bed on my stomach, and he stretched beside me, one heavy, hot hand resting on my backside. "Have I survived that, or is this the afterlife?"

I reached out and touched his chin, feeling the dark stubble under my fingertips. Reassuring myself that he was real.

"Did you ever think about this before we married?" I asked him.

A smile spread over his face. "I might have once or twice. Did you?"

"I might have," I said, returning his smile, "once or twice."

He chuckled softly, and his eyes closed. A moment later I could tell by his breathing he was asleep. I scooted closer and he lifted his arm, draping it over my folded wings.

When I woke, the chamber was brighter—light streamed in through the windows in the stern. Finvara was awake already and watching me. He reached out and pushed a strand of hair out of my eyes.

"It's hard not to think about how all of this could have been avoided had I not been such a headstrong ass," he said.

I considered this a moment, my mind waking slowly. I recalled how it had stung me that he had refused to honor Queen Isolde and my father's arrangement, and how I had vowed to make him pay for it.

"We can't know that it could have been avoided," I said. "My father was never interested in a lasting peace. Nor was I."

His answering grin was full of mischief. "You've no idea how charming I can be."

I gave a little snort. "I think I have an idea."

He laughed and rolled onto his side, fingers trailing down my arm.

"Do they bother you?" I asked him. "My wings."

His face softened as he studied them, eyes flowing from my shoulders down to my legs, and I found myself holding my breath.

"It's like they were there all along," he said, "and I just never noticed them. They suit you. And they're erotic as hell." His face lit up, eyes moving back to mine. "Can you fly?"

I laughed at the sudden boyish intensity. "I can, but it's exhausting."

He scooted closer to me and bent to touch his lips to mine.

TEAR YOURSELF FROM YOUR MARRIAGE BED, ELF MAID. DUBLIN CASTLE IS IN VIEW.

RECKONING

FINVARA

Like Knock Ma, Dublin castle was much changed. The basic structure was the same—a marriage of buildings constructed at different points in history, in different architectural styles. There were surviving medieval structures, including the defensive tower and great hall, a chapel built early in the nineteenth century, as well as living quarters and state apartments constructed in the eighteenth century. The Irish capital was a city of two names, with many citizens referring to it as Baile Atha Cliath. The name Dublin—more commonly used by city dwellers, officials, and foreigners—originated in the time of Viking settlement. It meant "dark pool," which referred to a peaty tidal pool at the confluence of the Liffey and Poddle rivers, and had the advantage of being much easier to say.

The Poddle river had been diverted under the city and no dark pool had been present in my lifetime—and yet there it was,

next to the castle where there'd once been a park. At its center was
a perfectly round island, over which was anchored a gas balloon,
brightly decorated in purple and gold. The cityscape surrounding
the castle had been invaded by forest, with trees sprouting right
out of cobbled alleys and tiled roofs.

"Where should we disembark?" asked Koli.

"There," I said, pointing to the medieval tower.

"Will they view us as invaders?" She peered over the rail at the
ship's gun ports. The cannons were tucked out of sight.

"Aye, probably so. We'll cause a stir anywhere we disembark.
And if we set down outside the city we'll lose time."

I unbuttoned and removed my shirt and began waving it
slowly overhead.

Corvus's sails had lowered, and we cruised along slowly under
power of the steam propeller.

Already guards clustered on top of the tower, shouting and
pointing. They had likely never seen a vessel quite like this
one, but at some point it was going to occur to one of them
that firing a hole through our balloon might very well bring us
down.

"Can I cast a fire-disabling spell without snuffing our burner?"
I asked Koli.

She closed her eyes and gripped the rail, and I realized my
question had forced her to communicate with the goddess. After
a moment she said, "She doesn't know."

"*Bollocks.*" Cupping my hands in front of my mouth, I yelled.
"Stand down! I'm Duncan O'Malley, the queen's cousin!"

There were indeed rifles aimed at us, and I repeated myself
until a few of the guards seemed to hear me, huddling to discuss
what I'd told them.

"King Finvara?" a voice called suddenly, and I noticed a young
gentleman standing against the battlements.

I craned my neck and narrowed my gaze. "Is that Mr. Yeats?"

He gave a short bow. "At your service, Your Majesty. I hardly recognized you."

Will Yeats had traveled with my father's ancestress Grace O'Malley in the Gap—where she'd been condemned to a kind of purgatory for misdeeds associated with *true* piracy—and he had been present for the Battle of Ben Bulben. If I recalled rightly, he was some kind of scribe—a soft-spoken and thoroughly odd young man who seemed to view the world through the wrong end of a telescope.

"Yeats," I replied, "could you explain to these jackeens that I'm the Queen's cousin, and make them understand that it would inconvenience us greatly were they to blow a hole through our balloon?"

"Certainly, sire," replied the young man.

He joined the circle of anxious guards, and I listened to the murmurs of their voices while *Corvus* moved into position over the tower. After a moment Mr. Yeats called up, "How many are your crew, Your Majesty?"

"Just the two of us," I replied. "Myself and my queen, *Koli Alfdóttir*."

The young man's eyebrows lifted, and then his gaze shifted to my bride. "Extraordinary."

"May we drop a ladder, Mr. Yeats?" I asked.

"Yes, of course, sire," he replied.

We found another ladder and tossed it over. Then we joined the others below. Once the introductions had been made, Yeats said, "Her Majesty was out early in the *Sea Aster* and had planned to rest until time for luncheon. Perhaps you and your queen would like to refresh yourselves and join us?"

Had *Sea Aster* referred to the garish balloon we'd seen on our approach?

"Aye, we would," I said. "We've come in a rush on urgent business, but we are sorely in need of a hot meal."

"Very good, Your Majesty," replied Yeats. "Follow me."

KOLI

At the base of the tower stairs, Mr. Yeats handed us over to a servant and went to inform the queen of our arrival. We were given a chamber in the living quarters and brought hot water. While Finvara washed, I considered the state of my hair. I could leave the plaits—along with the cloud of freed strands that had formed over the course of the last day, and somewhat resembled a swarm of midges—or I could remove them and risk a wavy and wild curtain. In the end, I opted for the latter.

"What is the queen like?" I asked him, lifting a brush from the vanity.

Finvara paused while drying his face, considering. He shook his head. "Izzy is better experienced than described. I'd like to say she is harmless, but that's not always the case. She and I have usually been on good terms, though."

This was not exactly reassuring. It had been less than two days since I'd considered myself the Irish queen's sworn enemy, and I had helped to spoil the peace she had so painstakingly created. My part in that could hardly be kept a secret. Isolde had a reputation in Iceland—headstrong and unpredictable.

"The two of you are close?" I asked.

He tossed aside the towel and began rolling down his sleeves. "We were for a time. I was a beast to her when we were younger. My brothers and I were great bullies." Frowning, he put on a waistcoat he'd found in the wardrobe. "We'd dare her to do things that might have killed her, but to her it was all a game. She always came back for more."

My anxiety must have shown—Finvara came over and took

the brush from my hands. He pressed me into a chair and began pulling it through my hair. I closed my eyes, wondering how it was possible the sensation could be so very different just because someone else wielded the brush. I felt myself begin to settle.

"All will be well," he assured me.

I glanced up at him. "I plotted to *kill* you."

He set the brush down and raised me from the chair, grinning. "*That* may very well go in your favor."

Sighing, I gave up trying to understand, and together we left the chamber. Most of the castle was of newer construction than Knock Ma, though the living quarters appeared very old, the bricks roughly hewn and laid in untidy rows. Still, the wall torches had been replaced by gas lamps, and thick carpets covered the floors of the corridors, muffling our footsteps.

Guards were stationed outside the hall, and as we approached the great doors, Finvara glanced at me and raised his eyebrows.

"Let's get on with it," I said.

The guards anticipated us and dragged open the doors. The hall was long and cavernous, its high ceiling vaulted and supported by wooden beams. A banquet table ran its length, and light was provided by great iron chandeliers whose candle brackets were fitted with tapered gas bulbs. The furnishings were an odd merging of modern and antique elements, though I would not have called the effect unappealing. The stark lines of the room had been softened by wall hangings in muted hues of blue and pink, and enormous vases of flowers. On the wall at the opposite end of the hall, behind a raised throne area, hung many stuffed heads of antlered beasts, including reindeer. An assortment of antique weaponry also hung there—swords, bows, spears, and shields—some of them clearly Viking-made.

"So it *is* you, Duncan," called the queen down the length of the table as we approached.

Despite the size of the hall, there were only a few persons assembled for the meal—the queen, Mr. Yeats, and a woman wearing a wine-colored military jacket with gleaming brass buttons. As we drew closer, the woman and Mr. Yeats rose to their feet.

The queen's smile was wry, her gaze sharply appraising. She too wore a fitted military jacket, though hers was of a more fanciful design—gold and green brocade, with a V-shaped opening that revealed the top of her corset. Atop an arrangement of dark plaits rested a matching officer's hat trimmed with feathers. Her skin was the palest I had ever seen, though she looked the opposite of unhealthy. Her eyes were bright and her posture stately. Despite the fact she'd remained seated, as was fit for her rank, I could see that she was tall.

"Your Majesty," said Finvara, bowing, "may I introduce you to my queen, Koli Alfdóttir of Iceland."

The queen's eyebrow lifted to a seemingly impossible height as she looked at me, and I curtseyed. "Your Majesty." Her gaze traveled slowly over me, and nervousness made my wings fidget—which caused the queen to give a quiet gasp.

"Good heavens, Duncan," she said. *Very encouraging.*

Nodding to her companions, the queen continued, "This is General Varma. Mr. Yeats, you already know. Sit down, all of you. Whatever it is you've come about will have to wait. I was roused at an uncivilized hour and am now famished."

I looked at Finvara, and he nodded. We took seats on a bench opposite Mr. Yeats and General Varma. The latter had glossy, dark hair that was streaked with white and pulled back in a severe bun. Both her skin and her eyes were brown, and her expression was cool.

The queen lifted a teacup to her lips, and at that moment servants walked through doors on opposite ends of the dais, each of them bearing a tray or covered dish. I could smell roasted meat and my stomach growled. I had not eaten since before my exhausting first flight, and I knew it had been even longer for Finvara.

As ordered, we held our silence as the luncheon was served— roasted fowl and venison, steaming bowls of vegetables, fresh spring greens, and fine, crusty bread, followed by a tray of pretty little tarts and bowls of cream. Aside from the tarts, it was all hearty fare like I was used to, and I ate everything placed before me, even accepting a glass of port from one of the footmen. Finvara also ate with relish, but refused the port in favor of a glass of whiskey.

The queen sipped her port and turned her gaze on Finvara.

"I must say, cousin," she began in a light and easy tone that sent a shiver down my spine, "my heart is aflutter in anticipation of this love story. I am on *literal* pins and needles as I wait to hear how you ended up blissfully wedded to the elf maid I so generously offered, and you so unceremoniously refused."

Without waiting for him to answer, she turned to General Varma. "You see, Bess, I said to Duncan that I thought it would serve all our interests to align ourselves with our near neighbors, who were once the allies of our greatest foes."

"A reasonable-sounding proposal, mum," replied the general, her expression neutral. She raised her glass. "One with many instances of historical precedent."

The queen shook her head, lifting her eyebrows in mock bewilderment. "Indeed, I did think so."

"His Majesty found fault with the plan?" Varma asked, as if we were discussing the weather. "Perhaps it seemed overly pragmatic?"

"So he did," Isolde replied, primly sipping her port. "Placed the whole armistice in jeopardy. But I have ever been fond of my cousin, so much so that I elevated him to an office beyond any he might otherwise have expected, having heretofore specialized in the arts of smuggling and roguery, so I—"

"Now just one minute, Izzy," interrupted Finvara, exasperated.

"I'll allow that you have reason to crow, and that I may in fact have behaved ungratefully, yet you go too far. I never sought the advancement you bestowed, and in fact encouraged you to look elsewhere for someone better suited. You *know* that I did."

The queen frowned—a far milder reaction to this fit of temper than I would have expected. "Perhaps you did," she replied crisply. "Would you care to explain to me what has caused the reversal of your attitude toward this woman that I believe you once referred to as a gob—"

"For heaven's sake," snapped Finvara, "punish *me* if you must. Leave my wife out of it. She has suffered enough for my mistakes."

This was more than generous, and I felt it keenly. But even having just met the queen, I could see that she was vexed with *him* and had not intended to insult me.

"That I do not doubt," replied the queen, sighing. "Very well, Duncan, I lower my rapier. Though I must say, I hope you thought more kindly of me when you discovered that I had not, in fact, expected you to marry either a hag or an ogre."

"I'm afraid my lack of faith in your discretion is the least of the errors I will have to confess today."

The queen set down her empty glass and folded her arms on the table. In a gentled tone she said, "I am very glad to see you, though not inviting me to your wedding was a cruel stroke. Tell me all that has happened."

FINVARA

We did indeed tell the queen everything, from Koli's first arrival at Knock Ma to the previous evening's escape. When I had explained about the Morrigan, Isolde's eyes widened and she glanced between us. Mr. Yeats, who had up to this point done nothing but scribble in his notebook, gasped and sat up.

"You're certain about this?" the queen asked my bride.

"I've never questioned it, Your Majesty," replied Koli. "Her presence is very . . ." Koli closed her eyes, and her brow furrowed. Her hands curled into fists on the tabletop, and I covered one of them with my hand.

"Is she speaking to you now?" asked the queen.

"She is," Koli replied faintly.

"What is she saying?"

Koli opened her eyes. "I'm afraid it isn't very complimentary, Your Majesty."

The queen pressed her fingers to her temples, muttering, "*Blast.*"

"So you see, I am outmatched," I said. "We thought it best to come to you, as more than Knock Ma is at stake."

Izzy laid her hands on the table, seeming to stare at the empty space between them. After a few moments, she looked at me. "I knew it was only a matter of time before Ireland's foes threatened again, though certainly I did not expect it to be so soon. But neither you nor any of us could have known the next threat would have come from within. Even our erudite Lady Meath did not see this coming."

"The threat has not come wholly from within, Your Majesty," Koli said. There was no need for her to remind the queen of this, though I knew her well enough to understand that she was not about to cower under the protective wing of her husband.

"Perhaps," agreed the queen, "yet your father's trap would not have been sprung so quickly without Doro's help." Her gaze came back to me. "You have been more vigilant than you realize, and you have come to me in time, or so I hope."

I had known Izzy for most of her life, and she did not inspire awe in me as she did in her subjects. Many believed she was at least half mad, yet which of us who had been touched by Faery did *not* seem so? There had long been true kinship and affection between us, which made me even less comfortable with the fact that I had failed her. Now she was absolving me, and it eased the weight in my chest.

"Bess?" She turned to her general. "The fleet is already in the Atlantic, is it not?"

Varma nodded. "It is, Your Majesty."

"We shall send you west as well, to reinforce our outposts and watch for Fomorian invaders."

At last something disturbed her general's composure—a flicker of interest. A sentiment I well understood. The queen was giving her a reprieve from court obligations and sending her into the field. Varma sat up straighter. "Aye, mum."

"As for you, cousin," continued Izzy, "you are to be commended for your quick action, as well as your bride's. Were Doro at large, things would be far worse. You are also to be commended for being your charming and chivalrous self, which is what has enabled you, no doubt, to win over such a competent ally. Your instincts are sound, and your presence has been sorely missed."

She frowned before continuing, and I braced myself.

"I do, however, expect you to tidy up your own mess." She leaned on her folded arms, eyeing me intently. "You have a ship to captain, a strong and resourceful partner, and an excellent opportunity to prove yourself."

Eyeing her dubiously, I replied, "My queen and I alone are to take on the Elf King?"

"It seems you have the assistance of the goddess of war, which would render my own involvement redundant—a state of affairs I could never endure. I will give you men, of course. And I do have something else which might prove useful. Consider it a wedding gift." She turned to the young scribe. "Fetch the device for me, will you, Mr. Yeats?"

Yeats jumped up and walked to the dais. Beside the throne

was a table that held a large vase of flowers, and next to it an item I had not noticed before but immediately recognized now. Yeats carried it back to the table, placing it before me.

It was the globe-shaped device that Grace O'Malley had used to navigate between Ireland and the Gap.

"Your bride mentioned that all Gap gates except Doro's first one have collapsed," said Izzy. "But you may be able to use the device to enter the Gap and—"

"Take them by surprise!" I finished. It was a worthy strategy. A ship with a navigator device had no need for Gap gates; it could nose into and out of the Gap at will. "Where did you get it?"

"Auntie left it behind, along with Mr. Yeats, when she crossed over, did she not, Mr. Yeats?"

The young man nodded, a wistful look in his eyes. "Auntie," who was in fact a much more distant relation than that, was not what I'd have called endearing, and she had heaped plenty of abuse on her young scribe. Yet he had seemed genuinely fond of her. Her assistance in the Battle of Ben Bulben had freed her to cross over to the Land of Promise, the afterworld of the ancients, which was open to her as a descendant of the first King Finvara.

"You know how it works, then?" I asked Izzy.

"I haven't the foggiest idea," she replied. "You're a captain. I am sure you will figure it out."

I stared at her. "Of a *regular* ship, Izzy. There is no device even remotely similar on the *Aesop*."

She frowned. "Well that *is* inconvenient."

Mr. Yeats cleared his throat, and all of us turned to look at him. "I believe that I may be of some assistance."

MANEUVER

KOLI

We agreed that Mr. Yeats would join us on our return to Knock Ma so that he might show us how to operate the navigator. It was a strange device—a glass globe filled with a kind of red vapor, and a miniature model of a ship inside. There were levers and gears for moving the ship. Mr. Yeats said that the device was more than mechanical—that there was some magic at work. It could be used to fold distances while inside the Gap, so our return trip to Knock Ma would be much shorter. It made me think of Doro—then I realized it could be his invention.

Mr. Yeats himself was a puzzle. He was quiet and polite, and just barely out of his boyhood. Yet from what Finvara had told me about him, he was more hearty than he appeared. He seemed to be always scribbling, although why or what about I could not say. I had never spent any more time at writing than my tutors had required.

The queen and Finvara agreed that two hundred soldiers would be sent aboard *Corvus*. He believed that no more could safely travel in a vessel of her size, especially since we would be cruising into battle. As I listened to them discussing plans for the siege, I began to worry.

My father had brought half his warriors—five hundred strong. I had left Treig behind at Knock Ma after she assured me she would be able to avoid the elves by moving in and out of Faery—while Doro had ordered the fairies to disperse from the castle at the king's request, it had not suited his purposes to cast the shielding spell that he had promised. That gave us hope that Treig would be able to speak to her people and unravel their alliance with Doro—and that the rest of the fairies would follow. But she'd had very little time.

The elves were fierce fighters—well-seasoned in hand-to-hand combat. We anticipated the Morrigan would be able to shield her Irish crew from spells, but once they disembarked, their rifles could be easily disabled. Finvara's fighting force would have only two advantages: the element of surprise—though even that was reduced by the fact my father would be expecting us at some point—and the Morrigan's cannons.

It would not be enough. Had the Morrigan's powers not been reduced by her transmutation, she would certainly have been a match for Alfakonung. As it was, I feared we would be charging to our deaths.

KNOCK MA HAS OTHER DEFENSES.

The voice exploded in my skull, shattering my thoughts and sending spasms down my body.

What other defenses?

THE TREES.

I felt a tear squeeze from the corner of my eye. The others were deep in their strategy discussions and hadn't yet noticed my distress. I wasn't sure how long I could endure the goddess's attention, but before anyone interfered, I needed to understand. What had she meant by "the trees"?

THEY ARE PROTECTORS OF THE HOUSE OF FINVARA.

But how?

ASK OISIN TO SPEAK TO THEM.

Odin's eye, if she would only speak plainly. *Who is Oisin!*

THE POET!

All of it was nonsensical, or so it seemed, and I knew that outwardly as well as inwardly I was beginning to fall apart.

Yet from the beginning I had been uneasy about the forest around Knock Ma.

The face of Mr. Yeats then rose in my mind unbidden.

OISIN, repeated the Morrigan.

The *poet*. It would explain the scribbling. But why was she calling him "Oisin"? And why did she think he could talk to the trees?

THE DRUID'S GAP GATE. IT LEADS TO THE FOREST.

It did! And the Morrigan—*Corvus*—using the navigator device, could take us to Doro's gate. But what would passing through it again do to me? And how could I lead another through it? Mr. Yeats was a red-blooded creature, so the experiments thus far suggested he would survive it. What would be the cost?

ASK HIM, insisted the Morrigan.

"Koli, what ails you?"

Finvara's voice came to me from a thousand miles away. I felt his hand on my cheek but my eyes would not focus on his face.

What the Morrigan was proposing—it would allow us to flank my father's army. If she was right about the trees, they could attack from the west while the elves were occupied with *Corvus* and the queen's army to the east.

The queen had told Finvara to tidy up his mess. These words might have just as fairly been spoken to *me*.

As my husband's face came into focus and I saw the worry plainly written there, I wondered how I was going to get him to agree to this plan—especially when it had been proposed by the

Morrigan. He didn't trust her. There was uncertainty. There was risk. I might be "comfortable with chaos," but could he be?

The affection and concern in his eyes—it was a warming balm. I had not felt this mortal, this *human*, in decades. Yet I had married him out of a desire to protect him, not so that he would protect *me*. And I had not made the dangerous decision to betray Doro and my father only to set up another man as my lord and master—however the intensity of his gaze might stir my blood.

Another tear slipped down my cheek. I could still feel the pulses moving through my body, though the pain was starting to fade.

"Is it her?" he asked, his thumb stopping the tear in its path. "What is she saying to you?"

Making a decision, I forced a smile. "I have gotten an earful about how she would make my father and Doro pay, were she her old self."

Thunderclouds gathered on my husband's brow, and I continued, "I think she will give me some peace now, but I would like to rest."

My request to retire ended the luncheon, and after I'd convinced Finvara that rest was all I needed, he asked to accompany General Varma so he might speak to the men who would return to Knock Ma with us. He left the navigator device in the care of Mr. Yeats.

Claiming to have forgotten the way back to our chamber, I asked Mr. Yeats if he would take me. The young man was happy to help, and as I took his arm, I noticed he was made of stronger stuff than his outward appearance suggested. Though he was not as tall as Finvara, his bespectacled brown eyes were on a level with mine. There was an awkwardness—an uncertainty—to his bearing that was not surprising in one so young.

"Mr. Yeats," I began, "may I ask what you are always writing?"

"Of course, Your Majesty," he answered brightly. "But please call me Will."

"And you should call me Koli. There are too many Your Majesties under this roof."

"You've a point," he said with an easy laugh. "Still, I'm only a Sligo lad, the son of a painter, and I would not choose to insult either you or your husband. May we compromise at 'my lady'?"

I nodded my assent. "Do you care to tell me about your writing?"

"Certainly, if it interests you. I write poems, and I collect stories about Ireland's ancient peoples."

"Were you writing a poem today?"

"Today I was simply making notes." He steered me down an adjoining corridor. "Someday I intend to return to my grandparents' cottage near Ben Bulben and write a memoir about the things I have experienced in the company of a number of Ireland's important personages. I hope you won't mind—there are quite a few passages devoted to Your Ladyship. I have always been curious about your people, and I am fascinated by the recent alteration to your physique. Perhaps on the return trip to Knock Ma I might ask a few questions?"

We halted at the door to my chamber, and I turned to him. "As many as you like." I wondered that he didn't seem to be anxious about the upcoming battle. "I have another one for *you*—have you heard of someone called Oisin?"

"Indeed! Oisin was a warrior of the Tuatha De Danaan, as well as a poet and historian. He wrote much about the people of Faery, and you can read it in the library at Trinity College. I had begun to write a poem about him before I joined Grace O'Malley's crew. Though so much has happened since then, I wonder whether I shall ever finish it."

"Oisin sounds much like yourself," I said, better understanding why the Morrigan might have referred to him this way.

A glimmer of mirth lit his large brown eyes. "I am no warrior, lady."

"Would you like to be?"

His brow furrowed. "I don't know that I am cut out to be one. I'm quite studious by nature. Why do you ask?"

Should I confide in him? What if he went to Finvara? But the Morrigan had directed me to ask, and without him my scheme had no hope of succeeding.

"I will be honest with you," I said. "I have a dangerous business to undertake. A business my husband knows nothing about, and which he would likely forbid me to pursue. Yet it is necessary, and I cannot do it without your help. The Morrigan has suggested you might be willing."

The poor boy's expression was utter shock. "*My* help? Are you sure you didn't misunderstand her?"

"Quite sure."

I explained to him what the Morrigan had proposed while he continued to watch me with wide eyes. Gradually other emotions took over the shock in his countenance. A spark of curiosity. A glint of excitement. And pride, unmistakably. After all, not everyone was recommended for a job by the goddess of war.

"I'm afraid you will have no time to consider it," I said. "We would have to leave immediately, pass through the Gap gate, and send *Corvus* back to Dublin so that the king may—"

"I will do it."

I studied him. He appeared in earnest, and quite determined.

"I can't imagine why she believes I can talk to trees," he continued, "but I am willing to try."

I laid my hand on his arm. "Listen to me, Will. Before you agree, it is very important that you understand—I cannot say what will happen to you when you pass through Doro's Gap gate. You are likely to be altered in some way, as I was. Some of the creatures that passed through the gate are no longer living, though there is reason to believe you will at least survive. I cannot even be sure what will happen to *me*. I am willing to undertake the risk to help my husband. You . . . you have no one to protect."

"Respectfully, my lady," he replied, straightening, "I disagree."

His thick, brown hair fell over his eyes and he swept it out of the way. "I have family in the west of Ireland. My home is there. I cannot but think that they will suffer, and so too all of Ireland, if you and your husband do not prevail. Besides, I like to think that I am loyal to both queen and country."

Relief washed over me. I squeezed his arm. "I thank you. I will do all I can to ensure your safe return. You have my word."

FINVARA

I had meant to check on my bride after leaving the soldier barracks, but General Varma suggested I accompany her to the armory. All the soldiers would need to be equipped with both modern and traditional weaponry—plus round shot for *Corvus*'s cannons—and Varma told me they had been struggling to replenish the queen's stores since the Battle of Ben Bulben. We sat down with the armory chief to hammer out requisitions for my men as well as hers.

Though there were many such details to attend to before our departure, which had been set for the following afternoon, I was increasingly uneasy about having left Koli alone. The castle was safe enough; it was the voices in her head that worried me. The more I thought over our last exchange, the more I suspected she was holding something back. What might the goddess have told her that she would feel she needed to keep from me?

By the time I had concluded my business with Varma, the sun had gone down and it was time to dress for dinner with the queen.

I stole into our bedchamber quietly in case Koli was sleeping. The lamps had been lit, so I called to her softly.

The chamber was empty. She had likely gotten tired of waiting and gone off to amuse herself until dinner. And yet my heart tapped out an anxious rhythm.

The queen had promised to send a servant with more clothing, and indeed the wardrobe stood open and stuffed to capacity. I selected a few items that looked like they would fit and carried them to the bed.

As I unbuttoned my shirt, I noticed that none of the bed clothes had been disturbed, nor was there an imprint of a head on any of the pillows.

Heart pounding, I grew impatient and ripped open my shirt the rest of the way, tossing it to the floor. I grabbed the fresh one and put it on, along with fresh trousers. I had just slipped on a jacket when I heard footsteps in the corridor, accompanied by a rising murmur of anxious voices.

My jaw clenched as someone rapped on the door.

"What is it?" I called, shoving my foot into a boot.

Rather than answering, the visitor pushed open the door—General Varma. "Forgive the intrusion, Your Majesty," she said urgently, "but I have it from my men that your queen and Mr. Yeats have absconded with *Corvus*."

For a moment I could do nothing but stare at her.

"A note was given to a servant," she continued. "I have opened it—I'm sure you understand."

I reached for the note and carried it to a lamp table.

Corvus will return for you and your men. We will see you again at Knock Ma. I have not betrayed you.

Koli

I wanted to trust her. With all my heart I wanted to trust her. How could I, when she so obviously didn't trust *me*? This message offered not even a hint of what she was planning.

And she had no real understanding of what the Morrigan was capable of.

MIND THE GAP

KOLI

So anxious had I been about my discussion with Will, I had given no thought to the difficulty of the task ahead. Stealing the ship had been easy enough. There were guards in the tower, but I had *arrived* in the ship and Yeats was trusted, so when we told them we were going aboard to make preparations for King Finvara's departure, no eyebrow was raised. We simply pulled up the ladder and left the rest to the Morrigan. We knew no one would dare fire on us without orders to do so. Most of the guards stood shouting after us, while others ran to sound the alarm.

Leaving Finvara without an explanation or even a proper good-bye . . . deceiving him again, after what we'd already been through? That had been much harder. There'd been no time to explain myself properly in the note I'd left him—putting it all down in Elvish would have been challenging enough, but English or Irish? A more thorough explanation would not likely have reassured him anyway.

Would he accept what I'd written in the note? In my heart, I believed that he would want to trust me. But had I been in his position, I wasn't sure that I could have. I had been his wife for a couple of days. I had been my father's daughter for nearly a century. Reflecting now on how much my life had changed in the time I had been at Knock Ma with Finvara made me wonder if risking the loss of that was worth it.

It was a fool's speculation. I could lose him forever with or without the risk. And his life was more important to me than his approval.

"Are you ready, my lady?"

I glanced at Will, and he raised the navigator device.

I nodded and followed him across the deck and up the stairs to the helm.

Will took a cord from his pocket and, setting the device on the rail that crossed in front of the wheel, he ran the cord through metal rings at the base of the device and tied it down.

"It's inelegant," he said, "but it will have to do. Now, to use the device to fold the distance between two geographical points, you need to know the coordinates of both points. Errors in configuring the device can result in missing your destination and even losing time."

I frowned. "Losing time?"

"Arriving a day later than you intended, for example. Or a week."

From his expression, I got the sense that he spoke from experience, and I offered a silent prayer to Freyja that he knew what he was doing.

He reached into the breast pocket of his jacket and pulled out a map. "So the first thing we—"

The navigation device suddenly issued a series of clicks, and its gears and levers began moving of their own accord.

STAND CLEAR.

"I'm not sure what's happening," said Will, sounding more curious than alarmed.

"It's the Morrigan," I said through clenched teeth.

"Oh!" replied Will, continuing to stare at the busy thing.

The vapor in the globe lost its color and began to look like normal fog. Glancing at the bow, I noticed a vertical line had appeared directly in the path of the ship. As we approached, the line widened to a slit, and finally to an oval shape—a dark opening filled with stars.

Will looked at me. "Mind the Gap, my lady."

He curled an arm around the rail, grabbing his fist to lock his hold. The boards beneath my feet began to creak and pop, and I followed his example. As we nosed into the opening, the bow of the ship lifted enough that I would have stumbled had Will not warned me. The tilt increased, and we soon found ourselves hanging from the rail.

"Is this expected?" I asked breathlessly.

"Aye," he replied. "I envy you your wings, lady."

I tightened my grip as the rail dug painfully into my elbow joint. The ship was now halfway through the Gap opening and halfway still floating in the sky above Dublin. Wings or no wings, the idea of a fall from this height was enough to turn my stomach. I was amazed by the lack of disquiet on my traveling companion's face. I was about to ask him how long we might expect to hold this position when the bow began to dip. By the time the stern passed into the Gap, the ship was again cruising levelly.

Glancing back, I watched the window of blue sky closing behind us. Then the balloon burner suddenly cut out.

Will released the rail and stood, tugging his waistcoat back in place. "Captain O'Malley herself could do no better," he said cheerfully.

The reference to Finvara's ancestress both stabbed at my

conscience and made me long for my own Captain O'Malley. Everything had seemed so clear back at Dublin Castle, but had I made the right decision? Should it not have been a decision we made together? I was grateful for Will's aid and company, but I would far prefer to have my husband by my side.

Finvara did not trust the Morrigan, and he had good reason for it.

I am terrified of my father's power, and I have good reason for it, I reminded myself.

We had been cruising through the Gap only a few minutes when Doro's *Black Swan* came into view. It was still positioned below the Gap gate. The decision to pass again through the gate was another one that had made more sense from the safety of Dublin Castle.

Turning to Will, I said, "Are you sure you want to do this? *I must. You still have a choice.*" In truth, I didn't know what I would do if he changed his mind. But I couldn't let him do this half-heartedly.

"I do, lady," he replied.

As we approached, I realized we would either have to board *Black Swan* or nose her out of the way, as there was not enough room for both ships beneath the Gap gate.

Something very like dark laughter rippled across my thoughts, and I heard the hum of *Corvus's* propeller.

"Hold on, Will," I warned as we picked up speed.

We approached the gate from a lower position than the *Swan*, as our vessel was much larger, yet we were still on a collision course.

I braced for the impact just as—*bang!*—the top of *Corvus's* figurehead clipped the bottom of the *Swan's* stern, and the smaller vessel lurched forward. As the *Swan* drifted, the portion of the ladder that stretched up to the cavern—repositioned since my escape—tore free. Instead of plummeting, it began drifting away.

"Have a care," warned Will, nodding at the ladder. "The physical laws inside the Gap are not what you're used to. Once we leave the deck, never lose contact with the ship until we reach the tunnel."

"And how will we do that?" I asked. He frowned, and I clarified, "Reach the tunnel."

Our eyes moved over the rigging—*Corvus* had no central mast. The square sales were floating alongside the ship, anchored by what looked like a kind of horizontal mast. The thick mast at midship served as a support for the balloon.

"We'll have to climb those," said Will, and I followed his pointing finger. Three side-by-side rope ladders had been affixed below the ship's rail and ran up into the rigging, along the side of the balloon, and presumably all the way to the top.

I had never much cared for boats, and I was beginning to *hate* ladders.

Best to get it over with.

Sighing, I started up, and Will left an empty ladder between us and took the third. I had to reassure myself that the ladder would not in fact flip over, much as it felt like it might. I kept my attention, on my hands and feet, on rails and rungs, and never looked down at the deck.

The climb took several minutes, and my heart was pounding by the time we reached the top. My feet still firmly on one ladder rung, I placed my sweat-slippery hands on the lowest of the stone steps and then carefully levered myself up, slowly transferring my weight away from the ship. Then I took a deep breath, climbed a few steps, and waited for Will to follow.

He joined me, mopping sweat from his brow, and we watched as *Corvus* began to coast away from the Gap gate. Per our agreement, she would return to Dublin Castle for Finvara and the others. At least I prayed that she would. She had yet to exact her vengeance, so I believed that she would follow the plan.

"No turning back now," said Will with a nervous laugh.

I glanced at him, and in that moment he seemed more boy than man. "I've not known many men as brave as you."

He laughed. "As brave or as foolish?"

I shrugged. "I think only those who measure us by our success distinguish between the two."

He gave a short nod. "Right you are. Tell me what to do."

I looked to the top of the stairs, at the watery opening there. "Follow me in. Let the water take you. Try not to be frightened."

He gave another nod, and we climbed up. At the top, I instructed him to wait a few minutes after I had entered the gate, afraid of what might happen if we went through together. Then, without giving myself time for further misgivings, I plunged a hand into the water.

I emerged on the other end of the gate coughing up water, and I clawed my way out of the shallow pool. I had forgotten how cold and wet it would be on the other side. I stood up and looked down over my body. I slid my hands over my face and head. I tensed my back muscles, raising my wings.

I breathed a shuddering sigh of relief—I seemed to be unchanged.

YOU ARE STILL A WINGED CREATURE?

The sudden peal of the goddess's voice knocked me to my knees.

She appeared able to examine my thoughts at any time she wished—why had she needed to ask? *She hadn't.* She had uttered it out of frustration. Out of desperation. I was beginning to glean more from her than the words she spoke to me, and the real reason for her question now came to me.

She had sent me back through the Gap gate because she wanted to know whether a second time would reverse the change. I was an experiment. Which meant *she* was no better than Doro.

Could something that size even pass through the gate? I recalled the Fomorian flagship had passed through a Gap gate at Ben Bulben, so it was at least possible. If I *had* returned to my original form, would she have followed me through and then abandoned us?

A splash followed by explosive coughing redirected my attention, and I waded back into the pool to help Will.

A quick and anxious survey revealed him to be unchanged, and relief swelled. I gripped his arm, steadying him as he staggered to a pile of loose soil, where he sank down, breathing raggedly.

"Are you well?" I asked, pushing wet hair from his face.

"Aye," he croaked, and then began coughing again.

I pressed his back with my hand. *Thank Freyja.*

When his coughing quieted, he lifted his head and looked around the cavern.

"This was a tomb," I explained, brushing sand and small pebbles from his cheek. "Doro reanimated the king that was buried here, and Finvara and I fought and killed him." He had heard this story already, at Dublin Castle. I was talking nervously, trying to use my voice to anchor him.

Still Will's eyes moved around the cavern like he was searching for something.

"What is it?" I asked him.

"That noise," he replied, "where is it coming from?"

I stilled, listening. But there was only an occasional drip of water, and the sound of a breeze blowing over the mouth of the tomb. "What noise?"

His hands came up to cover his ears and he said, "That infernal ticking!"

FINVARA

"I knew I'd find you up here."

Shifting my eyes from the horizon, I turned to Izzy. Her face was composed. The front of her hair was pulled back loosely, and a breeze teased the ends of her dark curls.

Wrapping my fingers around the compass in my pocket, I looked back to the edge of the sky.

"She's not to blame," I said. "I should have been more insistent about the Morrigan. You and I know how dangerous she is. Koli . . . she couldn't really understand."

"From what you've told me," replied the queen, "she understood perfectly. Back at Knock Ma, she took a calculated risk. Now she's done it again. You, my dear cousin, have never been risk averse."

I frowned. "I risk myself, aye. My ship and sometimes even my crew, if my hunch feels sure. But . . ."

"But now you are in love."

I gripped the battlement before me to ease the sudden sensation of falling.

The queen moved to stand beside me. "And that is the greatest risk of all."

TOO LATE

KOLI

Unease twisted my stomach. "Ticking?" I asked, watching the young man closely—studying him for signs of a transformation that I might have missed.

"Like a great clock," he said, wincing and shaking his head. "You must hear it."

"Will," I said softly. Raising his eyebrows, he looked at me. "I'm afraid I don't."

His eyes went wider. "It—it's *everywhere*."

I began to be alarmed but strove not to let him see it. "I think it must have to do with the Gap gate."

Seeming to recall it for the first time, he performed the same inspection I'd performed on myself after passing through.

"Nothing outward has changed," I assured him. "Though I wonder . . ." I hesitated, still worried I'd frighten him. But he deserved to understand what was happening.

His eyes riveted to mine. "Tell me."

"I wonder whether anything *inward* has."

I could see the fear rising in his eyes.

"Will," I said firmly, "you are sound. Your *mind* is sound. You know who I am. You know where you are. Whatever it is that has changed, it has left you very much alive and intact. I will do everything I can to help you."

I watched him wrest control of his mind from the fear. Nodding, he said, "Thank you, my lady."

"I think the best thing will be for us to continue as planned." I glanced up at the opening of the tomb, which served as a frame for the diamond-bright stars and a bone-colored waning moon. "We'll have the light of the moon to make our way, and also the cover of shadows. Let us proceed slowly and see what happens."

I had no real confidence after the Morrigan's deception, but I did not want to share my misgivings with him now. There was really nothing for us to do except carry on. If *Corvus* did not return with Finvara, he would find his way here eventually—if not for me, at least for his throne. And if the forest turned out to be a fool's errand, I would try to see Ulf and persuade him to help us. It was Finvara who had put it into my head that my bodyguard might feel more allegiance to me than was apparent. Still, I considered this a last resort.

"Do you agree?" I asked Will.

"I agree," he said, his teeth beginning to chatter.

"Come, then," I said. "We'll be warmer if we keep moving."

We crept carefully out of the hole, watching for movement before crossing the saddle to the hillside stairway, the one Finvara and I had repaired with our magic. We only needed to make our way into the trees without getting caught—I wasn't ready to let myself think beyond that point.

When we had climbed to the viewpoint, I led Will to the

north side of the hilltop and into the trees. Despite the bright moon, walking in the forest without the benefit of a path proved difficult. We stopped a little way in—no one would see us in the shadows, and *we* would see anyone who came up the trail from the grounds below.

"I know it's cold," I said to Will. "When we have finished our business here, we can gather some wood and return to the tomb. I think we can risk a small fire."

"What *is* our business, exactly, lady?" he asked.

I had told him all the Morrigan had told me. If there was any possibility of this working, it was up to him. But I knew he was cold and frightened and needed encouragement.

"Can you think of no reason why the Morrigan might believe you could talk to the trees here?" I asked gently.

He frowned. "None whatsoever."

I took a deep breath, studying the dark woods around us. Without their leaves, the trees were wraithlike—looming like the blackened skeletons of enemies my father had strung up along the path to Skaddafjall's gate. I could feel that they were ancient. Some of them so enormous I thought they must be older than time itself. We had nothing like them in Iceland, and I knew that my unease was at least partly due to a fear of their otherness.

"They are beautiful," said Will. His voice was calmer now, though he still pressed a hand over one ear. "I know of no other oaks in Ireland this old, and there has been no forest here in my lifetime. These trees have come from Faery." He scanned the branches overhead. "They must have great wisdom in them."

"You do have a kinship with them, it would seem," I said, growing hopeful. "I confess they frighten me."

He smiled. "You are descended from shield-maidens, lady. I would have guessed that nothing frightens you."

I shook my head. "Fearlessness is arrogance, and arrogance

can kill you. I have been an enemy of Ireland, and if these trees truly are protectors, my fear of them is only prudent." I shrugged. "Yet they neither move nor speak, at least in no way that we can understand, so it feels like the fear of a child."

"Oh, they move," countered Will. "In the wind, and in the stretching of their roots and branches over time." He turned to me. "As to their speech, I confess myself to be at a loss, my lady. I have never tried to talk to a tree."

I studied the trunk closest to me, with its knots and rough ridges. About halfway up, there was a bark pattern that looked like a face. I shivered.

"If it were me," I said, "I'd try a spell."

Will sighed and leaned his head against a trunk. "I have no magic. Lady Meath tried to teach me a wisp's light. It was humiliating."

I laughed. Then, thinking about what he'd said, I replied, "You have a different kind of magic."

He gave me a blank look.

"Have you written any poems about trees?"

He considered this a moment. "I have begun one. Though it's only about trees on its surface. Similar to all poems, I suppose."

"Why not see if they like it?"

He let his eyes move over the forest. Staring again into the lacework of branches overhead, he began to recite.

> "Beloved, gaze in thine own heart,
> The holy tree is growing there;
> From joy the holy branches start,
> And all the trembling flowers they bear.
> The changing colors of its fruit
> Have dowered the stars with merry light;
> The surety of its hidden root

Has planted quiet in the night;
The shaking of its leafy head
Has given the waves their melody,
And made my lips and music wed,
Murmuring a wizard song for thee."

When he finished, the air felt heavy with a silence that I had not noticed before. There was no wind to stir the branches, and no rodent rustled among the cast-off leaves. The peeping creatures that dwelled in the hidden springs and rivulets among these hills had also gone silent.

"I wish that I better understood your language," I said, "but I enjoyed the melody of your words."

He appeared not to hear me—in fact he appeared to be listening to something else. I wondered if the ticking was worsening. I watched him and waited, feeling a splinter of despair working into my heart. What was I doing here? I should be by my husband's side. Either by his side, or my father's, not wandering alone in the darkness with no purpose. I felt uprooted and isolated. Too far from my own ground.

"They have accepted my gift!" said Will suddenly, his eyes wide with wonder.

"What?" I asked. "How do you know?"

He gave a joyful laugh. "They told me so. They want to know what I'd ask in return."

My heart lifted. It seemed that at least some of what the Morrigan had told me had been true. "Tell them!" I urged.

He closed his eyes, his brow furrowing in concentration. Some minutes passed, and the silence held.

Finally he looked at me and said, "They tell me I have come too late. Or at least I think so. They don't speak plainly, like you and I. It's more like chanting, and it is indeed a kind of poetry."

"You mean too late to save Knock Ma? Are they sure?"

An uneasy smile rested on his lips. "I think I might be going mad."

No, no, no. Stay with me, Will.

"Is it the ticking?" I asked.

"In part. But there's something else. When they speak, they say many things at once. Some of it is . . ." He shook his head. "It's too difficult explain."

"*Try*, Will." Impatience crept into my voice.

He stared into the distance, blinking a couple of times. "They make one feel insignificant."

It was on the tip of my tongue to tell him he was thinking too much, and we needed to focus on the task at hand. Then I recalled the doubts that had reached into my own thoughts in the silence. Had they come from the trees?

"Have you any idea what they mean by 'too late'?" I persisted, trying to shake him from his melancholy.

His eyes met mine. "It makes no sense, my lady."

"*Tell me anyway*," I commanded.

He swallowed and stood a little straighter. "They mean that if we wanted their help, we should have asked centuries ago."

"Centuries!"

"Their lives are written in their bodies. In their pith, in their rings. In the water they absorb through their roots. It is not possible for them to act as quickly as we need them to."

I couldn't help wondering if this was the Morrigan's idea of a joke. She must have known. Or was it possible there was some way to give them what they needed? Blood magic could be used to see the future. Could it also be used to alter the past? And if so, would the price be worth it?

Will groaned, and I noticed his eyes had closed. I touched his wrist.

"Will, you're very warm. Are you well?"

His head fell back against the tree trunk. He didn't answer.

"Will!" I snapped, gripping his hand. "They told you what they need from us. Is there any way we can give it to them? Impossible as it sounds, *think*. Is there any way?"

He laughed feebly. "There is! We can travel back in time."

His laughter continued, a truly mad sounding chortle, and then his features began to blur. Suddenly feeling dizzy, I looked away—only to discover everything before my eyes was moving. I doubled over and was sick on the ground.

When my stomach was empty, I pressed my head against a cool stone, grimacing at the bitter taste on my tongue. Wiping the back of my hand across my mouth, I sat up.

I cried out in surprise—it was daylight, and the forest was much altered. Gone were the monstrous trees—most of the ones I could see were saplings. The light was strange and, looking up, I saw that the sky was as much green as blue. I could not see the sun.

"Will!" I shouted, looking around frantically.

I jumped at a rustling sound nearby. Something burst from an elderflower bush—a deer—and leapt clean over me before bounding away.

The forest floor was blanketed with fern fronds, and I bent and began shifting the greenery so I could see underneath. Finally, I found him.

"Will!" I helped him to sit up. "What has happened?"

Frowning in concentration, eyes closed tightly, he held out a hand to stave off my questions. "What day is it?" he asked. "Or *was* it, when we left. I need to know precisely."

I thought for a moment—the date of the ball had been that of the full moon. The next day I had married the king, and this morning we had arrived at Dublin Castle.

"I'm not sure," I said anxiously. "Very near the end of March, maybe—"

"No, not the calendar," he said. "They don't—how many days since—" He broke off, then continued, "How many days since the first day of spring?"

First day of spring—Finvara had mentioned it the morning we went into the forest together. The day we fought the wraith. I closed my eyes and counted back. "Six days, I think?" Suddenly it occurred to me why he might be asking—was he issuing instructions about the battle? The vertigo returned. I dug my fingers into the loose earth of the forest floor, retching again. Then I choked out, "Tell them *tomorrow*, Will! *Seven* days after the first day of spring!"

As he continued, deep in concentration, I noticed movement behind him. Next to one of the monster trees I saw a face, so dark and woody that at first I mistook it for another knot-and-bark illusion. But I *recognized* this face.

Treig! She was smaller, her features softer—the likeness was eerie. As I stood up, her wide eyes followed my movement. "Treig?" I said. She started at the sound of my voice, then her lips curled in a smile and she turned and ran off, leaving waggling fern fronds in her wake.

"I think I've done it," said Will, "or at least I've tried my best." He reached for my hand.

Before I could ask questions, the world was spinning again. I felt a jerking pain in my middle, and for a few seconds glimpsed the starry sky. Then I lost my balance and fell.

"Blast!" I swore, rubbing a bruised knee. The welts on my hips were throbbing too. "Have we just traveled back in time, Will?"

"And forward too, lady, or so it would seem."

I stared at him in disbelief, and a wild notion came to me. "You have a time travel device in your *head*. It is the reason for the ticking noise."

"I'm almost sure I have *become* a time travel device. And I'm not exactly sure how I feel about it."

The calm demeanor, the mild tone of voice—Will was himself again. Yet his reaction was so unlikely under the circumstances that I began to laugh.

"I'm sorry," I said, appalled at myself, "I am not—I don't mean to laugh. I just—I have never met anyone quite like you."

He smiled. "You're not the first person to say so, my lady."

"Tell me about the trees," I said. "What have you—"

"*Hrafn.*"

I jumped up, instinctively reaching for a weapon—I had none. The weapon display in Dublin Castle's great hall had provided an opportunity almost too good to pass up, but I'd been afraid to carry anything with me into the Gap gate lest I come out with it somehow attached to my body. Seeing Ulf now standing a few yards away with an arrow knocked and pointed at me, I decided it would have been worth the risk.

"So you have found your way home," growled my bodyguard. "Your father said that you would. Tired of the coward already?"

I tried to see behind him. Had he come with a patrol? I felt my furies stirring—the familiar pressure in my chest—yet I held them back. Though Ulf was no sorcerer, he had learned long ago how to counter the illusion. Releasing them would be a waste of my own limited magic.

"Finvara may not be ruthless," I replied, "but he is no coward."

"Then what are you doing here?"

I hesitated—there was no point in lying to him again. If he took me back to Knock Ma, my father would not be gentle this time; he would force the truth from me. All I could do now was try to forestall the inevitable.

"I am here to prepare the way for him," I said. "You may take me to Father, but Finvara will come regardless. Queen Isolde, too, has been alerted. No Fomorians will be coming to aid you."

Still eyeing me down the shaft of the arrow, Ulf replied,

"Alfakonung is not afraid of your husband, and he has guessed that you would go to the Irish queen."

"Then he must see that he is cut off and alone. He would be a fool not to return to Iceland while he can."

Ulf shook his head slowly. Will, somewhere behind me, had not made a sound—but Ulf would not have missed him.

"The queen has reinforced her coastline then," said Ulf.

"Father's allies will not get past her ships. The Fomorians are still limping after the defeat at Ben Bulben."

Ulf smiled. "Then it is good our strategy does not require them to. Now that Alfakonung is on Irish soil, he is no longer interested in dealing with the Fomorians. They involved us in a war that reduced our fighting force by nearly half. They negotiated a treaty that left us weak. He was left no choice but to make peace with the Irish, until he was approached by the druid."

I frowned, wondering at his confidence. "Father must see that it is pointless for him to hold out at Knock Ma. Even should my husband fail to remove him, the queen's army will eventually take up the task."

"Once Alfakonung has defeated your husband, we will march on Dublin. By the time we reveal our presence in the city, we will hold the queen and many of the families of the very men who would return to fight against us. We will welcome the rest of Alfakonung's army into Dublin. This queen is no sorceress. Without her army, she is no match for your father."

I began to fear our cause was more hopeless than I'd imagined. Only my father could be so bold, so arrogant, as to march on Dublin alone. The problem was that like Ulf, I believed he could take the city. And only my husband and I were in any position to stop him.

Now that the Morrigan had the information she wanted, would she honor her promise to bring Finvara back to Knock Ma?

Unless and until she did, Will and I, along with my furies and possibly the trees, were on our own. It would have been laughable had it not been so dire.

"I have a proposal for you, *hrafn*." Ulf at last lowered his bow.

I eyed him warily. "Go on."

"Fight me," he said. "If you win, I will join you against your father."

I stared at him—was he serious? Ulf had trained me in hand-to-hand fighting and we had sparred many times. I had even beaten him. *Twice*—in nearly eighty years.

"And if I lose?"

"You will come with me back to the castle."

I glanced at Will. His eyes were wide, and he shrugged helplessly. I realized he couldn't understand our conversation—we were speaking Elvish.

Turning again to Ulf, I said, "I am not going back to the castle, my friend. Not until my husband and I can return there together."

His heavy brows knit. "I *will* take you back, over my shoulder if I have to. I am offering you a chance."

I shook my head at the absurdity. Somewhere Loki was laughing. "Why would you suggest such a thing?"

He grinned. "Because I like you, *hrafn*. Because I respect you. And because it would be fun."

Fun. Ridiculous as it was, I thought I understood him. The fight would serve to reinforce the bond between us, and remind us what we were to each other and to my father. There was no question in his mind that he would win. There was hardly a question in *mine*.

What choice did I have?

"I have your word that if you lose, you will join me against Alfakonung."

"You have my word. But that fellow behind you must not scamper away or the deal is off."

I nodded. "I agree."

As we followed Ulf out of the forest, I explained to Will in Irish what was happening.

"If I win, he lets us go," I said. "I've promised you won't run, but if I lose, I want you to get away."

"Less talking," grunted Ulf in Elvish.

He drew two long-knives—*scramasaxes*—from sheaths at his waist. Stepping closer, he flipped one so the hilt pointed away and offered it to me. I took it, and we backed a few yards away from each other, bright moonlight glinting off our blades.

Then Ulf charged.

Though my heart was pounding, I easily danced out of reach of his first strike—it was only intended to get my attention. I knew no one better with a blade than Ulf. The only advantage I had over him was my size—it allowed me to move more nimbly—but he was well aware of it. Instead of chasing me and tiring himself, his strategy had always been to spend his energy in a slow and deliberate way, hoping I'd tire *myself* out. And I often did.

I feinted once, then twice. Ulf didn't take the bait, and we continued to circle each other. We were warming our bodies now, and thinking through strategy. I reminded myself not to hurry—it was my greatest weakness.

The first real strike I attempted was almost my last. I had not taken the change in my body into account, and the extra weight of my wings threw me too far forward. Ulf dodged the blow and brought his elbow down on my arm hard enough to knock the knife from my hand. In my panicked grab for my weapon, my wings lifted and the bony joint at the left wing's curve struck him hard in the face. He stumbled backward a step, and I grabbed the knife and put a little distance between us.

Grinning like an idiot, he wiped his nose and held up his hand for me to see. "First blood."

He motioned me toward him, but I held my ground, waiting for him to come to me.

When he did, he drove powerfully. I prepared to block, then at the last moment he tossed the knife into his other hand and dragged the blade across my waist, slicing through my dress and drawing blood.

The cut was not deep, but it hurt. I retreated to catch my breath. He granted me only a few seconds before reengaging, forcing me back into the dance.

I kept to feints for a while, conserving my strength for his strikes, which were coming faster. He had discovered I couldn't move as quickly as before. I was constantly shifting my wings to maintain my balance, and the extra weight and effort were wearing on me. Perspiration dripped down both sides of my face, and my back muscles were screaming from the strain.

"Do you yield?" he asked, punctuating the question with a fast jab.

I responded with a block and counter.

"*Hrafn*, you cannot win," he said, blocking, and this time he managed to lock up my arm. Both of us were panting now. "I will speak to Alfakonung for you. I will ask him to divide the punishment between us."

I curled in toward him and shoved my free hand up into his chin, jamming his head back. He cursed and stumbled, and I darted away, jogging a few yards further and doubling over with my hands on my knees, struggling for breath.

"You must know there are few I have ever cared for," I said, panting. "My mother, you, my husband. That is all."

"You have known him *days!*" he snarled, standing still and pointing his knife at me. "You have been with us at Skaddafjall for decades. Why did you do it? Why did you turn on us?"

Flipping the blade of my knife into my hand, I shouted, "Why did you let him *lash* me?" On the word "lash," I flung the knife. My question struck him like a slap, and his dodge came a second too late. The blade lodged in his left shoulder and he growled in pain.

"You chose Father over me, again and again. You were willing to protect me from everything except *him*. It was time I made a choice of my own." Tears rolled down my cheeks and I burned and shook with anger. "I didn't have to miss!"

I sounded like a child, but I wanted him to know I could have killed him. His expression darkened, and he reached up and pulled the knife from his flesh. Blood streamed from the wound, but I knew he could still fight—and he had both knives now.

Finally I released my furies, and they swooped out of me in every direction, shadows flitting against a moon-bright sky. I parted my lips to shout a challenge, and my voice came out like the ragged cry of a raven. I ran across the clearing, my furies gliding beside and ahead of me. I saw the uncertainty in Ulf's eyes as he realized these birds were *more* than shadow—my spell had grown stronger. He raised his arms to shield his face, and I crashed into him. He staggered backward, and the force of my attack carried us both over the rocky drop at the viewpoint—the same spot where Finvara and I had stood looking out over the green hills, both of us longing for the things we could no longer have. Our bodies crushed together—Ulf's limbs tangling with mine—and my wings folded around us. The ravens swarmed us like angry bees.

Focusing what strength I had left, I managed to extend my wings—Ulf was heavy, and I beat hard at the air. The thick cloud of ravens, too, lent us some lift, so that when we struck the ground in the lower clearing, near the tomb, it was not with enough force to break us.

The birds dissipated with the impact. I lay splayed across Ulf's chest, blood from his shoulder seeping into my hair, too sore and exhausted to move. It was hard not to think about how I'd lain like this with Finvara, though under very different circumstances. It gave me a hollow feeling in my chest.

"Loki's sack, *hrafn*," grumbled Ulf.

I raised my head and caught the glimmer of a knife blade, lying not far from Ulf's wounded shoulder. Grabbing the weapon, I pressed the tip against the underside of his chin.

"Do you yield?"

The fool began to laugh.

"Do you *yield*?" I insisted, drawing a bead of blood.

"I yield, but you might as well take that knife and slit both our throats, because your father will make us wish we had never been born."

I pushed myself to my feet, and I stretched my hand out to him. He grasped it, and I helped haul him up.

"We'll see about that."

PRODIGALS

FINVARA

The day that we had intended to return to Knock Ma dawned cloudless and warm. It was the first real day of spring. Preparations for departure were underway, and I intended to proceed as if there'd been no hitch in the plan. I started my morning on the battlements, waiting and watching.

The night before, Izzy had watched with me for nearly an hour. Unlikely as it seemed, her presence was comforting. She could needle and harp like no other—truly she took a perverse joy in it—but in a moment like that, I could not think of another person's company I could have tolerated.

Perhaps one other person.

Koli's departure had been a blow from which I was still reeling. Despite what she'd said in her note, it *felt* like a betrayal. Whatever she and the Morrigan had planned, there was something about it that made her feel that she had to sneak away. She still didn't trust me.

I was heartsore over it, but even worse was my fear that they might hurt her again. Was it possible she would pay with her life this time? Would Ulf allow that?

She had left me powerless to do anything but wait—wait for the Morrigan to return, wait to see whether Koli was alive and whole. I could neither rail at her about how ill-used I felt, nor help her if she found herself in trouble.

Before I was a husband, I was a king—and much as I might like to make light of it, a subject of the Irish crown. My country was again at war, and I would have to forge on. Even now, the queen and General Varma were hammering out details of a second strategy, should my wife and her patroness fail us. It was time I joined them.

I let out a sigh and swept my eyes over the horizon once more. There were guards in the battlements and I knew I would be notified of any change. Just as I was turning to go, I noticed a dark smudge in the sky over the far west end of Dublin. It could have easily been a flock of crows, stirred up by the mild weather. But I knew that it was not.

I confess that I had hoped to find my bride aboard *Corvus*, though in her note she hadn't said that she would return. And I had too much to do now to dwell on it.

We trusted that the Elf King would not anticipate a strike coming this soon after our escape, so there was urgency to our preparations. Because we would be outmanned initially—our reinforcements would have to travel west by train, then by horse and wagon into the very rural country around Knock Ma—the element of surprise was critical.

By late morning we had begun to load soldiers aboard the airship, as well as aboard *Sea Aster*. It had occurred to me that if *Corvus* towed the great gas balloon behind it, we could carry an additional one hundred men. Had we been forced to cover the distance in the normal way, it would have made for a ridiculously cumbersome and slow journey. But the shortcut through the Gap would save us that. And provided I could communicate our plan to the Morrigan, she could navigate out of the Gap at some distance from the castle, where the *Sea Aster* could lower with her passengers, who would disembark along with most of *Corvus*'s soldiers, and engage in an overland attack.

I would remain on *Corvus*. I hardly considered myself her captain—I merely served at the Morrigan's pleasure, and could not afford to forget it.

Our journey began inauspiciously, with me staring in bafflement at the navigator device lashed to the rail in front of the helm, while the queen and her attendants looked on from the battlements. I had assumed Koli only made off with Mr. Yeats because he was familiar with the device, and that she would return him along with the ship. The fact that she hadn't returned him made me worry that all had not gone according to plan.

Not knowing what else to do, feeling like an utter fool, I addressed the ship, explaining our plan, and asking her to carry us into the Gap. A moment later, the propeller fired up, the wing-shaped oars dug into the air, and we cruised away from the tower. I ordered all my men below deck for the perilous crossing, and I lashed myself to the rail.

KOLI

Will and I spent the night in the tomb, and an uncomfortable night it was. We gathered wood and managed to keep a fire going, but I worried about the smoke and never let it blaze out enough to really warm us. Though I was used to the cold, Will was not. Fortunately the temperature did not drop overnight, and the morning was the warmest since I had arrived in Ireland.

If the Morrigan had kept her word, Finvara would come today. His soldiers would arrive by land, and he and enough men to load the cannons would stay with the ship.

Ulf had returned to the castle to look for Treig and determine if she had made progress with the firglas. I told him to ask whether she remembered a strange woman calling her name in the forest when she was a girl—I hoped that she would, and that it would convince her to trust him.

Ulf had told me that he'd fallen out of favor with the king after my escape—Alfakonung suspected he had been negligent out of overfondness. As punishment, Ulf had been left out of my father's war council for the first time in many years—it was how he had ended up alone in the forest. When Ulf found us, he'd been on his way to the tomb. He thought that I might try to return to Knock Ma using the Gap gate—he knew me well—and also that he might regain my father's trust if he brought me back.

Something changed after our fight. It was more than just losing, and having to make good on his promise. The fight had served its purpose in reinforcing the bond between us—and it had forced him to choose between my father and me.

Ulf was supposed to return to us by midday whether or not he'd spoken to Treig. When he didn't, I began to worry.

"I'm going back to the castle," I said to Will.

He looked up from the fire. "Is that wise, my lady?"

"I'm not sure. If Ulf was caught, they may come for me. Then they will have *you*, and that we cannot afford."

"I can't say that I would choose to be taken by the Elf King," he replied, "but I don't see how my liberty is more important than yours."

"It is far more important. We have no idea what the results of our visit to Faery will turn out to be. We need someone here who can talk to the trees."

"Lady, mightn't your father use you against Finvara?"

Will was right, and I was taking another big risk. But I felt useless waiting in this hole, and I could not leave Ulf to his fate after he had turned his back on Alfakonung for my sake. I felt sure that something was wrong. If Finvara came, the attack would provide me cover. If he did not, all the more reason I must try to help Ulf.

"I will not let that happen," I said.

I bade Will stay where he was—Ulf had told me the elves were just as wary of the tomb as the fairies. Then I set out for the castle, keeping off the path and moving among the trees. As the day wore on, clouds gathered and it now began to look like rain. Mist had collected in the low spots and hollows, which made it easier to keep hidden, but also more likely I would surprise a patrol.

As I drew nearer the castle, I had to track more closely to the path. On the last hill of the approach, the path wrapped around a large boulder. There was no way to walk between path and boulder without being visible, so I wound around the outside—cautiously, as it was the perfect spot for a patrolman to watch the path. What never occurred to me was that there might be someone standing on top.

I felt the impact as he landed behind me, and strong arms snaked around my chest.

"Let go!" I shouted. I was accustomed to being obeyed by my father's men, and they were accustomed to obeying—things had changed.

"We have been waiting for you," the warrior growled in my ear. "Alfakonung will be pleased."

My fingers brushed the hilt of the knife Ulf had given me, and I stretched my hand, grasping for it. Suddenly it was snatched out of its sheath—a second warrior had joined the first. I tried calling my furies—already my wrists were being bound with *brisingr*, halting my spell. For a moment I continued to fight, but finally there was nothing to do but go with them—and dread the meeting with my father that I could not avoid.

Inside Knock Ma, the patrolmen turned me over to guards, and the guards took me directly to the prison tower.

Descending the stairway into the dungeon, I made two discoveries. My father and Ulf were below—my friend had been bound wrist and ankle to the outside of a cell. And the other cells were no longer empty—Finvara's kin, the family members that had visited Knock Ma, were locked inside. Had Finvara not said they'd started for home? But my father had many spies in the castle—it would not have been difficult to intercept them on the road.

Elinor O'Malley stepped forward, wrapping her fingers around the bars of her cell. "Lady!" she cried.

One of my father's men banged a spear against the bars and she jerked back with a frightened cry. It was then I noticed a solitary inhabitant of one of the other cells. Her face was much changed from the last time I'd seen her, peeking between the trees in Faery.

"Treig!" I called to her. She nodded faintly, and I saw that she was not well. The lump Ulf had given her at the cottage was freshly opened, and one eye had been blackened.

Alfakonung waited at the bottom of the stairs next to a blazing brazier, in the open area where the little machines had been stored. The flames licked at the air and cast a huge, undulating shadow on the wall behind him. The whites of his eyes were vivid against the dark stripes painted across his face—so white I could see the movement of his irises as they followed my descent. I shivered when I noticed he held a *scramasax* in one beefy hand and a whip handle in the other. Both were carved from obsidian and had been made especially for him by a sorcerer. The whip handle had no actual whip attached—none was needed. My father only used it to direct his magic. It was what he had used to punish me before I left Knock Ma, and the marks on my body burned as my eyes moved to Ulf.

He, too, was watching me, and I saw the bitter disappointment in his eyes. Horizontal slashes had been made across his chest, several on each side, from his neck to his waist. His face was a mask of pain and he was covered in blood.

"What have you done?" I demanded, glowering at my father though my heart was racing.

"I've been waiting for this traitor to tell me what he was doing in the forest, and how he came by his wound. I think I have an answer to both questions now."

"Ulf has served you loyally for centuries," I said. "It is me you want to punish."

One corner of my father's lips twisted up—he said nothing.

For all my outward show of anger, I was terrified. I had truly broken with him now, and I had no idea how far he would take this. He would have to make an example of me at the very least.

Alfakonung sheathed his knife, and he motioned to the guards who had brought me down. "When I have the full story of this treachery—and make no mistake, I will have it *all* this time— we will send you back to your husband with a message from his family."

My father raised the whip handle as the guards grabbed my arms and dragged me toward Ulf. I began to tremble. It would be worse this time—for Finvara's benefit.

"*Brisingr*, release your prisoner!" Ulf cried out in a ragged voice.

The chain dropped from my wrists.

Instinct took over—I conjured my furies, and my guards staggered back as the birds burst out of me, swarming my father. He cast a blocking spell in a voice so deep and loud it shook the tower. For the space of several heartbeats, *my* spell held, and I planted a foot in the groin of the nearest guard. He dropped— and three others approached. The angry cloud began to disperse in obedience to my father's command. I grabbed the fallen guard's spear and danced backward, wondering what my next trick would be. I would never defeat them all.

The door at the top of the tower flew open, and someone yelled, "The Irish are marching from the east, sire!"

Isolde's men! Finvara!

My father roared in rage. He spun around, waving the whip handle at me, and the force of his angry lash sent me crashing into the bars of Treig's cell, knocking the wind out of me. Dizzy from the blow, I raised my head and watched my father as he launched up the steps, taking them four at a time.

"No one gets out!" he shouted. At the top, he slammed and bolted the door.

"*Hrafn!*" Ulf muttered a spell to release his arms from the ropes that bound him, but it failed.

Two guards hoisted me to my feet. My chest finally released and I sucked in a breath. My father's strike had been wild and unfocused, but it had still singed my bodice—as well as the skin over my ribs on my left side.

The guards opened Treig's cell and thrust me inside.

"Finvara is coming," I said quietly to Treig in Irish. "We need to get out."

She was in pain, I could see it in her eyes—still she got to her feet. I saw her slip her own *brisingr* into a pocket. To prevent the spell release from affecting more than one *brisingr*, you had to touch the chain as you spoke the words—Ulf's command had released hers too.

"We served you faithfully," growled one of the guards, moving close to the bars of our cell. She had a blood-red band painted from temple to temple. "If your punishment was not reserved for Alfakonung, we would deliver it ourselves."

Dark goat horns curved out of the warrior's ropes of gray hair. I didn't recognize her—she had not served at Skaddafjall in the time that I was there. My father's warriors ranged all over Iceland.

"You would come to regret it," I spat. "I am now mistress

here, and that is my husband outside knocking on the walls. Alfakonung has broken his treaty with Ireland. He has brought down punishment on you *all*."

The guard looked like she would have struck me had the bars not been between us, and she did grab for the lock before one of the others restrained her, muttering, "No, Eld." The other guard I recognized as one who had served at court. He was Grimm, a captain like Ulf, and the two of them had not been friends.

"Lady, can you tell us what's happening?" called a tremulous voice—Elinor.

"Finvara is attacking the castle," I called to her in Irish. "Queen Isolde has sent soldiers. There is reason to hope we will be freed."

"Thank heaven!" she said.

"My son is leading the attack?" asked the earl, his eyes bright.

"Quiet!" shouted Grimm, raking his spear against the cell bars.

"We need to take her outside," urged Eld. "I heard Alfakonung say she has married this king. If he sees her, he will stop his attack."

The captain shook his head. "You heard him. We were ordered to remain here."

"But it is a good plan, is it not?" demanded Eld.

The other two guards were mumbling, their gazes moving between her and their captain.

Eld swore and jammed the butt of her spear against the floor. "Maybe *you* want to remain trapped down here while the fighting goes on above. I do not. What if we are killed in a collapse during the battle? How will we be received by Odin and Freyja?"

Will had warned me I might be used against Finvara. Still, was it not better to be outside where I could aid him, rather than locked in this cell?

I let a chuckle escape my lips, and the guards turned to glare at me. "Can you hear it announced in the hall of the fallen?" I covered my mouth with my hand and laughed through my fingers. "'These are Eld and Grimm, mighty elven warriors, crushed to death by falling stones!'" I glanced to the top of the stairs. "Finvara has cannons. The towers are always the first to go."

The muttering of the other two guards grew louder.

"We cannot leave Ulf down here unguarded," insisted the captain, but his protests were weakening. "Not even locked in a cell."

"Then we will kill him!" said Eld, her eyes wide and bright. "We will tell Alfakonung that he broke free and we had no choice. Then we can leave the others in their cells and join the battle."

I held my breath. They all looked at Ulf. One of the others said, "Alfakonung would have killed him in the end, anyway. You know it, Grimm."

The captain drew his *scramasax*. "I will kill the traitor."

"No!" I shouted, gripping the bars. "Alfakonung will—"

Suddenly there was a bang, followed by a rattling impact that I felt in the iron bars. Some part of the castle had taken a heavy hit. Another impact came, then the sound of an avalanche of stones.

Corvus! The Morrigan had returned.

"What is your command, Your Majesty?" I whirled at the sound of a rasping voice so close behind me.

Doro had appeared in the cell.

I stared a moment before recalling my last words to him: *Should you leave my chamber by any means, you must come to me at once.*

He had an ugly cut across one cheek, and he held one arm against his chest. His eyes were angry and hard, and I could see by his rapid breathing that he was in pain. The cannon fire must have cracked open his hiding place—and the protective enchantment along with it.

Outside, thunder rolled, and the goddess bellowed inside my head.

BRING HIM TO ME.

"We need to get out of this cell," I said. *"Now."*

CORVUS

FINVARA

By the time we left the Gap, arriving a couple of miles out from Knock Ma, the clouds had returned. Mist had even begun collecting in the low areas. All of this would work in our favor.

Corvus's balloon vented and the *Sea Aster* released gas, and both vessels descended into an open field. I kept only enough men onboard to load the larboard guns. Then, with a roar of the burner, *Corvus* lifted off again.

We used the navigator device to return to the Gap—my plan was to cross the rest of the distance and then appear without warning in the sky over Knock Ma. It would require precise navigation, but if the Morrigan couldn't do it, no one could.

When we slipped out of the Gap high above the eastern wall, frightened shouts went up from the battlements. Just as I was about to relay the command to my crew, two of our guns fired.

The southwest tower, where Koli's bedchamber had been—and where Doro had hidden—took a direct hit.

The goddess is having her revenge. The round shot took out part of the turret and also blasted a hole through the tower wall.

I quickly scanned the forest to the east and found Isolde's soldiers on a ridge just below the castle. They were waiting on *Corvus*'s cannons—and the ones we'd left behind in the field—to breach the walls. There was the moat to contend with as well, but that could come later.

"Fire!" I shouted, for all the good it might do. My men were loading the shot and readying the powder, yet clearly the Morrigan was in control.

Two more of *Corvus*'s guns fired—two more direct hits to the tower. What was left of it collapsed outward, spilling stones over the western wall into the moat below.

"The *east* wall!" I shouted at the ship in frustration. The elves had spells powerful enough to disable both rifles and cannon—we were running out of time.

Then came a blast from the cannons in the field—which were firing from a much greater distance—and a slice of the eastern wall collapsed.

Movement directly below us caught my eye—an enormous elven warrior had climbed to the top of the turret above the prison tower. A bright orange ball spun in the air above him.

The Elf King.

"Fire on him!" I shouted.

The air felt strange, as if the sky around us was hollowing out. I recognized it as a gathering of magic. I had felt it at the battle of Ben Bulben, where, with my ancestor's help, I had called the wind to aid Queen Isolde's becalmed fleet.

"Fire the guns!" I shouted again. What was she waiting for? The Elf King's fireball was the size of a hay bale, and still growing.

I heard shouting below, and then my man on deck relayed, "The powder has stopped lighting, Your Majesty!"

Bollocks! The Elf King's spell was gobbling up fire. How long could the Morrigan's burner hold out?

I heard the distant cannons fire, but the Elf King held up his hand, and I watched three balls stop dead in the air beyond the wall before dropping into the trees below.

"Into the Gap!" I bellowed. "Before he blasts us out right out of the sky!"

I grabbed the railing, bracing for the rough passage, but nothing happened. No window opened in the sky, and *Corvus* maintained her position.

The fireball was now a bright sun hanging over the turret atop the prison tower.

I felt frozen in time, and utterly powerless, as the staggering spell continued to grow. One desperate thought presented itself: *Where is Koli?* It broke my heart as it dawned on me I wouldn't see her again. I would have given anything to touch her one more time.

KOLI

Doro reached toward the back of the lock mechanism on the cell door, quickly scratching a symbol on the metal with the inch-long nail of his smallest finger. The fingernail began blackening from the tip, and the lock transformed from a rusty, blood red color to a tinny silver. Then he punched his fist through the lock, pushing open the door. He'd somehow changed the strong metal to a weaker one. *Alchemy.*

Treig and I rushed out of the cell as the guards moved to challenge us.

"Release the others!" I shouted back at Doro.

Suddenly Ulf gave a loud grunt of exertion, and one of the

bars he was tied to broke away from the frame at the top of the cell. Outside, cannon fire sounded and another part of the castle was hit. Our guards froze, unsure which threat to contain—I swung a fist at Eld. She easily dodged the blow, but Treig was waiting with a punch to the big warrior's throat. Eld fell to her knees, holding her neck and gasping.

Grimm lunged for Treig, but Finvara's father, now free of his cell, ploughed into the captain from behind. Ulf too was free, and wielded the bar from his cell like a pike against the other two guards.

Together we herded and battered all the guards into an empty cell. While Ulf eyed them with menace, I took the *brisingr* from Treig and used it along with my own to bind the guards to each other as well as the bars.

With the guards contained, I forced my mind to consider strategy—it was all I could do not to run up the stairs and look for Finvara.

"Did you have any success with your people?" I asked Treig.

"I spoke to as many as I could," she replied, "until I was caught. I think some will help us."

Touched by her loyalty, I laid my hand on her arm. "The drawbridge will have been raised," I said. "We need it lowered, and we need to drive the elves out onto the grounds west of the castle. Into the trees. Do you think there's any way to do that with only a small number of helpers?"

Treig lifted her eyebrows. "Fire?"

"Fire," I agreed. "Burn everything. Finvara's men are laying siege from the east and will discourage them from fleeing in that direction." I looked at Ulf. "Will you help her?"

The two exchanged an unfriendly glance, and I recalled that Ulf had given her the lump on her forehead. Yet he replied, "*Já.*"

"If you trust him, Your Majesty," said Treig.

"With my life."

"We'll go with them," said the earl. He and his eldest son had joined us. Elinor and his daughter-in-law clung to each other just outside their cell. Lady Mayo looked terrified, but in Elinor's eyes I thought I caught a glimmer of excitement. The earl continued, "Duncan needs my help."

"He does, my lord."

"Is there anywhere Elinor and Margaret will be safe?" he asked.

I had very little patience left for remaining here—I looked for Doro. He was standing outside our circle, watching us closely. I shivered.

"I know you cannot leave Knock Ma unaccompanied," I said to him, "but you may pass into Faery?"

"I may, Your Majesty," he said icily.

"Take the earl's kinswomen to Faery. Leave them someplace safe and return to me at once."

"Faery!" said Lady Margaret, eyeing me fearfully.

"You will be safer there than here," I replied.

"Can the creature be trusted?" asked the earl, giving Doro a wary glance.

Not generally. "He is magically bound to me and must obey." I turned to Doro. "Go now."

He moved close to the ladies and lightly touched Elinor's back. All three of them vanished.

"What will happen in the forest?" asked Ulf.

"I don't know," I admitted. "I have reason to believe the trees will help us. You must all keep clear of it if you can."

"What will *you* do, *hrafn*?"

"Find my husband," I replied, starting for the stairway.

The others followed me up. Outside, they ran down the stairs to the parapet while I stopped to look up at *Corvus*—and the carriage-sized fireball that my father had conjured on the turret above me.

Return to the Gap! I used my thoughts to scream at the Morrigan.

The ship did not respond, and I tried again. *Please save my husband!*

Everything had gone impossibly still. Alfakonung's men were silent, waiting and watching from the battlements. My father shifted his position so the fireball hung in the air over both of his outstretched hands.

Doro reappeared beside me, and I grabbed his arm. "I need a soft landing for Finvara!" I told him in Irish, so there would be no possibility of misunderstanding. "I don't care what spell you cast, but cast it *now!*"

My father intended to destroy his enemy in a single stroke. Did he know it was the Morrigan he faced, or had anger driven him to use all his power to destroy one Irishman?

I waited feverishly for Doro's answer, my fingernails digging into his flesh. What if it wasn't in his power? How much elemental magic had been spent already? Yet he was the only one who could help me—everything the Morrigan had done for us was in exchange for her chance at punishing Doro. Her revenge was more important than our lives, and that was what my husband had been trying to tell me all along. If he died because of her, I would never forgive myself.

My father let out a roar that vibrated the stone beneath my feet, and he hurled the fireball at *Corvus*.

"*Doro!*" I screamed.

He had closed his eyes and begun to chant. I ran up the stairs to the top of the prison tower, and I climbed into a crenellation in the battlement.

Then I leapt from the castle.

This time my wings were ready and caught the air quickly. I conjured my furies.

They are of earth magic, I realized, the most ancient of the elements. My father's fire magic had not diminished them. I recalled what had happened with Ulf in the forest and I sang to them as we flew, binding them close to me.

Finvara's gaze met mine the moment the fireball struck *Corvus.* Liquid fire—hot as the volcanic blood that had once spewed from the Laki craters—splattered over hull, balloon, and sails. The slack sails immediately caught fire, and a dozen men emerged on the deck—my stomach twisted as one of them jumped from the railing, choosing to fall to his death rather than be burned alive.

By myself, I could only save one of these men—if that.

"Finvara!" I shouted as I approached the burning wreck.

My heart lurched as he rose from beneath the railing, where he had fallen on impact. Smoke rose from holes in his clothing—he had been burned. He glanced at the deck behind him—the rest of the crew had followed the first.

There was a *whoosh* of hot air as liquid fire finally penetrated the balloon, and the ship began to plunge, her wings digging frantically at the air. Finvara too climbed onto the rail and jumped.

I swooped down and met him in the air, throwing my arms around him. Like Ulf, he was too heavy for me to carry. I managed to raise my wings a few times but was soon unbalanced by his weight, and we began to tumble, my furies swarming around us. We had *so* far to fall—we could not possibly survive it.

"Save yourself!" Finvara shouted. "Let me go!"

We stopped rolling for a precious split-second, and I glimpsed something miraculous. A circular ribbon of water hung in the sky just below us. I could not make sense of it, and there was no time to question. On our current path we would shoot through the open middle of it.

The water! I screamed at my birds. I shook my wings free and began to pump them, my fists knotted in Finvara's coat. A thousand feathered bodies pressed close against him, their wings whacking at him and the air and each other, helping to support his weight.

With the smack of flesh on a surface more yielding than earth or rock, we plunged into icy water, dark as a subterranean lake. I stopped fighting and let my exhausted body float. Finvara, too, went still, and his hands came to my waist. My heart jumped as an enormous silvery fish with a huge gaping mouth went streaking past us. Finvara tugged me to his chest, and I felt a bubble of laughter escape his lips. It was the happiest sound I had ever heard.

FINVARA

To laugh in that moment was a ridiculous thing, but I had learned from my mother that if you can laugh, not only are you still alive, but life is still worth living.

Koli had come for me, and the fact that we were somehow swimming in Knock Ma's moat at least a hundred feet from the ground—along with pike that were large enough to swallow us—was not going to steal the joy of this moment.

Running out of air would indeed steal the joy, however, so I grasped Koli's arm and we began to kick for the surface.

Our heads burst from the water. Before we had caught our breath enough to speak, we were suddenly falling again—I threw my arms around Koli's waist.

"Doro's spell!" she sputtered.

So Doro had raised the moat—and now it was returning to the castle.

"Kick!" I said. "Don't slip down below the water line!"

Our descent was slower than if we'd been tossed from a bucket, but still we landed with a sloppy splash, and I lost my grip on her. I flailed around for a moment, confused about which end was up.

The lighted end, idiot.

I felt a hand on my back, and together we swam for the side of the moat. Much of the water had been lost in the splash, and it was not at all apparent how we were going to scale the slimy walls.

While I was looking for a vine or rope, Koli shouted, "*Corvus!*"

She was engulfed in flames and falling out of the sky like a ship of souls bound for hell. Even aflame, her wings continued to rake through the air. At the last, there was an explosion and the ship lurched violently—the fire must have found the black powder. Koli gave a cry of surprise as the burning wreckage slammed right into the turret where her father had stood.

Spell-borne fire splattered out from the ship and across the courtyard. Shouts of alarm and confusion filled the air. Elf warriors and panicking horses pounded over the drawbridge and fled down the hillside into the forest. Flames licked at holes in the castle walls.

"Come with me," I said.

We swam under the drawbridge, and from there were able to climb an abutment and haul ourselves out. Then we ran for the gatehouse.

There was no one inside, and we climbed the stairs to the top, where we would have a good view of the forest and the castle.

With the collapse of the prison tower, the wreckage of the ship rested partly on the east wall. Several other sections of wall had been taken out by cannon fire. Dark smoke curled from the burning bailey, and even from the windows of the keep.

Suddenly Koli threw her arms around me. Warmth spread out from my heart, filling my chest.

"I thought I had killed you," she said, her voice thick with emotion. "I should never have left you like that. You were right about the Morrigan."

I pulled her close. "You did what you thought was best, and who can say that it wasn't? But can you now tell me why, *acushla*?"

She drew back to look at me, but before she could answer, we heard the distinct call of a crow—about a hundred times louder and more shrill than any crow I had ever heard . . . save one.

Looking out, we saw the enormous bird circling above the burning rubble.

"She's survived," I said.

Koli shook her head slowly. "How can that be?"

I shrugged. "She's a goddess."

Koli stared at me. "She must not have known. If she had known she could become her old self simply by destroying her new self, she would not have needed us."

I smiled, thinking how Lady Meath would appreciate the situation—the Morrigan, goddess of death, decay, and renewal.

"Her revenge might not have been so spectacular, though," I said. "It was a good thing for us, because we needed *her*, as much as it pains me to say so."

The great crow suddenly dived into the rubble. A few moments later she emerged with something draped across her back.

"Doro," Koli said with such certainty I looked at her. "He was standing outside the prison tower with me when my father threw the fireball."

I frowned. "Can he have survived?"

"I wouldn't have thought so. I wonder what she'll do with him."

Shuddering, I said, "I hate to think."

The Morrigan left the sky above the castle, flying off north with her prize. I sighed. "And now she abandons us with the battle half fought."

We watched her fade into the backdrop of cloud.

Koli turned. "At least we no longer have my father to contend with."

I studied her. "How do you feel about that?"

She moved in close, pressing her cheek to my chest, and I put my arms around her.

"I don't think I really feel anything yet."

I stroked her hair, and I kissed the top of her head. "I suppose we should—"

Suddenly I felt a trembling through the floor, and I glanced at the castle. The rubble against the east wall began to shift and slide.

"Father!" cried Koli.

SORCERESS

FINVARA

"It's just the debris settling," I said. "Don't worry."

Still, I continued to watch the rubble with her—it stayed put.

"Koli." She looked at me, and I took her hand. "Let us go."

We left the gatehouse and plunged down the hillside into the forest, heading for the lines of fighters that were forming on a flatter stretch of ground to the southwest. Knock Ma was an unusual fortress when it came to defensibility, possessing not only a moat and drawbridge but a hilltop position. Yet the strength of those assets was undermined by the proximity of the forest, which made it easier for an enemy to get close to the castle before being seen—as my men had today. None of it had mattered in the end—the castle had been all but destroyed by magic, and the two armies would now clash in the field.

My men had circled around south of the castle, pushing westward and forming a line that stretched north to south. The elf warriors had formed a shield wall about thirty yards directly west of the line.

"It's going to be bloody difficult," I said as we reached the Irish line. The forest was sparser on this ground, but not by much.

"*Hrafn!*"

Ulf took long strides toward us, and I looked frantically for branch or rock or *anything* I could use to defend us. But my bride hurried to meet the big elf, and he threw his arms around her, lifting her from the ground.

A change had certainly taken place, and I confess I did not rejoice at it.

"I was sure that you were dead!" he roared.

"So was I," she said, laughing.

"Ulf," I interrupted, with a tentative lift to my voice that annoyed even me.

She slipped down from his embrace, and he answered my greeting with a grunt. It was probably the best I could hope for, considering the last time I'd seen him, he'd punched me in the face.

Koli turned to me, explaining how Ulf had defected and aided us. He took over to tell how he and Treig had smashed the gearworks after lowering the drawbridge, then joined the elven warriors running from the plummeting hell ship.

I had railed against him for not taking Koli's side. Now that he had, it did not sit well.

"Where are the others?" she asked. "Treig? The earl?"

I looked up sharply. "Earl?"

"Your father," said Koli. "The elves went after them—he and the others were in the dungeon at Knock Ma."

I scanned the line of men, but there was too little visibility and too much movement. "What about the others?" I asked. "What about Elinor?" As if the poor girl had not suffered enough. "Were they harmed?"

"Finvara," said Koli, squeezing my arm. "They are well. Elinor is well. I ordered Doro to take her and Lady Mayo to Faery until it's safe." I saw it dawn on her that Doro was gone—her eyes went wide. "We will find them," I reassured her. "It was the right thing to do." Ulf uttered a stream of Elvish, and I looked up—his gaze had been drawn behind us. We turned in time to watch the Elf King duck through the entry arch and cross the bailey toward the drawbridge.

A command was shouted from behind our line, and I recognized the voice of my father. A volley of arrows fired at the drawbridge. The Elf King waved his hand, batting them off course like a swarm of gnats.

I called the nearest soldier over to me. "Give me your blade," I said.

"*No.*" It was the strongest voice I had ever heard Koli use. She glared daggers at me. "It is impossible, husband. He will snap you in two."

Before I could mutter something childish and unhelpful about her confidence in me, I remembered the barrow-wight, and how we had worked together that day.

"Do you remember the stones?" I asked her. "How we repaired the path on the hillside, after we defeated the barrow-wight?"

She gave a quick nod.

"I know he is powerful. But do you think that together we could make a blocking spell strong enough to prevent him using magic? It would give us a chance."

Her gaze darted to her father, who was trudging across the bridge. He raised a sword, the edge of it burning with green flame. After shouting at his men in Elvish, he raised the weapon higher and swung at our infantry line. Green flame jumped from the blade and struck down half a dozen men.

"The block would work on everyone!" she said. "I know of nothing except *brisingr* that can block magic in a limited way."

"It doesn't matter!" I said. "Could we do it?"

With a grim expression she watched her father strike down another half dozen men.

Finally she shook her head. "My magic—it's not that strong. I'm a warrior, not a sorceress."

"Koli!" I cried in desperation. "That's not *true*—what about your furies?"

KOLI

It had always been a source of secret shame for me, and of open disappointment for my father. How could I be descended from Gunnhild and Alfakonung and possess no more than middling magical ability? Instead I had cultivated the skills of a warrior, and I had offered unquestioning loyalty.

Yet my loyalty had *not* been unquestioning. Out of the seed of anger sewn by my father's coldness to both me and my mother, my furies had grown. Until I had come to Ireland, I'd never had any real control over them. They possessed solid forms now, and there almost seemed to be an unlimited number of them. Finvara was right—they had become my most powerful spell.

It was as if they'd become more real as I'd discovered things in my life worth fighting for.

THEY WERE NEVER CONJURED, ELF MAID. The voice came like an echo, a fragment of the Morrigan remaining in my mind.

What did she mean? If not conjured, then . . . they must have been *summoned*. It meant they *were* real, and if I could call hundreds—I could call thousands.

Alfakonung lashed Finvara's line again, and men screamed and fell away burning.

"Call them now!" urged Finvara. "It will be like the stones, except I'll feed my magic to *you*."

My lips parted, and I murmured a prayer to Loki, the father of my people—and the god of earth magic. If any god could forgive me for turning against my own kin, it was him.

Then I spoke the first words of a summoning spell.

FINVARA

The Elf King had struck down more than half the line of infantrymen. With each strike, the men behind the fallen moved up to repair the line. The soldiers fought with bayonets and daggers, the elves with long-knives and shields, and both sides had bowmen. Isolde's men were skilled fighters, as the warriors of Ireland had always been, and so were the firglas that had chosen to fight with us. But we were now badly outnumbered. If we couldn't stop the Elf King, we wouldn't last.

I had finally glimpsed my own father in the melee, acting every inch the commander he was.

"Mayo!" I shouted. It was what everyone except his sons called him, and the only sure way I could get his attention. He heard me and looked up. "Keep driving forward!" I said. "We'll deal with the king."

My father was born a gentleman, but the O'Malleys had been warriors all the way back to the Fianna, the fighting men of the Tuatha De Danaan. Our ancestor Finvara, too, had been a warrior before he became the fairy king. The former earl of Mayo, my grandfather, had kept a fighting force that my father had taken over, and my father had served the queen at the Battle of Ben Bulben.

As he began shouting orders to my men, I thought I saw the beginnings of a smile on his weathered old face. He was in his element, I supposed. Or maybe I'd finally done something to make him proud of me.

I turned back to Koli and found her watching her father with a distant expression. Her lips were moving, but I couldn't hear her voice over the fighting. I closed my eyes and tried feeling for her magic.

It didn't take long to find it—she was swimming in it. *Earth magic.* Earth spells were as ancient as blood magic, and they could be extremely powerful. The Elf King had shown himself partial to the fire of his homeland, yet I had sensed the earth magic in him. He would have had to use it to get free of the rubble. I wondered whether Koli understood how much power was building in her now.

I began a conjuring spell, but I couldn't make it link with hers—it was like trying to use the wrong knot to join two lines. Then I realized she wasn't conjuring at all—she was summoning. A conjuring spell called upon the elements to create something. A summoning spell made an opening and called something through it.

There was a reason her furies often felt real—they were *trying* to be. Whether she knew it or not, she had been suppressing her power—summoning and blocking at the same time. *No longer.*

I had very little experience with summoning—perhaps because the original Finvara had thought of it as "woman's magic"—but I reached for her hand, threading our fingers together, and I copied her spell.

When the ravens poured out of her, it nearly knocked us to the ground. Their wings blackened the air around us, shutting out the light. Their huge and very real bodies swept forward onto the bridge and formed a living net around the Elf King. I could hear him bellowing counter-spells, but to no avail. Koli's spell—*our* spell—was stronger.

It had almost become too strong for me to hold—I tried softening my grip and allowing her to control it. As soon as I did, the swooping creatures tightened their net and pulled the Elf King toward the gatehouse. He stumbled, shuffling to keep from being dragged, swinging his sword into the angry mass. He felled them by the dozen, but their beaks and claws raked into his flesh as well.

He staggered from the bridge onto the forest path. I hoped Koli would force him to our side of the line. When our magic was spent, our men would at least have a few precious seconds to set on him with mortal weaponry.

I had no chance to suggest it—suddenly our spell was finished. I could feel it shorn clean through as if with a knife. Koli let out a cry of surprise and lost her footing. She fell against me and then we were both on the ground—the expenditure of power had weakened us.

The vengeful flock dissipated, and fresh shouts of fear went up from the battleground. I saw that that the Elf King had raised his weapon again. He was clawed and bloodied, yet it hardly seemed to have slowed him, and I began to despair.

He took up a position in front of an ancient oak tree that might very well have been the only living thing that could make him look small. As I wondered whether he would kill us all or whether there would be an opportunity to negotiate, I noticed something—odd.

Someone was *standing* high up in the tree. I was almost sure it was Mr. Yeats.

The still winter-bare boughs of the tree began to *move*. Not like they were caught in the wind, blowing one direction or the other, but inward toward each other, until they made contact with the Elf King's body.

Startled, the king shook himself free and hacked off a bough with his sword. A deep groan came out of the tree, and the king tripped, dropping the weapon, as a root ripped itself from the ground in front of him. Another root snaked toward him, coiling around an ankle, and the king let out a furious roar. He uttered a line in Elvish, and a fireball began forming above him.

A wind rose, snuffing the fireball and stirring the tree branches more in the way I was accustomed to—except now I began to hear voices.

Northman, you should not have come, should not have come.
Northman, you should not have come.

Next came raking and scratching noises. These grew loud,

and louder still, until the men around us covered their ears—even the Elf King stopped fighting and covered his.

Then all of it stopped—the breeze, the creaking, the groaning—and a half-relieved, half-dreading silence descended. I glanced up at Will, still perched like a lookout in the crow's nest. He had curled each arm around a thick bough.

"What's happening?" I whispered to Koli.

"The *trees*," she hissed back.

A chorus of deep groans rose from the forest, vibrating branches and twigs, seeming to come from the very bones of the trees. The giant oak was growing taller, I thought, until I noticed that in fact its roots were pushing it up out of the ground. Huge clods of dirt fell from the great woody snakes as the trunk continued rising, until the base of it stood a full six feet off the ground.

The warriors of both sides uttered fearful cries as the oak's roots wound up and around the Elf King's arms and legs. He shouted at his men to aid him, but those who weren't frozen in terror were watching the trees around them wide-eyed, while inching the opposite direction.

Our men, too, appeared frozen, watching the horrifying spectacle unfold—even my father.

"Look alive, Mayo!" I shouted, startling him out of his trance. "The line is breaking!"

Seeing now that the elves were falling back on his position, he rallied the queen's men to begin their attack.

The Elf King continued to bellow, but his deep voice cut off suddenly. Looking back I saw that a thick root had twisted across his face. The smaller roots snaked around him too—tightening, strangling—and his body was slowly dragged under the trunk as it lowered. The root ends began digging into the soil, returning to place, pulling the trunk down until once again it rested snug against the earth.

THE BEGINNING

FINVARA

Some of the elves fled toward the outer edges of the forest. Others fled toward the relative safety of the castle and were rounded up by my men. The rest surrendered. What else could they do? The Elf King had been defeated by his daughter, who was mistress of the castle they had stolen. They were terrified she would feed them to the trees.

My father, my bride, both her bodyguards, the time-traveling poet, and myself—the king of this ruin of a castle—all gathered at the gatehouse to survey the damage. One of four towers remained standing. The walls were in shambles. The keep was half-collapsed, and the stables had burned to the ground.

And somehow it was fitting. I had not been ready for this responsibility. Maybe I was now. My father was right that I had needed a partner. This was my chance to start again.

I reached for Koli, pulling her close to my side. I wanted

to ask how she was feeling about the death of her father. About suddenly being a queen in two countries, as well as a powerful sorceress. And especially—selfishly—how she was feeling about *me*. Instead, I had to figure out how to conjure food and shelter for ourselves and the men who had survived.

There were many firglas moving about the grounds, and some of the less earthy fairy creatures were already cavorting in the rubble of the castle. The redcaps, who had joined the battle on the side of the elves but switched when they saw the tide turning, were sullenly foraging for abandoned weapons—I had ordered them to leave the fallen soldiers alone. When the light was gone, which wouldn't be long now, there would be banshee keens for the dead.

It was a kingdom not many would claim, but it was growing on me.

"What has happened to my wife and Elinor?" asked my brother as he joined us.

I sighed. "My steward took them to Faery and then got himself killed by the Morrigan." My father and brother stared at me, alarmed. "Right," I said. "I'll find them."

I glanced at Koli, hoping she would want to come—she had slipped into a whispered conversation with Ulf and was making a noise that if I had not known my wife better, I would have called *giggling*.

A jaunt in Faery was the very last thing I wanted right now. Or *ever*, really. I hadn't gone there since before Ben Bulben, when I was still under the control of my ancestor. At the time, Knock Ma castle had only existed there, while it was hardly more than a pile of stones in Ireland. Would the merging of worlds mean it had been destroyed there too? Was there even a "there" *there* anymore? It was something I should have looked into—another responsibility I had shirked. I was done with all that now.

"All right, then," I said, feeling rather sorry for myself. Then came a deafening grinding noise.

Bollocks, what now?

The ground began to quake. Everything left standing within the fragments of castle wall, along with the fragments themselves, tumbled into the moat.

"Into the forest!" I shouted.

My relations looked at me like I'd gone mad, but I could think of no better place to go.

They did as I'd ordered, and we watched from a safer distance as what was left of the castle collapsed. Yet it was only getting started. The ground *beneath* the castle began to give way, or so I assumed, because the stone heap was sinking. The earth around us quaked more violently and we grabbed at the trunks of the trees for support, praying they felt more friendly toward us than they had toward the elves.

When the rubble had gone, there was nothing left—only a massive well in the top of the hill. We had just a few moments' respite before stones began sprouting from the ground. Not single stones, but oddly neat groups of them, popping up and arranging themselves like puzzle pieces.

Koli exclaimed something in Elvish. I slipped my arm around her waist, and I kissed her forehead. "It's all right," I said. "It's happened before." Not two days after the Battle of Ben Bulben in fact, when the seal between Faery and Ireland had been no more and Knock Ma had pushed up from the ground, whole again.

By the time the sun had set, a new castle stood on the grounds of Knock Ma—a new castle that was exactly like the old castle, except its towers were all standing and nothing had been blackened by fire.

"We won't have to sleep out of doors after all," I said.

No one found this as funny as I did, except maybe Koli, who was eyeing me in a way I very much hoped boded good things for the evening to come.

"Is it safe, son?" asked my father.

"As safe as it ever was," I said. "Doro, at least, is gone. There won't be monsters in the lily pond. Or so I hope."

Koli was laughing quietly now—we were in very real danger of frightening off the mortals. At that moment two figures passed through the new castle gate and made their way toward the draw-bridge.

"Here's your wife, brother," I said.

"What?" said Owen.

The two women were running now, and my brother and father hurried to meet them.

I turned to look for Mr. Yeats, who'd been unusually quiet since the ordeal in the forest—even for *him*. He hung back a little, his arm around the trunk of a tree. He looked more boyish than ever with dirt smudges on his face and twigs in his hair.

"Are you whole and well, Mr. Yeats?" I said.

He straightened and cleared his throat. "I am, Your Majesty."

"And how's the ticking?" Koli had told me what happened to him in the Gap gate, and how he'd developed some kind of rapport with the trees. Still I could hardly understand it.

"Diminished," he said, "I thank you."

"Excellent. I need to thank *you* for your valiant service, and for taking good care of my wife."

He gave a short bow. "I think it was she who took care of me, sire."

I nodded. "As she does of us all. Can I make one more request of you?"

"Of course, Your Majesty."

"Look after the others? Help make them comfortable? The queen and I are passing the night . . ." I looked at her, and she gave me a puzzled smile. Ulf, on the opposite side of her, was frowning. "*Elsewhere*," I continued. "We'll return in the morning. Ulf and Treig will help you. Are you up to it?"

I could feel Ulf's glare, but Treig gave her lady a knowing smile.

"I am, Your Majesty," said Yeats.

KOLI

Just outside the new guardhouse, a group of soldiers had been rounding up the horses that had fled the burning castle. After claiming one of them, Finvara fashioned a halter and reins from a long coil of rope.

"Where are we going?" I asked, though I had already guessed.

He climbed onto the horse and then gave me a hand up. "You will see," he whispered into my ear.

With night coming on, our journey was not leisurely. Yet I was content to relax against my husband's chest, as I had on our first ride to the cottage. How much had changed, and in such a short time. The despair I'd felt then had been replaced by an alien emotion—*joy*. Along with a fuller sense of who and what I was. The loss of my father—I had yet to really feel it, beyond my new sense of freedom. There was a legacy that I must think of, but that could wait.

Though it was too late for hunting by the time we reached the cottage, the clouds had cleared, and Finvara declared there was enough moonlight to travel to a nearby farmhouse. "I'm sure they've food to spare," he said. "I'll be back soon."

When he'd gone, I went around to the stream in back of the cottage. Kneeling on the moss, I splashed cold water over my face and neck, and I combed out my hair with my fingers. Then I sat on the bank, listening to the small night creatures and the gurgling of the stream.

I am home.

It was a strange realization. I knew I could never forsake my own country, but because of Finvara, there was room in my heart for this one. And I was eager to know it better.

I got up and went inside, where I cast a tiny fire spell to light a candle. Then I used it to light the others, and by the time I got a fire going in the hearth, Finvara had returned.

"Unfortunately they weren't expecting a night visit from the fairy king, and I frightened them half to death." He unloaded a feast—a round of yellow cheese, fresh bread, a pastry of some kind, and a bottle of spirits.

"It was worth it," I said, and he laughed.

When the table was set, he came over to me.

"How are you, wife?" he asked tenderly, tucking my hair behind my ear. Running his finger up and over the backward-curving point that we did not have in common.

"Very well, husband."

He frowned. "I am sorry about your father. I know that you weren't close to him, but it can't have been easy."

I nodded, resting my forehead against his cheek. "I wish . . ."

Finvara waited patiently, and finally I looked at him. "I wish it could have been different. My mother was soft. She cared for me." Moisture stung my eyes. "He saw no value in those things."

"Aye."

After a moment, he cleared his throat. "You had Ulf, at least. He cared for you, and you for him."

I studied him. I had seen that Ulf's change of heart had made him uneasy.

"Yes," I agreed.

"I'm glad about that," he said. "Glad that someone was there for you in that cold, hard place. How is it between you now?"

He watched me closely, and I began to tremble. "Ulf has changed," I said, and I thought I saw something in his face shift. "We fought. We almost killed each other. I don't know that you can understand it, but after that, we were different—*he* was different. My father tortured him because of me."

Finvara took a step back, and my belly went cold. "I do understand," he said, "or at least I think I do. I don't know if it has dawned on you yet—your life is really just beginning. You don't have to be queen here. You can be queen in Iceland. You and Ulf—you can rule together. Or you can rule alone. You have choices."

I hesitated, unsure what to make of this speech.

He let out a sigh, and he ran a hand over his head. "I don't mean to confuse you. I only mean to say I wish you to be happy."

He was right about all of it. My father's people—they would accept me. Things were different with the elves. I had killed their king, or so they would understand it, and that would make me strong in their eyes, not a traitor.

"I cannot go back to Iceland," I said finally. "Not to live, anyway."

He lifted an eyebrow. "Can you not?"

I shook my head. "Ulf is family. He always will be. But it is *he* who must go back, so he can mind the kingdom in my absence."

His gaze held mine. "And why is that?"

The wings of my furies beat at the walls of my chest. "Do you not know?"

"I do not," he said. "All I know is that I love you, and I would be lost without you."

I closed the distance between us, wrapping my arms around his neck. He pressed his forehead to mine.

"I would have to be a cold and heartless thing to leave you to such a fate."

He smiled, and his hands came to my waist. He kissed my cheek, my nose, and finally my lips. "That you could never be."

ACKNOWLEDGMENTS

As I write this, my family is dealing with the aftermath of a mudslide that cut off access to our neighborhood in a rural area of western Washington. The last week has been long and stressful, but thanks to members of my community, I have been able to focus on the final steps for getting this book out to the world. Huge thanks to community road board members Samantha Idle, Korren Karahalios, and my husband, Jason Knox, as well as all the other neighbors who are putting in huge effort and long hours to help resolve this crisis. You guys are my heroes.

THANK YOU . . .

To my agent Robin Rue and her assistant Beth Miller (who is also a terrific agent) for so many things—FOR ALL THE THINGS. Also to Mandy at Blackstone Publishing, who has done a terrific job supporting the first book in this series, *The Absinthe Earl*, as well as to all the great marketing, editorial, and production folks at Blackstone.

To my wonderful, kind, and enthusiastic editor, Corrina Barsan, for seeing things I couldn't and helping to enrich this story and make it the best it can be. And my copyeditor who worked on both books, Ember Hood, for her great work and for being a fan.

To authors Lorraine Heath, Mary Jo Putney, Maria V. Snyder, and Amanda Bouchet. Also bloggers Tammy, Riley, Justine, and Has (and so many more), as well as all the enthusiastic bookstagrammers out there.

To Jeff Lilly, my trusty language and Celtic expert, who knows his stuff and also always has an encouraging word.

To poets everywhere, but especially those I was inspired by and have quoted in this work: W. B. Yeats ("The Two Trees"), William Blake ("Little Boy Lost"), Samuel Taylor Coleridge ("The Rime of the Ancient Mariner"), and Catherine Martin ("ErlKönig's Tochter").

All my love to friends and family for continuing to support my work, especially Jason, Selah, Talia, Debbi, Dominic, Lisa, Mark, Diana, Laurie, Donna, and Melissa.

Finally, to the person or persons I know I have left out: forgive me, and know that I couldn't have done this without all of your wonderful help and support.